The Woman at No. 3

ALSO BY REBECCA COLLOMOSSE

STANDALONE
He's Gone
The Woman at No. 3

THE WOMAN AT No. 3

REBECCA COLLOMOSSE

JOFFE BOOKS

Joffe Books, London
www.joffebooks.com

First published in Great Britain in 2025

© Rebecca Collomosse

This book is a work of fiction. Names, characters, businesses, organisations, places and events are either the product of the author's imagination or are used fictitiously. Any resemblance to actual persons, living or dead, events or locales is entirely coincidental.
The spelling used is British English except where fidelity to the author's rendering of accent or dialect supersedes this.
The right of Rebecca Collomosse to be identified as author of this work has been asserted in accordance with the Copyright, Designs and Patents Act 1988.

No part of this book may be used or reproduced in any manner for the purpose of training artificial intelligence technologies or systems. In accordance with Article 4(3) of the Digital Single Market Directive 2019/790, Joffe Books expressly reserves this work from the text and data mining exception.

Cover art by Nick Castle

ISBN: 978-1-80573-144-3

For Sam and Lydia

PROLOGUE

I watch them through my window. They are almost obscured by the big white van parked in the drive. But I can just about see the woman, directing the men as they lug furniture into the house. She's smiling. Her husband walks over and slips an arm around her. They hug for a second. There's a big grin on his face too. Well, I guess they would be happy, wouldn't they? Moving into a lovely new home in a leafy neighbourhood, a stone's throw from the river. Their little girl runs over and clutches the woman's leg with one arm. The other arm is pulling along a rainbow-coloured mini suitcase. They stand for a moment, picture-postcard perfect, before the woman pulls away and starts waving her arms at their movers. Seeing that little family unit, I feel more alone than ever, my nose pressed against a glass door that won't open. They thought they were going to have an idyllic life in their new house, watching their daughter grow up happy and contented. I take one last look, before forcing myself to turn away. Should have been me.

CHAPTER 1

"Now, this — this is the jewel in the crown!" Tom the estate agent takes in the room with an expansive sweep of his arm.

I make a sharp intake of breath and clutch Mike's hand. I've dreamed of a kitchen like this. Slate tiles, a huge island, an Aga and skylights. Gleaming marble worktops. Room for a large table, a corner sofa and an armchair. *Tick. Tick. Tick.* All on my wish list.

"Amazing, isn't it? And deceptively large," Tom continues smoothly, pulling at his tie. "The owners — not actually the current ones but the previous ones — built this extension. They've transformed the space."

He walks over to a door in the corner and pushes it open. "But alongside this fantastic modern kitchen, we still have the original 1930s pantry."

I want to scream with delight as I peer inside, every shelf full to bursting with food. There's even room for vegetable and wine racks.

I'm sure Tom clocks my wide-eyed delight as I try my best to keep my expression neutral, all the while calculating an offer. Could we afford to offer over asking price?

Mike looks impressed too, although he's better at hiding it than me. He gives my hand a squeeze.

"Right, let's take a peek at the utility room before going upstairs." Tom's delivery is as slick as you would expect.

A utility room! I've always wanted one. And this one's large, with plenty of room for drying clothes.

We head upstairs. I beam at Mike. He shakes his head slightly. *Keep your cards close to your chest*, he'll be thinking. He's right, of course, but I've fallen in love.

Upstairs, Tom takes us to a bright room with large windows, pale pink walls and a built-in wardrobe. It's perfect for our two-and-a-half-year-old daughter, Poppy. It's already a child's room, with toys stacked neatly in boxes and a *Frozen* duvet cover.

The main bedroom has a huge bay window, with a comfy-looking chair taking pride of place beside it. I want to sink into it, to gaze out of the window, taking in the trees. There's even a glimpse of the river. I wander around the en-suite and the family-sized bathroom. More boxes neatly ticked.

Tom shows us two more decent-sized double bedrooms. I smile as Mike nods appreciatively at the original open fireplace. This would make a great study, or spare room.

"Has there been a lot of interest in the house?" I burst out, as we head back down the stairs.

"There has," Tom says. "It's a great-sized family home, at a decent price. If you're interested, I would act quickly."

My heart quickens and I bite my tongue to stop myself making an instant offer.

The front door opens. A tall, thin woman with a sheet of gleaming chestnut hair appears in the hall.

"Sorry," she says quickly. "I've had to come home to collect my son's swimming gear before we head to his lesson from school. I was in such a rush this morning I forgot!"

She's flustered, sliding past us to get up the stairs.

"Oh, no worries, Helen," Tom says easily. "We're just finishing the viewing."

"Actually," Mike cuts in. "It's good to see you. I had a couple of quick questions. I was going to ask Tom but as you're here . . ."

Helen suddenly freezes, but her voice is relaxed. "Sure."

"How long have you lived here?"

"A year," she says. Before I can feel alarmed that the family are moving so fast, she moves on quickly: "We love it — the house, Twickenham — but my husband's been offered his dream job in another city, so . . ." Her voice trails off.

"Where to?" Mike asks.

Don't be so nosy. I eye Mike, embarrassed. But Helen looks unperturbed. "The Midlands. Birmingham," she says easily. "We have family links there anyway, so it all works out really well."

"And what are the neighbours like — do you get on well?" Mike persists.

I know he's just being thorough and sensible, but I cringe. I don't care what the neighbours are like. I just want this house.

"No issues at all," says Helen, taking a quick glance at her watch. "There's Mabel Jackson on one side, she's on her own — recently widowed, sadly. In her late seventies. Very pleasant. And in the house adjoining ours, there's Josie and . . ." She changes tack. "Actually, just Josie. She's been friendly and helpful. She's lived here a while, and Mabel has been here for ever."

She starts moving up the stairs. "Anyway, lovely to meet you but I'm running a bit late. I need to get my son's stuff." She gives us a smile as she disappears into her son's bedroom.

"We'll be in touch," I say to Tom as we leave the house.

He shakes my hand enthusiastically. "Great. Well, like I said, it's gathered a lot of interest, and we have a good number of viewings tomorrow."

I clutch my bag. *Please let us get to it first.* I stare at the house: 1930s. Semi-detached. Set back off the road, with a wide drive and beautiful rowan tree at the front.

OK, it's not detached. But it's still a serious step up from our cramped maisonette in Tooting, South London.

I glance at number three, the house it's attached to, and see a pale face peering out of the front window's shutters. I notice very blonde hair, almost white. As I start to raise my hand tentatively in greeting, the face disappears.

Mike links arms with me as we head to the car.

"Oh my gosh! I know I shouldn't get too excited, but I love it," I gush. "Oh please, we have to have it. It's just glorious!"

Mike laughs. "I knew you'd be like that," he says, pulling on his seat belt. "I like it too, very much. I just wonder a bit about them leaving so soon. A year is no time at all, really."

"Oh, Mike!" I'm frustrated. "Helen explained that. Stop looking for problems."

"Just being sensible." Mike pulls the car out of the drive and we both look back at the house.

"I know." I sigh. Mike is more cautious than me, but I don't want anything to stand in the way of us and this house.

"What if someone gets in first?" I fret.

"I'm surprised the house is so reasonably priced," Mike continues as if I haven't spoken. He taps the steering wheel. "I mean, this is prime Twickenham."

"Don't look a gift horse in the mouth," I snap. "They need to move quickly due to his job. Remember?"

"OK, OK! Look, I really like it too. We'll put an offer in — but not asking price, not yet."

I wring my hands. "But we might not get it. You said yourself how reasonably priced it is."

"Don't let the estate agent worry you. He's going to push for our best price. Let's discuss it at home."

The lights turn red, and Mike slows gradually to a halt. "Do you think there are any issues with the neighbours, though? Helen stumbled a bit when she spoke about the second one . . . Josie, I think she said her name was?"

I roll my eyes. "You don't half overthink things. She was nice about both Josie and the other neighbour, Mabel.

Anyway, you have to declare if you have a dispute with your neighbour when you're selling your house."

I sit back, pleased with myself. But there's something nagging at me, right in the back of my mind. "I think I saw Josie at the window," I murmur. "Just quickly, and then she was gone."

I pause.

"You don't think she was watching us, do you?"

CHAPTER 2

"Hello," says Mabel coolly, her voice crisp and clear.

I was expecting an elderly-looking woman, frail and vulnerable. Mabel is, however, anything but. She is tall and glamorous, with a ramrod-straight back. A razor-sharp silver bob frames her big, brown eyes and prominent cheek bones. She's wearing skinny jeans, a tight turtleneck jumper and her make-up is perfectly applied: scarlet lipstick, emerald-green eyeshadow and delicate pink blusher.

I clear my throat. "I'm so sorry to bother you, but my husband and I have put in an offer on the house next door. I just wanted to knock on a few doors and see what it's like to live here."

We put an offer in yesterday. I was desperate to offer asking price, but Mike was adamant that we should offer five per cent below, to allow room for negotiation. Sensible, practical Mike. Usually I love that about him, but now I could almost shake him.

Working from our cramped maisonette in Tooting, but unable to stop thinking about the house, I sneaked off for a few hours to take another look. My old university friend Layla lives in nearby Richmond and, as luck would have it, has a day off work. At Layla's suggestion, we decided to knock on one or two doors to do a little more digging.

We tried Josie's door first and, finding nobody at home, moved to the property on the other side. This time, the door opened immediately.

Mabel smiles, her severe, suspicious countenance fading a little. "Well, I've lived here for thirty years," she says decisively. "My daughter grew up here and I love it. There's a lovely family atmosphere. Do you have children?"

"Yes, my daughter's two — well, two and a half." Despite my initial anxiety, I'm now glad I took the plunge.

"Well, she'll love it round here." Mabel's chilly demeanour has largely vanished now. "There's so much for children to do. There are lovely parks, there's the river. Then we have Kew Gardens and Richmond on our doorstep."

"That's great to hear," I respond. "I love the feel of it around here." I feel that sense of excitement again, until I remember Mike's concerns about the current owners leaving so soon. I hesitate, wondering how best to tackle it.

"I guess it's a little surprising that Helen and her family are moving so quickly," I say in a rush.

Mabel's smile fades. "Is it?" she says thoughtfully.

"Well, they've only been here a year," I push on. "Helen says that it's because they're relocating for her husband's job."

"Ah yes, that's right, so they are." Mabel shrugs her shoulders. "Well, it's a shame, but what can they do? They're a nice family, that's for sure."

"They must be sad to leave such a lovely home." I cringe inwardly as I clumsily carry on the conversation. As far as Mabel is concerned, the matter is closed, but I want an answer.

Mabel steps back inside her house. "I have no idea," she adds firmly. Layla exchanges a quick glance with me.

"What's the lady on the other side of the house like?" she asks. I'm glad my friend is bold enough to ask, as I was ready to call it a day.

"You mean Josie?" Mabel stiffens. "I don't know her that well, if I'm honest. She has lived here for a while, though — over a decade."

Layla presses on. "Does she live on her own?"

Mabel draws her brows together. "She is — or was — married, but I believe there have been some issues. Look, it's really not my place to say. I must be going. I'm going to meet my friend for coffee shortly. Best of luck with the house."

Mabel starts to close the door. "It was lovely to meet you." The lightness of her tone feels at odds with her obvious earlier discomfort.

"Thanks ever so much," I say quickly. "Sorry to bother you, and I really appreciate it."

Layla nudges me as we retrace our steps, back down the drive.

"*Shhh*," I mutter. "Don't say anything yet, in case she hears." We turn away from the house.

"Well, her reactions were a bit odd — about both neighbours," says Layla. "What do you think?"

I consider. "I almost wish I hadn't knocked now."

We're briefly silent, and I'm lost in thought. "Now I'm worried about why Helen's leaving," I confide. "Mabel definitely didn't want to be asked, did she? I wonder if Helen really is leaving because of her husband's job. Maybe she's not happy in the house, or the area."

"Well, she was a bit evasive," says Layla. "But maybe she feels uncomfortable saying anything about the neighbours, particularly to complete strangers."

"You're right," I nod vigorously. "I shouldn't have asked. I'm not going to think about it anymore."

No need to tell Mike about my exchange with Mabel. He would only worry and start analysing the neighbour's motives. I want that house and a neighbour being slightly cagey isn't going to stand in my way.

"The other one, Josie, I'm actually less concerned about." I'm thinking aloud. "It sounds like she's having some issues in her marriage, that's all. Obviously very sad for her but nothing that should make us hesitate about buying this house." I stare at the house as we pass it. I still want it so much.

"It's very nice," says Layla, reading my thoughts. "Don't let that woman put you off."

She pauses suddenly and looks around. "I'm sure I recognise this street and the house, but I'm not sure from where. It's been niggling at me since we arrived."

"Maybe you've been to this street before," I suggest. "It's not inconceivable, is it? Since you live close by."

"Maybe." But Layla doesn't sound convinced.

We walk past Josie's house. The door is open, and a woman stands on the step. I recognise the same pale face I saw yesterday. Her hair is almost white and she's wearing a billowing blue dress. I halt and take a step towards the drive, wondering whether to introduce myself.

When I look again, the door is closed. I step back, surprised.

"Layla!" I exclaim, "Josie was at the door, but now she's gone. Did you see her?"

"No," says Layla. "I thought she was out. She must have come back. Shall we go and knock?"

I'm not altogether sure we would be welcome. That door closed swiftly.

"No, let's leave it. I don't even know if we'll get the house anyway."

I take my phone from my bag. Perhaps I've missed an update from the estate agent? I sigh as the blank screen stares back at me.

CHAPTER 3

"Me not want to go to bed." Poppy frowns and flings a teddy angrily into the corner of her bedroom. I sigh and sink to my knees.

To say Poppy is difficult at bedtime would be an understatement. I've managed to undress my daughter, coax her into the bath, wash her, persuade her to climb out of the bath and into her pyjamas. I'm exhausted. As Mike doesn't usually return home from work until at least seven o'clock, this job always falls to me.

"Come on, darling." I try to adopt a soothing tone. "Let's get you some milk, and then Mummy will lie down with you and read stories."

"No!" shouts Poppy. She hurls her beloved cuddly dog towards the bedroom door.

I hate this part of the evening. The Graveyard Shift, I've taken to calling it. It's not Mike's fault, of course, but I can't help feeling a little irritated with him when Poppy behaves like this. Couldn't he ask his boss for more flexible hours?

It feels worse tonight too. Ever since Mike submitted our first offer for the house, I've been on tenterhooks. And since then, nothing.

I hear the sound of a key turning in the lock. *Mike! Thank Goodness. Now he can damn well help me out with Poppy.*

"Thank God you're back!" I rush to him. "Poppy is being a nightmare."

Mike has a funny look on his face. He places his rucksack carefully on the floor.

"They got back to me," he says slowly. "They want asking price. There's a lot of interest, the estate agent says. But then again, they would say that."

Poppy screams but I ignore it. I clutch Mike around the neck, whispering, "Oh, please let's offer asking price and get it done! I want it so much. I walked past it again today with Layla and, oh my gosh, we'd be so happy there. Please!"

Mike has that cautious look on his face again. Usually I like his sensible side, but this time, I just want to slap him. If we lose this house, it will feel like a boyfriend breaking up with me. The emptiness of a broken heart. *Pull yourself together.* I give myself a shake.

To my surprise, Mike's shoulders relax. "Look," he begins, taking a deep breath. I know how much the house means to you. And I want it too, I really do.

"I love the house. It's a reasonable price, and it would be perfect for our family." Another pause.

"I agree." Mike pulls out his phone. "I'll call the estate agent now."

I fling my arms around his neck. "Oh Mike! I'm so glad!"

"Me want cuddle." Poppy clutches at Mike's legs. I feel guilty. In all the excitement I've forgotten that Poppy is still not in bed. "Me want Daddy," she moans.

"Is it too late to call?" I fret. "It's gone seven."

Mike bends down and swings Poppy into his arms. She beams and clings to his neck. "No," he says. "I've been dealing with Tom on his mobile, so he'll have it on him. Do you want to call? I'll get Poppy to bed."

"OK." I'm relieved that Mike is taking over the Graveyard Shift. I am, however, nervous about speaking to Tom.

"He's in my call list — 'Tom estate agent'."

"Night, darling." I bend to kiss Poppy but she's already turned away, wrapped in Mike's arms. A proper daddy's girl.

I go into the living room and close the door. My heart skips a beat as I press *call*.

I'm so nervous I almost don't want him to pick up, but he does so after three rings. "Hello?"

"Hi there, this is Clara, Mike's wife. I know you've been dealing with Mike." My voice trembles slightly. I shake my head crossly. For goodness' sake, I interview CEOs of global companies in my job as editor of a shipping magazine. Surely I can manage to speak to an estate agent? *It's just, I want this house so much.*

"We've been dealing with you about number five, Lunn Road." I take a deep breath. "We'd like to offer asking price for the property."

"OK, great." Tom sounds businesslike. "I'll speak to the sellers and come back to you as soon as possible."

"Thanks. Bye!" I squeak. I pace around the living room. *As soon as possible* . . . What the hell did that mean? In an hour? Two? Tomorrow? And if this offer is rejected, how will I persuade Mike to go above asking price?

"OK, Poppy's down." Mike opens the door with a triumphant grin. "Have you called?"

"Yep. And he says he'll get back to us as soon as possible." I hand Mike's phone back. "I'm so nervous! It's likely to be tomorrow, isn't it?"

"Let's see." Mike is calm. I like his composed demeanour. It works well with my nervous energy.

I've been with Mike for ten years, since I was twenty-five. We met at a press function. Mike is a shipping analyst, and we bonded over container ship volumes, trade lanes and freight rate predications, before realising that we shared more than the maritime world in common. We both lived in Balham, London. Our families even live just a few miles apart in Surrey.

Our relationship took the usual course — dating, moving into a rented one-bed flat in London, before deciding we wanted to get our foot on the property ladder and moving slightly further out to Tooting Broadway.

Then came engagement, marriage and Poppy, our blonde-haired, blue-eyed toddler, whose cherubic looks hide a forceful personality.

"After all this, I think we can both do with a drink," Mike says. "Glass of wine?"

"Yes, please." I fiddle with the TV remote and decide to distract myself with the news.

I hear Mike's phone ring and jump up — could it be Tom, but surely not so soon? I strain to hear.

Suddenly, Mike is back in the room. He beams from ear to ear. "Offer accepted."

I fling my arms round him and we're hugging and laughing and smiling.

"This calls for champagne," Mike declares.

CHAPTER 4

I watch as the men unpack our furniture into our new house.

"We own a house!" I breathe to Mike. "I can't believe it."

Poppy proudly scoots her mini suitcase along and grabs our legs.

"Fam'ly hug!" she shouts. Mikes slips his arm round me and the three of us cling together.

I cannot believe that this is our home now. I stare at it, sniffing appreciatively at the honeysuckle round the door, enjoying the dappled sunlight through the rowan tree's huge branches.

"Let's go in," I say. "I can't wait to see it again."

"Let me get some of our suitcases from the car," Mike says. "You take Poppy in, show her her new bedroom."

"My bedroom!" screams Poppy excitedly, her chubby legs gathering speed as she hauls her suitcase behind her to the house.

"The most important room," I smile.

Even though Poppy is only two and a half, I'm a little anxious about how the move will affect her. She's been living in our Tooting flat since birth, and loves her nursery.

To help her with the transition, we've been making a big deal about her lovely new bedroom decked out in pink — Poppy's favourite colour.

As we run up the stairs, I remember Poppy's room is on the right. I fling the door open.

Without all the furniture in it, the room looks a little bleak and lost, but I expect that. I remember how desolate our flat had seemed when we arrived, but that it took us next to no time to make it feel like home.

Poppy cries with delight at the pale pink walls, then points. "Mummy, what's that?"

I look and gasp. Bright blue felt tip has been scrawled all over the wall next to the wardrobe. It covers a huge area and I'm certain it wasn't there when I first viewed the house. Then at once I remember: there was a bookcase in that spot, which would have hidden the scribbling. A tall, imposing bookcase, with all the books neatly aligned. What a contrast, I thought ruefully, with Poppy's — a haphazard affair to say the least.

I feel a sudden surge of anger. Who would leave a wall in that state? It's bang out of order. Couldn't Helen have painted over it, for goodness' sake? Poppy isn't thrilled either. "Mummy! It's not pink. Me want pink walls!"

"Oh darling, it'll be the little girl who used to sleep in this bedroom! She's only a baby," I improvise. Then again, I did ask the estate agent the ages of the three children who lived here. How old had the youngest been? Five? Too old to be turning the wallpaper into a Banksy piece, that's for sure.

Poppy roars and flings herself on the floor. "Get it off my wall! Get it off!"

I sigh. I hate doing this but sometimes it's necessary. I pull an Oreo out of my handbag. "Come on, sweet, have a biscuit and calm down," I coax. "I promise that Daddy and I will get it off of the wall as soon as we can."

Poppy's screams subside to a whimper and she takes the biscuit, biting into it.

I hug her. "And just look at your gorgeous room, it's huge and so pink. We've got a special new pink duvet for your bed as well, just wait until we show you."

Poppy allows herself to be cheered up and a small smile forms on her lips. "Pink," she breathes.

"Excuse me!" shouts Rich, one of the removal men.

"Hang on," I call. I haul Poppy to her feet. "Come on, Poppy, we need to go downstairs to help the removal men."

But Poppy buries her feet hard into the carpet. "Me stay here," she pouts, with a spray of crumbs.

I hesitate, then shrug. I'll only be a minute and it will give Poppy a chance to become more comfortable with her new bedroom.

"I'll be right back." I dash down the stairs.

Rich is standing in the hallway with our coffee table. "Where's this go, please?"

"Um, living room." This is my favourite room and I can't resist a peek before dashing back to Poppy. It's so cosy, with the open fire and window seat. I can't wait to curl up on it and gaze out of the window at the swaying green branches of the rowan tree.

Taking a closer look at the parquet floor, I step back, startled. It's caked in dry mud, with leaves dotted here and there.

"Honestly!" I mutter irritably to myself. *Did the removal men really have to make all this mess? Did they really . . . ?* My train of thought is interrupted when I notice the room is bare. The removal men haven't even been in here yet.

Helen's family, then. First the mess on the wall, and now this. I grit my teeth, trying to stay calm. Mike and I cleaned our old place from top to bottom just this morning.

"Whereabouts?" Rich plods in holding the coffee table. I wave my hand to near the middle of the room.

"Around there. Thank you."

He plonks it down and thuds out. I notice that his boots don't leave a mark on the floor.

"Poppy!" I had better get back to her. I dash up the stairs and into her room. The blue marker pen sticks out like a sore thumb, burning into the wall.

But Poppy is not there. Nor is she hiding in the wardrobe. She must be exploring. *Better find her.*

"Mummy!" squeals Poppy. And there is my daughter, halfway up a ladder leading into the loft. The ladder has been left down and the loft hatch open.

I gasp, and stepping on the first ladder rung, manage to grab Poppy and pull her down.

"Goodness, Poppy, that's dangerous!" I snap. But it's not my inquisitive toddler's fault. It looks like another careless mistake. Having emptied the loft, they obviously forgot to close it. I tut loudly. *What the hell is going on?*

"Come on, love, let's go and find Daddy," I coax.

Poppy dances downstairs, holding my hand.

Two of Rich's colleagues are edging into the hall heaving Poppy's bed.

Anticipating their question, I say, "In the room to the right." *The one with the blue scribble on the wall*, I want to add.

Turning right, I pull Poppy towards the kitchen diner/family room. I can't wait to take it all in again. Wow! From our telephone box of a kitchen to this.

"Hello," I beam as I see Mike. With all this to look forward to, I can't feel angry for long.

But Mike doesn't return my smile. He's staring at the inbuilt black hob, frowning.

"Daddy! Cuddle!" Poppy leaps into his arms but Mike is distracted.

Mike points at the hob. There's a large crack in the glass. I see red. This is the final straw.

"Oh my God!" I slam my hand down on the worktop. "This is not acceptable."

Mike presses the controls and all the circles light up. He forces a smile. "At least it still works."

"It looks horrible," I say. Poppy shuffles down from Mike's arms and scoots off to explore the rest of the kitchen.

"And Mike, this isn't the only thing." I barely know where to start. "There's felt tip scribbled over a substantial chunk of Poppy's bedroom's wall. There was definitely a bookcase there before — they probably positioned it there to cover the marks. I'm really upset. It looks so unsightly. When I went back upstairs to check on Poppy, I found her halfway up the ladder leading to the loft. The living room floor was covered in mud — and no, it wasn't from the removal men's boots."

"Right!" Mike looks grim. "We're going straight to the solicitor. You're obliged to leave the house in a decent condition, and they clearly haven't. They'll need to pay to fix this hob, or else replace it. And I want them to pay the decorating costs for Poppy's room."

I grip his arm gratefully. Usually, I don't like to kick up a fuss, but in this instance I feel it's warranted, and I'm glad that Mike is a doer. On my own, I probably would have just stewed over it, rather than acted.

Rich appears in the doorway. "We're almost finished." He rubs a sweaty hand across his face. "Just a few more bits and pieces . . ."

Mike directs Rich on where the last pieces of furniture are to go. I glance around the room, suspicious about any more defects, and spot an envelope addressed to me and Mike on the worktop by the sink.

I open it and read:

Dear Clara and Mike,

Welcome to your new home! We really hope you'll be happy here. While we've only been here a year, we've loved it. A few pointers: Bins on Tuesdays. Recycling, food and green waste, and then general rubbish, alternate weeks. If you need a cleaner, try Kathy on the number below. She's cleaned for us weekly since we moved and is brilliant. And finally, please enjoy the token that we've left and use it to raise a glass to a truly happy family home.

With best wishes, Helen, Jim and family.

The letter seems at odds with how Helen and Jim have left the place. It seems a little cheeky, to be honest. Still, nice to be left something. I guess Helen means a bottle of fizz. Yet there's nothing on the worktop, nor in the cupboards. Well, that seems a bit rich — offering us a present and then not bothering to leave it.

Still, it seems to sum up Helen's personality. *Careless and slapdash*, I think primly. She probably meant to leave it and forgot.

Mike comes back. I wave the note at him. "Take a look at this."

He scans it. "We're still going to get them to pay out for the stove and the wall," he says.

"Absolutely." I don't miss a beat. "I just thought it was a bit of a cheek. Plus — where is this 'token' they've left for us?"

Mike rereads the letter and takes a look about. "Most likely forgot," he shrugs. "We've got our own bubbly anyway. We don't need theirs."

Poppy is singing and skidding over the wooden floor. I'm relieved she seems happy. I catch sight of the crack on the hob and turn away.

"Right, the men are gone," Mike says. "Let's see this mark on Poppy's wall, then." My heart sinks a little. Maybe I shouldn't have made such a big deal about it. I don't want it to cloud what is meant to be a turning point for us.

I link arms with him. "Come on, Pops, let's show Daddy your lovely new bedroom."

Poppy gives a little scream then frowns. "Those horrible marks on my wall!" she wails.

We go upstairs and enter Poppy's room. Poppy makes a beeline for the wall and waves her hand around.

Mike shakes his head. "Yeah, they're paying," he says.

"Come on," I say. "Please, let's try and look at the good things too. Let's look round the top floor. I haven't seen it properly yet."

We move to what will be our bedroom. Our double bed looks too small for the room. Time for a king size, perhaps? We peer into one of the spare rooms. The afternoon sun floods the room and I smile. This will be the bedroom for our second child. If we're lucky enough to have one.

"What's that noise?" Mike tilts his head.

It's coming from the bathroom. We head there. I look approvingly at the traditional roll-top slipper bath, and then see the leaking tap.

Drip, drip, drip. Relentless. Poppy dips her fingers underneath and sucks the water. *Drip, drip, drip.*

"Oh, for God's sake," Mike rolls his eyes. "We might have to get a plumber in. Happy bloody new home."

* * *

I pour the champagne into my glass. It fizzes over the top and I catch it with my fingers and suck. It's been a long time since I've had champagne. After all, what have I had to celebrate? But how could I help myself? The bottle was there, on the gleaming worktop, next to the note. No doubt full of syrupy praise for the house. It took only a moment to swipe it and stick it in my bag. Anyway, maybe I do have something to celebrate now. I enjoyed today. I had fun sprinkling the dried mud and carefully picked rowan leaves on the living room floor. I felt like a kid again when I scrawled in felt tip in the pink bedroom. I'd definitely done it as a youngster. I remember Mum and Dad telling me off. Like they always did. And I enjoyed poking about the loft. Damaging the cooker had taken more effort. I smashed my bottle of olive oil over it. Result. But then it took me a while to clear up the greasy liquid. I thought that it would have been a step too far to leave it. I raise my glass. "To new beginnings," I say aloud. "For them and for me."

CHAPTER 5

We clink glasses, surrounded by boxes. The remains of a fish-and-chip supper lie on the coffee table in front of us. Poppy has finally gone to sleep.

"To new beginnings," says Mike. I'm glad to see the stern creases around his eyes have eased. He has already fired off an email to our conveyancing solicitor to complain about the hob and the wall. That seems to have calmed him. And the dripping tap has stopped — for now. I cross my fingers.

Despite the hiccups we've encountered, I'm so happy to be in this house.

"I hope our new beginnings include a new addition to our family soon," I murmur.

"Me too." Mike squeezes my hand briefly.

"In fact, tonight is a good time to try," I say, gazing at him meaningfully. I hadn't wanted to take the risk — as blunt as the phrase sounded — in our old flat. What if our move had fallen through and we had been stuck in a small flat with two children? But as soon as our completion date was in the diary, I had sprung into action. Folic acid, vitamins and ovulation kits. All systems go.

Mike sighs. "I'm so tired," he groans. "We've got loads of time to get going. Do you mind if we give it a miss tonight? I honestly think I'll have to go to bed really soon, and I'll be fast asleep as soon as soon as my head hits the pillow."

A spark of irritation flashes through me but I try to ignore it. Of course he's tired. I need to calm down.

"Of course," I say. "I'm just eager to get going but I totally understand."

Mike stifles a yawn.

"So, you're still pleased we moved?" I ask. "Despite the hob and all the rest of it?"

"Of course," Mike replies instantly. "I mean, the stuff with Helen and her husband . . . it's really annoying, but it's one of those things. We'll get things sorted and it'll all soon be forgotten."

I give his shoulder a squeeze and inch closer towards him. "I think we'll be really happy here." I smile.

* * *

I trudge toward the front door and sigh. Even though it's barely midday, I'm exhausted. It's our first full day in our new house and there's still so much to do. Will we ever finish unpacking these bloody boxes? With Poppy at the local nursery for a settling session, we should finally be able to make some progress.

"I'm back!" I call, dumping my coat over the banister. We haven't put up our coat hooks yet.

"Just in the kitchen putting crockery away," Mike shouts back.

I'm about to join him when the sound of the doorbell stops me in my tracks. I sigh. *Who is it?*

I open the door, and a woman returns my gaze. Her shoulder-length hair is so blonde it's almost white. Big pale blue eyes. Skin almost translucent. I recognise her. *The woman next door.*

"Hi, I'm Josie Sanders. I live next door. Number three." Her voice is low and quiet. She smiles slowly.

I'm about to say *I know* but stop myself.

"Come in!" I adopt a welcoming tone. "I'm Clara. It's nice to meet you."

Josie steps in. With her petite frame and that pale skin, she almost resembles a China doll. She wears a floaty green dress that almost drowns her.

Josie proffers a Tupperware box. "I've made you some banana bread and cupcakes for your little one." Her voice is so quiet that I strain to hear.

"Mmmm, delicious," I gush. "Thank you so much." I take the Tupperware box, my heart sinking. I've always struggled with my weight. My mouth waters. I'll have to get Mike to hide the banana bread.

"Poppy will love these cakes!" I exclaim.

"That's a pretty name," says Josie. "How old is she?"

"Two . . . oh Mike, meet Josie. She lives next door and has kindly brought us some homemade goodies."

Mike appears in the hall. He bounds over to shake Josie's hand. Josie smiles at him shyly. A pretty dimple appears in one cheek. Mike appears to find it attractive as he stares at it, his hand still grasping Josie's.

I'm starting to inwardly bridle when Mike quickly drops Josie's hand, looking awkward.

"Is your daughter here?" she asks Mike.

"No, she's at her nursery settling-in session," I answer curtly.

"Oh." Josie's face falls. "I'd been hoping to meet her."

"Would you like a coffee?" I hope Josie says no. Mike and I desperately need to crack on with unpacking.

Josie hesitates. "If it's not too much trouble."

* * *

Sipping coffee in the living room, I eye Josie. There is a large single sapphire on her ring finger, and a wedding band underneath it. I wonder how I can ask Josie about her life without seeming too nosy.

"It's a shame I missed Poppy," Josie says again. "I really want to meet her. I love children."

Feeling unsettled but unable to work out quite why, I change the subject. "We're so happy to move here," I begin. "After our small flat in London, all this space is wonderful."

Josie smiles thinly. "It must be."

"So . . . how long have you lived here?" I press on.

"Twelve years." A long pause. "My husband inherited some money at a relatively young age, so we moved here when I was twenty-three. I guess we were young to move to a house such as this. We skipped the starter home."

Josie must be thirty-five. My age. I wonder if she has children, as unlikely as it feels.

"Did you know Helen well?" I ask.

"Not really. She didn't seem interested in getting to know the neighbours." Josie ponders. "But of course, she was very busy with three children and a full-time job," she adds quickly.

"She left after only a year," I continue to probe.

"Yes."

"I guess that they had no choice, with Helen's husband's new job in the Midlands."

"Yes."

No use. *If she won't open up*, I think crossly, *let's get rid of her*. Time to drop a rather heavy hint.

"Gosh, we have so much to be getting on with. So many boxes still to unpack!"

Lost in thought, Josie seems not to hear me. "I bet Poppy likes her new pink bedroom," she murmurs.

"How do you know that's Poppy's room?" The words are out before I even realise I've spoken.

Josie smiles.

"Well, it was Amy's room — that's Helen's youngest daughter — so I gathered that was probably the room that Poppy would have."

Fair enough. But there was that uncomfortable feeling again, an unpleasant fizzing sensation in my chest.

I resolve to let it go. "You must have been round to see Helen a few times, then?"

"Of course! We were neighbours."

"I thought that . . ." I stop. That was an about-turn. Josie said just a few minutes ago she didn't know Helen well, because Helen wasn't interested in getting to know the neighbours. I shake my head. I'm being too pedantic. That's the problem being a journalist. I pick up on the slightest thing.

I drain the rest of my coffee and Josie appears to take her cue.

"I must be getting on. If you ever want someone to babysit Poppy, I'd be more than happy. I bet you don't get out much, with a little one, and I love children."

I don't want you babysitting Poppy, I say to myself as we wave her goodbye. Mike's cheery tone halts my train of thought.

"How nice she offered to babysit. We must take her up on that."

I open my mouth and close it slowly. Now isn't the right time to say anything, but I'm uncomfortable with the idea of Josie being alone with Poppy.

"I find her odd," I choose my words carefully. "Like a closed book. Monosyllabic answers. Why come over if you don't want to chat?"

"I thought she was pleasant," Mike says distractedly.

I noticed. Aloud I falter, "Yeah, but . . ."

I'm unsure how to explain my unease over seemingly inconsequential details. Before I can ponder further, Mike breaks the bad news.

"So, the solicitor got back to my email about the damage." Mike's voice is even but still I can sense his anger rising. "Helen and her husband are adamant that they did not leave scribbles on the wall or crack the hob."

He slams his fist down angrily on the hall side table.

"What?" My heart sinks. "But they must be lying."

"Exactly," says Mike. "How could they miss that scribble on the wall — it's the first thing you notice when you walk in. And the crack in the cooker! It wasn't us, and the removal men didn't touch it."

"Look, if it's going to get nasty, I don't think it's worth pursuing." I'm surprised at how calm I feel. Perhaps I'm just glad to have my mind taken away from Josie. "It's annoying, but maybe it's quicker and easier if we sort it out ourselves."

Mike has other ideas. "It's the principle of the matter," he snaps. "I don't want them getting away with it. Luckily our solicitor agrees, and he's going to go back to their solicitor hard."

I sigh. I need to leave in fifteen minutes to collect Poppy. Running upstairs, I grab handfuls of Poppy's tops and shove them haphazardly in a drawer.

The doorbell rings. *What now?*

Mabel stands there, ramrod straight. A tight jumper shows off her sinewy frame. In one hand is a bunch of daffodils.

"Oh. Hi, Mabel. Thank you," I stutter as Mabel thrusts the flowers at me. She makes me feel nervous and clumsy.

"I won't stay," Mabel replies immediately. "I just wanted to give you the flowers and a card. I hope you'll be happy."

"Thank you so much," I say, but Mabel is already heading down the path. Flinging the flowers down on the hall table, I rip open the envelope.

On the card, a bouquet of flowers frames the backdrop to a house. I scan the message. A generic "Good luck in your new home." Then "Here's to happier times. Best wishes, Mabel."

I stare at it. "Happier times"? What on Earth does she mean? My heart sinks. Do I even want to know? It's an odd thing to write. I open my mouth to call Mike and show him the card, then think better of it.

I toss the card on top of the flowers. It slides to the floor.

Mabel is elderly and probably a bit confused.

It will be that. She wrote the wrong thing. She must have meant "happy". I exhale, grab my car keys and open the front door.

Mabel's card lies face down on the floor.

CHAPTER 6

"What the . . . ?" I jump from my chair. The lights have gone out. It's 4.45 p.m. and, as this is mid-January, the house has been plunged into darkness.

In my makeshift office in one of the spare bedrooms, I was on a Zoom call with my managing editor, Jake, to discuss a redesign of the magazine.

"What's going on? I can't see you," says Jake irritably.

"Sorry, I think I've blown a fuse. All the lights have gone out," I reply swiftly. "Can you give me five minutes to get to the fuse box?"

"OK," says Jake. "I hope you can sort this quickly. We have quite a bit to get through."

I grab my phone and switch on its torch. Even in midwinter, I can't believe how dark it is.

I'm approaching the stairs when I hear a bang above the ceiling. And another. *Thud, thud.* A third. *Thud.* My heart is racing now. I glance at the loft hatch. Firmly closed.

Another bang. *Keep calm, for God's sake!* Bats? Too loud for mice, that's for sure. One of my friends had once found a squirrel in her loft. *Please not rats.*

The fuse box is in the garage — or at least I think it is. More in hope than expectation, I flick the light switch but nothing happens. Shining the torch, I locate the box on the wall in the corner and turn that switch too. Nothing. I want to scream. It really is pitch black in the garage, despite the glow on my phone. *Thump, thump, thump, thump.* There goes my heart.

Deep breath. Turn off the whole fuse box and try again, I tell myself. That's what IT workers always advise for a computer that doesn't work. *Reboot.* I flick the switch on again. Nothing.

I think I hear another thump up high in the house. *Ignore, ignore, ignore.*

I call Jake, who sounds grumpy but agrees to reschedule our meeting for the following day, and hurry into the street. My heart sinks when I see the lights are on in Josie's living room. No power cut in the area, then. What is it with this bloody house? I'm already preparing myself for Mike to lose his rag.

As I turn to walk back indoors, I catch something moving from the corner of my eye. Behind the half-open shutters at number three, a ghostly face peers into the street. Josie.

Why is she looking out of her window?

When I look again, the face has gone. I feel that unpleasant fizzing sensation in my chest again. Why does this woman unsettle me so much?

"Everything OK?" I'm surprised to see Josie standing only six feet away from me. She had been at her window only seconds earlier, but now . . .

"All our lights have gone out," I reply brusquely. I tap my watch, stressed. "I thought it was a neighbourhood power cut, but obviously not. And I have no idea what's wrong."

"Oh dear, that's annoying," Josie sighs. "I have the number of a really good electrician that we use. Would you like it?"

"Yes, please. Thank you." My annoyance turns to gratitude. I wonder if Josie is going to ask me in while she seeks out the number. I hope so. It's nosey but I'd like to see what Josie's house is like. There appears to be no sign of a husband. But no: Josie pulls out her phone.

"Here we go — Keith," she says. "What's your number and I'll WhatsApp it."

I hesitate. I don't know if I want Josie to know my number. *Why don't I want that?*

"Do you mind just reading it aloud and I'll tap it into my phone? Sorry, I sometimes have a few problems receiving messages from unknown numbers."

"Sure," says Josie. I thank her and walk back into my dark, silent home. I hear the drip of the leaking tap in the bathroom. It makes me feel even jumpier.

I give myself a mental shake. I'm thirty-five, not five. What on Earth do I think is in the loft? Ghosts? I tut at my unchained imagination. As I do, there it is! A faint rumbling noise like an underground train passing below. The house is bathed in light once more.

I blink at the contrast. *Phew.*

Time to collect Poppy. I slip on my shoes and reach for my bag — then stop in my tracks. There is another scuffling sound in the loft. I frown. Maybe we need to call pest control.

***

Mike finally comes down the stairs. It has taken a long time to settle Poppy. Even now, I can hear her singing.

Mike shrugs. "She seems happy enough, so I took my chance to escape."

"Good. Look, shall we get a takeaway tonight? I can't be bothered to cook and I'm sure you can't after a busy day."

"Good idea."

I pull up the local Indian takeaway menu on my phone, as Mike says: "By the way, good news. Our solicitor got back in touch and Helen and Jim have agreed to pay for the cooker top and the wall. Apparently they're still adamant they're not responsible. But still, they've agreed to it."

I'm relieved Helen has finally given in, more to appease my husband than anything else. He's smiling now. I haven't seen that for a while. I'm going to have to burst the bubble.

"I had quite a shock today." I take the plunge, the words tumbling from me. "All the lights went out in the house. I was on a Zoom call to Jake about the magazine redesign. He was pretty annoyed."

Mike's face darkens instantly. "Not another thing," he sighs. "And we still have to sort out that dripping tap too." He makes to bang his fist on the arm of the chair but stops himself just in time.

I'm unnerved at how quick his temper has come. A couple of months ago, something like this would have barely registered. Now it looks like it's ruining his evening.

"Luckily, everything came back on again after about half an hour, so I'm hoping it's just a one-off glitch." I try to sound reassuring. "Josie gave me the number of an electrician. If it happens again, we can ring him."

"That's very nice of her. She seems a good neighbour."

"Yes." There it is: that sense of unease in my chest once more. *Why?* I can't put my finger on it. I dive in again.

"The other thing is, I heard thuds in the loft, like something moving about. I think we need to call pest control."

Mike harrumphs. "Tell me why we bought this house again?"

I turn to him, smiling, and expecting that familiar grin in return. Instead, Mike doubles down. "And which of us wouldn't take no for an answer, because she 'just had to have it'?"

Before I can reply, Mike is striding away from me towards the front door.

I stay put, waiting for it to slam.

* * *

Tap, tap, tap. What now? I never used to mind having visitors, even when I was working from home. Now all they seem to bring are stress and problems.

I've just finished a Zoom call with Jake and am feeling happier than I have for weeks. Not only is Jake delighted with my ideas for the magazine redesign, but he's also encouraged me to apply for the position of deputy managing editor.

A promotion and a pay rise! What's not to like? Something to take the edge of our increased mortgage payments. I'd been about to text Mike the good news when I was interrupted.

Tap, tap, tap. Yes, definitely someone at the door. Maybe the doorbell isn't working. I smile bitterly. *Add it to the bloody list.*

Josie. Again. With her hair scraped back, she looks paler than ever. Prominent cheekbones and milky complexion. Petite figure enveloped by a flowing red dress. Bangles on her tiny wrists.

I try to hide a grimace with a wide smile. I go to say something, then check myself. *Let Josie speak first.*

Josie gives that shy half-smile that I've come to expect. "I just thought I would pop by and see if you fancied a coffee," she says softly. "I know you work from home and figured you could do with some company."

I frown. *How does she know I work from home?*

* * *

Click. Josie closes the door behind her. The sound of her footsteps fades. I take a deep breath and lean against a wall, trying to come to terms with what has just happened.

The mask slipped, all right. Wrapping her hands around her coffee mug, and completely unprompted, Josie laid bare her soul.

She and her husband — his name is Steve — are on a trial separation. They had been desperate to start a family. Yet, try as they might, they could not. Five rounds of IVF. One miscarriage. "All for nothing," Josie said, her tone even.

But that wasn't all. "I can't give Steve a baby. So, he doesn't know if he can still be with me."

Hoping to comfort her, I placed a hand on Josie's shoulder — and was shocked at the reaction. Josie's features, usually so impassive, twisted into a snarl. She shoved my arm so hard that I staggered backwards.

"I'm dealing with it!" she hissed. Just thinking about it again makes my breathing quicken a little. My hands are still shaking.

Even more extraordinary was that the moment passed in a flash. The snarl gone; the even tone restored. Not even an apology. It was as though Josie herself didn't realise what had happened. As though she'd momentarily lost control of her senses. She thanked me for the coffee, offered again to babysit Poppy (*Is she for real?*) and left.

Woman desperate for child takes off with neighbour's daughter.

I laugh out loud, my tension easing. Honestly! I've been a journalist for too long. Though Josie has alarmed me, I'm prepared to give her the benefit of the doubt. IVF, miscarriage, no baby, husband leaving. No wonder Josie told me that she's been signed off with stress from her job in a PR company, I reflect. What strain she must be under. *Wouldn't we all act a bit oddly under those circumstances?*

I resolve to forget about it. Right, back to work. I sit again at my desk. The afternoon brightness has disappeared from the late winter sky. I get up to switch on the light. Nothing happens. I try a couple more switches. No use. "FOR GOD'S SAKE!" My anger gets the better of me.

I grab my mobile and call Keith the electrician.

"OK, fine, I'll be round tomorrow afternoon," he says.

Relieved, I hang up. I check my watch and at that moment, the light returns. At the same time as yesterday. Almost to the second.

Almost like someone has planned it.
Don't be ridiculous. I give herself a shake.

* * *

"It's a bit of a pain for sure." I've just finished telling Mike about the latest mishap with the lights. "But I'm sure the electrician will sort it out tomorrow."

I'm relieved that he doesn't seem too dismayed by it.

"Poppy is, amazingly, asleep," I say. "So, at least that's good. Nursery must have tired her out."

Mike is holding a bottle of prosecco. "Great! Now we can get stuck in," he smiles.

I suspect it's Mike's way of apologising for storming off the previous night, though he insists it was simply an impulse buy. I know Mike doesn't really do spontaneity, but I decide to play along nonetheless.

We are settled in the living room clutching glasses when I tell Mike about Josie. "I must admit, I didn't warm to her, but how awful that her husband left her because she can't have children."

"We don't know the whole story," says Mike, then seeing my expression, adds quickly: "It is awful, though."

"I just don't know what it is about her," I say. "She's offered to babysit again, but I don't want her to. I'm not sure why, it's like I have this reflex reaction."

Mike sighs. "She seems perfectly pleasant. And I would love to go out to dinner one evening, child-free."

My thoughts change direction. "I heard noises in the loft again today. Please can we get someone in to sort it out? Do you mind doing it? As I've arranged the electrician."

"I haven't heard anything up there," Mike says. "But obviously you're here more than me. I'll find a pest control firm tomorrow."

CHAPTER 7

The cries echo around the house and jolt me awake. I open my eyes wearily. Mike snores quietly beside me. *Typical.* He sleeps through Poppy's night awakenings the majority of the time.

Poppy screams louder and higher, catapulting me out of bed. I dash into her bedroom and find her crouched on the bed.

"Go away!" she shrieks, pointing to the corner of the room. I look. Nothing there. I suspect she's half asleep.

I gently touch her arm. "Shhh, darling, come on, calm down." I place my daughter's elephant night light on the pillow next to her. She slaps it away.

"Tell her to go away!" she shouts, gesticulating at the bedroom corner. I try to snuggle down with her. I sigh as my limbs rub against the narrow angles of the child bed. But Poppy lashes out, pushing me.

"Light on, light on, light on," she moans.

I hesitate. The bright light will wake her, but I must do something to soothe her. To my relief, it seems to do the trick. Poppy is calmer now, though still pointing at the corner of the room.

"Milk! Milk!" she wails — though when Poppy is half asleep the word sounds more like "murg" or even "mugger".

I rummage around for her sippy cup and rush downstairs to refill it.

Night terrors. I'm sure my mum told me I'd had them as well, and that they'd started when I was two. I must remember to ask her next time we speak.

Poppy grabs her sippy cup and I tiptoe away. Back in our bedroom, Mike is still sleeping like a log.

* * *

"Mummy!"

I heave myself out of bed with a sigh and pad back into Poppy's room. It's already 7 a.m. and Mike has gone to work.

"Milk!" she thunders.

"*Please.* Milk, *please*," I say more sharply than I intended. I remember the electrician is coming and my heart sinks. Much as I would like the problem fixed, I could do without the disruption.

Ruffling Poppy's blonde curls, I take the sippy cup. "You had a bad dream last night, sweetie," I say. "Do you remember?"

Poppy digs her fist into her eye and doesn't respond. I'm not sure whether she understands what a dream is yet.

"You thought there was someone in the room, over there." I point.

"There was a . . ." Poppy pauses. "A big girl in my room, Mummy." She pulls the duvet over her head. "She has no face." The words are muffled.

"What?" Unsure if I've heard correctly, I pull back the duvet. "What did you say, darling?" But Poppy just stares at me. I decide not to pursue it, not wanting to unsettle her further. I pick Poppy up and cuddle her, trying to dispel the disturbing image her words have evoked from my mind. "It was a bad dream, darling. That means in your sleep, you thought there was someone in the room. There was nobody here, I promise."

36

I'm surprised Poppy remembers her dream and wish I hadn't brought it up. Poppy clings to me.

Then: "Milk . . . *please*."

***

Keith the electrician cracks his knuckles. "It's odd," he says. "I can't see where the problem's coming from."

I sigh, irritated. The lights flicking off every day is a pain, and I had wanted it sorted out today. Now Keith is talking about a return visit, and not until next Tuesday.

"OK," I say, sounding shorter than I had intended. "No chance it could be sooner?"

"No, sorry," Keith moves to the door. "But we'll be round in the morning."

I open the door. "But isn't it strange it's happened at the same time each day, and the lights have come back on again at the same time?"

Keith shrugs. It looks like he's lost interest. "Coincidence," he says, grabbing his car keys. "See you next week."

I slam the door and stomp down the hall. While I love the house, I'm sick to death of these problems. Poppy's wall. The oven top. The lights. *Just another thing*. And Mike better have called pest control.

I run upstairs and settle in front of my laptop in the study. With a promotion on the table, I need to be on top of my game. I lose myself in my feature and then glance up quickly at the clock — I need to get Poppy from nursery. Five past five. I realise with a jolt that on the previous two days, the lights had gone off by now. At 4.45 p.m., to be precise.

Relieved, I grab my car keys. Maybe Keith was right. Just a coincidence.

***

Poppy clings to me. "Me want another story and milk," she says aggressively.

I feel like I'm going to explode. Tiredness. Frustration. Stress. It's well past 7 p.m. and I want to scream.

And when the doorbell rings, I nearly do.

"Fucking Hell!" I mutter. I'm surprised at myself. I rarely swear.

"Ducking Hell!" chortles Poppy. I cross my fingers that she doesn't repeat it at nursery.

I take a moment before opening the door. *Please not Josie.* "Who is it?" I call.

"Layla!"

I quickly pull open the door and eye my friend with concern. "What's happened?"

"Can I come in? It's freezing." An icy wind blows into the hall and Layla steps in, unravelling her scarf and peeling off her gloves. "Shall I take my shoes off?"

"Um . . ." I feel dismayed. I'm exhausted. Poppy isn't asleep yet and I don't want to hear about the latest episodes of Layla's love life. But I can hardly turn her away.

"Mummy!" Poppy roars. "Where are you? Come upstairs."

Layla quickly unzips her rucksack and hands a bottle of wine to me. "Here, have a glass and relax. I'll deal with Poppy."

Before I can reply, she has bounded upstairs. "Layla!" Poppy cries and gives a high-pitched giggle.

I shrug. If Layla is offering to handle it, who am I to argue? I pour two glasses. Maybe it isn't so bad after all that Layla has turned up.

"Asleep!" Layla announces, standing in the doorway of the living room.

"Wow, well done. You should come round more often," I say, sipping my wine appreciatively. "She's much better behaved for you than me."

I head to the kitchen. "Thanks for bringing the wine. Here's a glass for you. Is spag bol OK?"

"Oh, you don't have to cook for me," replies Layla, following me. "I was only dropping in."

But I'm starving and need to eat and can hardly just cook for myself with you here, I'd love to say, but do not. Sometimes Layla can be a little thoughtless.

I wave towards the island. "You sit on one of the stools so you can talk to me while I chop."

The next twenty minutes go exactly as I predicted. After plonking herself down with a heavy sigh, Layla plays all the old hits: bad dates, no luck, everyone married with kids while she is divorced and single. And so on. To make matters worse, Layla mentions that our mutual friend Rosie is expecting a second child.

In spite of myself, I feel bitter envy. Rosie has a daughter around the same age as Poppy. How I would love to be expecting a baby brother or sister for my little girl. *Bloody Rosie. Some people have all the luck.*

I try to tell myself not to be so uncharitable. *Stop feeling sorry for yourself.*

I look at Layla and smile. She really is a good friend. The least I can do is try to make her feel better, especially as Layla has been through a terrible time. She's currently going through a painful divorce after her husband Max left her for a work colleague.

"You're wonderful, Layla! You're a great person: witty, intelligent, lovely-looking. You're a catch. You will meet the man who deserves you. I know you will." I inject as much feeling into my voice as I can. I'm sincere and I want Layla to know it.

Layla smiles faintly. "Thanks."

I put the mince on to simmer and perch on the stool next to Layla.

"So, how are you settling in?" asks Layla.

I've secretly been dying for Layla to ask this. Layla is a couple of degrees removed from the situation and may be able to give a different perspective. I would also like someone to reassure me that I'm not going mad.

I dive in. Just talking about it makes me feel better. I tell Layla about the lights, the broken cooker, the scribbles on the wall and the noises in the loft. Eventually I come to the matter bothering me the most: Josie.

"Creepy!" I've been searching for the word that sums up Josie and settle on this. "She stares at me and barely says a word. She seems to know when I'm working from home, even though I've never mentioned anything about it. Despite claiming not to know the previous owner, she knew which bedroom was their daughter's."

I come to the crux of the matter. "She's so keen to babysit Poppy, and I don't know why, but I don't like it."

"That is unusual," agrees Layla. "She doesn't have children, does she? Has there been an issue there perhaps?"

"Yes, a big one, actually. She hasn't been able to have children and she and her husband have separated as a result."

Layla frowns, a dark cloud settling on her face. I've said too much.

"She must be devastated," she says finally, her eyes glistening.

I know what Layla is thinking. How dare I, with my husband, daughter and wonderful new home, be so thoughtless? I'm frustrated with myself. There's no point discussing Josie further.

"But if you don't want her babysitting, I'd be more than happy to." At least Layla has broken the ice. "And it's so easy now we're neighbours."

I perk up. "Now, that I would like, thank you."

"The other lady acted a bit strangely though," Layla muses. "Mabel, wasn't it? She was a bit secretive about this house. It made me wonder if there was more to Helen and her family leaving than meets the eye."

I walk over to the built-in shelves in the family part of the room and pluck out Mabel's moving in card.

"Read this." I hand it over to Layla.

"*Happier times*." Layla scans it again. "Not 'happy' but 'happier'. Very strange."

"Surely you wouldn't put something like that on purpose," I say. "I tell myself it's a mistake. She's getting on, you know. She might have memory problems."

"She seemed pretty switched on to me," Layla interjects.

"Thanks, Layla," I snap. "I'm trying not to go down a rabbit hole here."

"Sorry, sorry!" Layla holds up her hands. "I didn't like her when we spoke to her, she seemed cold and hard. Maybe she's trying to scare you, takes a pleasure in it. I'd ignore it."

"Well, I hope it's not that." I'm unsettled again. "I don't want two strange neighbours."

A key grinds in the lock in the front door. Mike. His cheeks are flushed, a sure sign he's had a drink or two. I'm glad. He needed to relax and let his hair down.

"Well, hello," Layla drawls. "Sorry, you weren't expecting me, were you? Now I'm a neighbour, I thought I'd drop by. Expect to see quite a bit more of me."

Mike moves over to hug her and claps her on the back. "Great," he says warmly. "And that reminds me. Now you're living so close, would you take a spare key for us? Just in case we lose ours or need you to pop round while we're away."

"Sure, no problem." Layla takes the key and stands up. "Well, I'd better get a move on. I need my bed."

After a flurry of hugs and goodbyes, she's gone.

"So, you had a good time?" I probe.

Mike smiles and gives my hand a squeeze. "Yes, it was nice to catch up with Clive. It's been a while, and I could forget about the issues with this house." He frowns slightly and smiles. "Joke! All fixable stuff."

He knows I get worked up easily. I brighten at his hand in mine, kissing him on the cheek.

"Let's cuddle up in bed," I murmur.

Mike pauses on the stairs. "Oh, love, not tonight. I'm exhausted," he says.

I grit my teeth. "But this is the right window for us to try to conceive," I say. "You were tired last time. We need to act now, or we'll need to wait another month."

"Last time, we had literally just moved in, of course I was tired," Mike retorts. He lets go of my hand and stomps up the stairs.

I screw up my face in frustration. As soon as the words are out, I regret it. Putting his back up like that and pressurising him is a passion killer.

I follow him into our bedroom. A soft snore emanates from Poppy's room.

"Tomorrow, then?" I cringe as I speak.

Mike rips off his socks. "Clara, please, can you drop it? We've had loads going on. I'm not full of the joys, if I'm honest."

There's a lump in my throat. We're meant to feel closer than ever, laying the foundations of our forever home. Instead, the few inches between us feel like a mile.

Mike is soon breathing heavily, yet try as I might, I cannot drift off. My heart pounds as I hear a creak in the loft. I stiffen. *Bloody mice or squirrels.*

There is a soft thud, then silence. Then the drumbeat of more thuds. *Bump, bump, bump.* It sounds like the footsteps of a person, walking across our loft. I want to scream. *Don't be stupid.*

Rats? I've always been terrified of them. In the dead of night, though, rats feel like the least of my worries.

* * *

Poppy reminds me so much of myself at that age. Feisty, bossy and loud. I loved seeing her strut with her mini suitcase when she moved in. I want to see more of her. It's probably not a good thing, as it sends me back to my past, to things I don't wish to remember. But maybe I do. Otherwise, why am I here? Poppy is not the only one. I'm drawn to Clara and Mike. Most of all, I'm drawn to this house. I can't seem to give it up. I wonder what my life would be like if I had this lovely, normal existence, full of opportunity, like Poppy has. I look at her mum, with her impressive job, lovely husband and wonderful daughter, and my life feels so barren in contrast. And then the jealousy grows, spreading through my whole body. My insides are on fire. Things are starting to get to Clara, though. I'm starting to peel away the layers of the house. Mark my words, it won't be long until I get all the way to its rotten core.

CHAPTER 8

Mike opens an eye and looks at me sheepishly. He squeezes my shoulder, remembering our argument. "Sorry," he murmurs.

I dreamed he left the house, piling luggage into his car as I begged him to stay. He pulls me to him and I cling on, the dream fading.

"I'm sorry too," I reply quietly, half listening out for Poppy's awakening cry.

"I shouldn't have snapped at you like that. I do want another child, I really do."

I snuggle up closer to him, my limbs relaxing. I hadn't realised that I've been holding myself so tightly. *Relief.* Hopefully I'll be in Rosie's position soon.

"I'm sorry about the problems we're having in the house. I feel bad, as I really pushed to move here."

"Don't be silly," Mike says instantly. "And I'm sorry I made such a big deal of them. People often get niggles in new houses, I'm sure. We'll get it all sorted."

I smile. He's right. The house is perfect for us, and the problems will soon be fixed.

A large rodent with big human feet plodding around the loft pops into my mind and I smile inside. My nerves were all on edge last night. No need to mention to Mike I thought it sounded like a person walking up there. I just hope that it *isn't* rats.

Mike stretches and pulls back the cover. "Speaking of which, the pest control firm are coming this afternoon."

Our cosy state of sleepy wakefulness is rudely interrupted by Poppy's war cry. "Mummmyyyy!"

I scrabble out of bed, pushing aside my drowsiness, and head to Poppy's bedroom, bending over her bed to cuddle her. She rubs her eyes sleepily. "Me like Layla. Can she come tonight?"

I laugh. I'm not at all averse to the idea. Layla worked wonders at getting Poppy to sleep.

"Of course, darling. Maybe not tonight though. But very soon."

Poppy frowns and pushes a golden curl out of her eye.

"Don't like big girl."

I'm surprised that Poppy still remembers her bad dream. "She won't come again," I say after a pause.

Poppy nods gravely. "Big girl wants to get me, Mummy."

She buries her head on my shoulder.

I stroke her hair thoughtfully. It's easy to overlook how the recent changes in our lives might have affected Poppy. Perhaps this dream is the consequence of so much upheaval. I resolve to speak to the staff at the nursery if Poppy mentions it again. They must have plenty of experience of dealing with these situations.

"Right, let's get you dressed and to nursery." I determinedly change the subject and get Poppy ready.

For the first time in a little while, I feel genuinely happy. I grab Poppy by the hand and coax her out the front door towards the car.

As I wrestle her into her car seat, an electric smart car pulls into Mabel's drive. A tall woman, perhaps a few years younger than me, angles her long legs out of the car. She has a severe auburn bob and the same chiselled bone structure as Mabel.

We catch each other's eye. I smile tentatively. The woman half returns the smile before striding swiftly to the front door.

***

With Poppy safely at nursery, I drive home, focused on my day ahead. I have to report on a webinar this morning and need to do some prep. Jumping out of the car, I spot Mabel leaving the house with the woman I'd seen earlier. Mabel clocks me immediately and moves towards the low hedgerow that divides our drive.

"Hello, Clara," she says in her deep, rich voice. "How are you settling in?"

"Good, thanks. It's a lovely house. I mean, obviously there's a lot to do still. We're trying to juggle sorting everything out with work and there are a few problems," I babble on, feeling that I'm talking too much. Mabel makes me nervous. It's the way she holds herself in that haughty manner and stares at me with those glacial eyes, as if she can see right through me. The woman I believe is Mabel's daughter clearly thinks I'm droning on. She gazes over my head and taps her foot on the pavement.

"Clara, meet my daughter, Belinda," Mabel interjects politely.

Belinda smiles and shakes my hand limply. "Hope you're enjoying it here," she says blandly.

"Oh yes. I mean, apart from all these problems." I cringe. I'm oversharing but can't seem to stop.

Belinda's expression is pained. "Right, well, hope you sort it out soon . . ."

"Belinda, of course, knows it like the back of her hand here. She was born and brought up in this house, in this street," Mabel says proudly. "And even now, she lives just down the road, in Egham, with Teddy and my two lovely grandchildren."

Belinda bobs her head up and down like a nodding dog toy. "Come on, Mum. We're going to be late!" She ushers Mabel towards the car.

Mabel allows herself to be steered away, but not before she turns and stares straight at me. "Well, I do hope there are happier times ahead." *Happier.* That word again.

"Mum! Come on!" Belinda is practically yelling, wiping sweat from her brow even though it's another chilly morning.

"I'm sure there will be!" I put my bright, happy voice on and wave enthusiastically, trying to suppress that familiar sense of dread.

I hurry to my front door and shut out the world, my heart feeling heavy again. *What is it with this place?* It's not just the house. Why are the neighbours so strange? I scoop coffee into my cafetière. I didn't warm to Belinda at all. *Rude, frankly.* And I let Mabel unnerve me again.

Here's to happier times. I try to push the words from my mind.

I fill the cafetière with boiling water. Belinda's face flashes in front of me. It wasn't just boredom and scorn behind those eyes. There was unease, even fear. Her clammy forehead looms large.

"Alexa, play Greatest Hits Radio," my voice booms around the silent kitchen. The DJ's friendly voice fills the room. I want to hold it close. *Don't stop talking.* I want to inject the positivity into my veins.

Here's to happier times.

* * *

I'm batting at the keys on my laptop, focused on writing up the webinar I listened to this morning. The doorbell rudely interrupts me.

Sighing, I push my laptop away and head downstairs.

"Hello, Tony from Pest Control." The stocky man steps in and points to the badge on his shirt.

I take him up to the loft opening. "I'm glad you're here, to be honest. I think there could be something big up there. Last night, I could hear huge rhythmic thumps. It was like a person walking above us." I give a self-conscious laugh.

Tony lays his case of tools down. "Could be rats," he says thoughtfully. "They're much larger than mice."

I never thought I'd be pleased to hear that there could be rats in our house. But it's better that than a person. I flinch at the thought.

I prod the hatch with its stick, and it falls open. I hook the stairs down.

Tony starts ascending the ladder. "Right, let's see the beasts up here," he says jovially.

I'm back at my computer when there's a flash and then I'm plunged into darkness.

"Oh, for goodness' sake!"

I slam my palms down on the table.

"Hey!" shouts Tony. "The lights have gone up here."

I hasten to the hatch. "Sorry," I call. "We've got a glitch. I thought it had rectified itself, but it hasn't."

"Hang on, let me put my phone light on." There's a scuffle and a flash of light and Tony's face looms out of the loft opening.

"I'll do what I can, and I can lay traps down, but it'll be hard for me to look properly for evidence of a pest."

"Have you managed to see anything at all?" I ask, grimacing with frustration. The main priority is to extinguish whatever it is up there, but I also want to know what "it" is.

"I haven't, and the light isn't the only reason. You do know that the loft is full of furniture?" asks Tony.

"What? I had no idea. I haven't actually been up there yet." My anger boils at Helen and Jim again. I know that when moving house, the previous owner is meant to remove all items in the property. Another thing they've disregarded.

"What's up there?"

"Oh, loads of stuff, a table, chairs, old suitcases, a bookcase, and stacks of old books and board games. Let me do my best to have a look and I can at least lay some poison down."

Tony disappears and I can hear him thumping around.

I'm sure the lights will come on as they have done previously, but Tony will be gone by then. I flick the torch on my mobile and stomp back to the study. Keith's arrival tomorrow can't come quick enough.

Tony clambers down the ladder twenty minutes later.

I meet him in the hall with a wave of the torch on my mobile.

"I found some mice droppings," he confirms. "I've left six lots of poison, that should sort it. I'll do a follow-up call in around a week's time."

"Great, thanks." I'm both relieved and agitated. At least I'm not going crazy. There is something up there making noises. But could mice really create the thuds I heard last night?

I can't help myself. I watch the clock, unable to tear myself away. And sure enough, at 5.15 p.m., the lights flash on again.

CHAPTER 9

I run out of the front door, grabbing my keys and bag, once again racing to make nursery pick-up time.

As I reach the car, I hear shouting from next door. There's a van in the drive with *S. Sanders, Builders* emblazoned on the side. I can clearly make out the voice of a man and a woman. Josie? I pause. I can see the shapes of two figures through the shutter slats in the front bay window.

One is big and solid and still. The other is moving around, arms waving frantically. I'm rooted to the spot. I can't tear my eyes away. Then I remember I must collect Poppy and jump in the car.

I manage to collect her just in time, breathing a sigh of relief. I hadn't wanted her to be the last one collected, to add to her possible feelings of insecurity.

"Did Poppy mention a lady or a 'big girl' in her room?" I ask Poppy's key worker, Fiona. Fiona is lovely. Big-hearted, sparkling eyes and smiling happily, nothing is too much for Fiona when it come to her charges.

"She had a nightmare about someone in her room the other night and mentioned it again today. I wondered if it was a sign that she was unsettled," I explain as Poppy buries her head against me and flings her arms around me.

"She hasn't mentioned anything," says Fiona. "But you're right, dreams like that can be a sign of stress. She's had a lot going on — new home, new area, new nursery. No doubt it's quite a lot for her to come to terms with. I'll let you know straightaway if she says anything."

She ruffles Poppy's hair and Poppy transfers her affection to Fiona, flinging herself at her. Fiona strokes her hair tenderly.

"She's honestly settled in so well. She's warm-hearted and looks after her friends and loves to play baby dolls with them. She also loves to set the table for lunch and tea and helps me hand out cups of water. She's very nurturing. I don't think you have anything to worry about."

* * *

Back home, I reach into the back and unbuckle Poppy from her seat. As I do so, I notice a man standing in Josie's drive. Over six feet tall, he's puffing on a cigarette, staring into the distance. I put two and two together. *S. Sanders, Builders.* Steve. And presumably the owner of the man's voice from the argument I heard earlier.

He gives me a brief smile of acknowledgement. Walking to the edge between the two driveways, holding Poppy's hand, I say, "Hi, I'm Clara and this is my daughter Poppy. We've just moved in."

The man I think is Steve nods briefly. In his own way, he's as unfriendly as Belinda. There's a spark of anger in me as I recall that he left Josie because she couldn't have a baby. *Bastard.*

Steve — if that is who it is — has very short, cropped light-brown hair and large eyes. I can't tell what colour they are due to the darkness. Although broad, there appears to be not an ounce of fat on him.

It's left to Poppy to break the ice.

"Me want a smoke ring!" she chatters excitedly. "My grandaddy does them!"

I smile to myself. Poppy is fascinated by Mike's dad's cigarettes and smoke rings, even though she knows it's "bad" to smoke and that Mike and I would like him to stop.

"Hello, sweetheart." The look on Steve's face changes. He crouches down to Poppy's level and he says gently. "Take a look at this."

He blows a huge smoke ring. It wafts slowly up. Poppy screams with excitement. Steve laughs — a carefree, spontaneous sound at odds with the shouts I heard earlier. He comes closer to the hedge separating our houses.

My heart softens towards him. He likes children and is kind to Poppy. Then I remember again why he left Josie.

"Your wife has been very kind. She's been round a few times," I say, trying to keep my voice steady and not emphasise "wife".

Steve's gentle expression hardens. "Ex-wife," he says.

"Oh, I'm so sorry. Josie said you were on a trial separation," I say without thinking.

"Trial separation?" Steve's eyebrows shoot up. "Is that what . . . is that what she said, is it? Well, it's a bit more final than that. We're actually getting divorced."

He flings his cigarette on the ground and stubs it out.

"She's bad news," he mutters.

I'm not sure I've heard him correctly. "Pardon?"

"Do another smoke ring!" shouts Poppy.

Steve smiles at Poppy. He stands up slowly.

"She is bad news." He enunciates every syllable and glances again at Poppy. I notice a restlessness in his eyes, as though he knows he's already said too much but finds it impossible to stop.

"She's obsessed with having a baby — and so was I. So am I, more like. It's all I've ever wanted. But it wasn't to be and she's never forgiven me for that."

"More like you haven't forgiven her!" I clamp my hand over my mouth — too late. Have I really just accused a man I've never met of telling such an appalling lie?

"What the hell are you talking about?" Steve's face tightens and he shakes his head. "I can't have children, OK? It's me, not her. I can't believe I'm telling a stranger this but . . ."

He glances at Poppy, who's staring expectantly at him, and lowers his voice.

"My sperm count is too low. We tried IVF again and again. But there was nothing anybody could do."

Guilt pricks at me. First Belinda, now Steve. I'm usually so reserved — almost deliberately bland — in encounters like these. Now here I am, arguing with one stranger and sharing the intimate details of my new home with another. What on Earth am I thinking?

"It's destroyed Josie, and that I can understand," Steve went on. "It's been heartbreaking for me too. But she blames me. I can't cope anymore with her anger or wild mood swings. For my own sanity I've had to leave her."

"But . . . but . . ." I stutter. Josie said the opposite. *She said that she couldn't have children and so you left her.*

"Do you want to see my cuddly bear, Huggsy?" Thank goodness for Poppy.

I'm about to jump in but Steve's expression relaxes. "Sure," he says softly. "Huggsy sounds amazing."

"Oh, er are you sure?" I can't recover my composure. "I'll need to go to the car to get him."

Steve stares at me. "Absolutely."

He bends down to Poppy and whispers in her ear.

I open the car door and glance over to Josie's house. The familiar pale face is at the bay window. This time though, the blinds are pulled back and I can clearly see the flaxen hair, white face and eyes that stare straight at me, drinking me in.

I raise my hand in a half-wave, and Josie is gone. I blink and slowly bend down to collect Huggsy. Josie might not be thrilled that I'm talking to her ex-husband.

Poppy grabs her teddy and thrusts him towards Steve. "Wow, what a cool little chap he is," he says, stroking his worn head and patchy ears. "I can tell you love him lots."

Poppy is listening entranced. "You've got a fan there," I laugh.

Steve smiles bashfully. "I've got nieces and nephews and love spending time with them." His smile fades.

"I've been very tactless, and I'm ever so sorry," I jump in hurriedly. "It's really none of my business."

Steve shrugs and his expression softens a little. "Ah, don't worry. You're obviously a good person sticking up for Josie."

"Can you cuddle Huggsy?" Poppy interrupts, staring adoringly at Steve.

"I can do more than that!" Steve plants a giant kiss on Huggsy's nose. As Poppy laughs delightedly, Steve leans close to me.

"Be careful of her." And then he's kneeling down.

"Right, Poppy, I have to go. I've loved meeting you and your amazing bear."

"Owww." Poppy's face falls, but she soon brightens up when Steve gravely gives Huggsy a high five. "Your turn!"

Poppy smashes her hand into Steve's.

"Right. Well, Poppy, I hope to see you again, and good to meet you, Clara." He pumps my hand up and down.

"Do you live there?" interjects Poppy, pointing to next door.

There's a brief pause. I open my mouth but Steve gets in there first.

"I used to." He flashes us a smile and then he's striding off to his van.

It's funny, in this one brief meeting with Steve, I feel I know him better than Josie, I think as I take Poppy's hand and walk to our front door.

They've given contrasting reasons for their split, but my gut feeling is that Steve is telling the truth. My train of thought is halted when I see the lights twinkling in the hall and sitting room. I frown. I'm fairly sure I turned the lights off when I went to collect Poppy. In fact, I'm absolutely certain.

* * *

"What are you doing here?"

I'm shocked to see Layla standing in the hall. She's holding a mug and her boots sit neatly by the stairs.

Poppy gives a scream of delight and flings herself at Layla. "Can you put me to bed again?" she shouts excitedly.

Layla laughs and picks up Poppy, holding her tightly.

She then looks at me, a flash of concern in her eyes. "God, I'm sorry! I didn't mean to scare you," she exclaims. "I actually did WhatsApp you about twenty minutes ago but you obviously haven't seen it. Mike contacted me this morning to say he was a bit worried about you."

"Worried?" My hackles rise. *Bloody Mike! Taking liberties like that.*

"You know, you've both had a stressful time with the move," Layla blusters. "He suggested that perhaps I could pop by again soon. He said it really cheered you up when I came the other night.

"So, I thought I'd come by this evening. I forgot you'd be picking up Poppy and, when there was no answer, I remembered I had your spare key and thought you wouldn't mind if I let myself in. It's so cold out there."

Layla gives a dramatic shiver.

I step into the house. "Oh, no problem," I say hastily. "I totally understand. And it's great you've come over."

Inside I'm cursing. Why can't I be honest and say what I really think: *You are crossing a boundary letting yourself in to our house without our permission.*

I don't want Layla turning up unexpectedly and letting herself in.

"Right, you go and relax," Layla orders. "I'll get Poppy to bed."

She sees me looking at the mug she's placed on the floor. "I made myself a cup of tea, I hope you don't mind — I was bone cold." She gives another shudder.

"Right!" Layla bustles to the door pulling Poppy by her hand. "We are going to get ready for bed, and read stories and cuddle . . ."

I jump up. "I'll get her sippy cup ready. You'll need some pyjamas; they're in the—"

Layla holds up her hand. "All under control." She flashes a smile. "When I arrived, I found her cup and filled it with milk and got fresh pyjamas from her drawer, plus I got her a nappy. See, it's a good thing I let myself in!"

She chases Poppy out of the room.

"Goodnight, Poppy," I say weakly, my voice drowned out by my daughter's joyful chatter.

I sink onto the sofa. I should stretch out, read my Kindle and relax. Instead, I sit stiffly, clasping my hands. Though the room is in darkness, I make no move to switch on a light. I wonder what Josie is doing on the other side of the wall. Is she relaxing? Watching television? Or motionless, like me? Sitting and thinking.

"Right, all done!" Layla bursts into the room, flicking on the light as she does so. "Poppy's almost asleep. She went down like a dream!" She's pleased with herself.

I emit a groan. "Why can't she do that for me?"

"She's used to you. Trust me, when I'm no longer a novelty, it won't be so easy."

I open my mouth. This is my moment to draw a line, establish my boundaries, imply politely that I would prefer Layla to remain "a novelty". As I search for a way to make my point without sounding ungrateful, Layla says gaily, "And you don't need to worry about dinner either — ta da!" She drags her rucksack in and pulls out pizza and garlic bread. "And there's a bottle of wine chilling in the fridge."

Moment gone.

* * *

I bite into my slice. The combination of supermarket margherita and sauvignon blanc has calmed my nerves. Layla means well. I'm probably reading too much into it.

"Are you OK?" Layla asks. "I thought Mike seemed quite concerned, not that he gave away any specific information. I hope he doesn't mind me mentioning this."

She bites into garlic bread with gusto. Butter trickles down her chin.

"Some funny things have happened," I begin. I describe bumping into Mabel's daughter Belinda and Josie's estranged husband Steve. Layla doesn't seem particularly interested and glances at her phone.

"I know I've only met him today, but I think I believe Steve." I pick up another piece of pizza, trying to suppress a pang of guilt as I do so. I really must go for a run tomorrow.

"But I don't think it's black and white." Layla has stopped fiddling with her mobile. "It must be awful, not being able to have children when you desperately want them. Then with their relationship breaking down, they'll be blaming each other. It won't be a case of one lying and the other telling the truth. It'll be somewhere in the middle."

Layla flicks through her phone again, changing the subject. "Look, I want to show you this guy's profile. His name's Matt. We've been messaging and he wants to go out for a drink tomorrow. You know what, I'm actually excited!"

I suppress a smile. So it wasn't just worry about me that propelled Layla over tonight. If things go well with Matt, I doubt my friend will be turning up for a while.

CHAPTER 10

"So, I get home and there she is!" I'm packing the dishwasher as I tell Mike about Layla's impromptu visit. "I love Layla, but I feel funny about her letting herself in without us knowing."

"It's because of my message," Mike says. He's back from his work meeting and surprisingly relaxed, leaning against the counter smiling.

"But I certainly didn't mean her to let herself in."

"Oh, I'm sure it'll be OK." I feel the tight muscles in my back relax. I click my neck and it lets out a satisfying snap. Mike moves behind me and massages my shoulders. He kisses my ear. "I missed you today."

I'm tired and about to push him away laughingly but then I remember how much I've missed this connection (not to mention how much I want a baby). I turn round slowly and kiss him on the lips. Mike responds eagerly. It's been a while.

* * *

I lie in a post-coital daze, happy, dreamy and excited. Maybe tonight will be the night I conceive. Mike emits a soft snore and I relish his arm draped over me.

A scream tears sharply through my cosy thoughts. Snapping my eyes open, I sigh. *Please Poppy, go back to sleep.* I hold myself rigid, heart pounding, as if a bomb is about to go off.

Poppy roars, a low-pitched sound before screeching. I'm catapulted out of bed. Never has my daughter sounded so distressed. It even wakes Mike. I rush to Poppy's room. Poppy is sitting upright in bed. She continues her high-pitched wails, but as I gently move closer, I see that Poppy's eyes are three-quarters shut. I stroke her damp hair. Sweat trickles down Poppy's forehead. Poppy twists violently as Mike hurries into the bedroom.

"I'm sure it's night terrors," I say loudly, over the wails. "I don't think she's even awake, or at least not fully."

Mike leans over and bundles Poppy into his arms. She's still writhing as he carries her out. "Let's go into our bedroom," Mike bellows above the din. "It might calm her down."

He sets Poppy on our bed and tries to cuddle her. No joy. Still she screams and thrashes, unable to settle.

"Daddy, Daddy, Daddy," she howls.

I wince. Usually, I don't mind that Mike is Poppy's favourite — a proper daddy's girl. But tonight, it hurts that my daughter does not want my comfort.

"Stop it. She's half asleep," I whisper to myself.

"Daddy, Daddy, Daddy." Poppy's screams get more frantic. "Her, her her, her."

"Who is 'her'?" Without thinking, I glance at the ceiling. *Don't be silly! We know it's mice,* I remind myself. *Tony said so.*

"You, I assume." Mike is stressed. He grapples with Poppy, trying to pull her onto his lap, but that makes it worse. She kicks out.

"Can you get some milk!" he shouts above the uproar.

I fight an urge to stick my fingers in my ears. Poppy's screams are like fingernails down a blackboard.

I dash downstairs, grabbing Poppy's cup from her room. Milk slips over my fingers as I impatiently pour it.

"Hurry up!" Mike shouts.

"I'm coming!" I yell fractiously as I pound up the stairs, almost flinging the cup at Poppy, who hurls it across the room. It smashes against the wardrobe, spraying droplets of milk.

Ding-dong.

I wonder if I imagined it.

"Doorbell," says Mike. He's clenching his fists, his mouth set in a straight line. "Who the hell is that?"

"Don't answer!" I speak louder than I intended as tension fizzes through my body. "No one calls at this time. Not unless they're up to no good."

My breath comes fast as Poppy continues her screams and moans. She pounds her little fists on the bed covers.

"No, I'm going to answer. It could even be the police. Something could have happened to our parents." It's unusual for Mike to catastrophise. "Don't worry, I'll be careful. I'll ask who it is before opening the door."

I wish he hadn't said that. My anxiety grows. Between the doorbell and Poppy's incessant screaming, my heart feels like it's going to burst through my chest.

Mike hotfoots it out the room and I once again try to comfort Poppy but again she wriggles free. In desperation, I try with the milk again and this time Poppy grabs the sippy cup and sucks frantically at it. *Silence truly is golden.*

I strain to hear what Mike is doing downstairs and who is at the door. *What if he opened the door and someone grabbed him and hit him over the head or pushed him out the way and they're in the house now?* I shake my head. Of course there isn't someone roaming the house. I'm tired and Poppy's screams have set every nerve on edge.

Poppy lets out a small whimper and her breath is ragged. A tiny teardrop hangs from her eyelash. I hold her protectively. *If this continues, maybe I should call the health visitor.*

Again, I strain to hear, but nothing. Poppy's whimpering has stopped and her breathing has become steadier. I inch away slowly, wincing as a floorboard creaks, and move down the stairs. The hall is in darkness, but a light shines underneath the sitting room door.

I can hear the low murmur of voices. I push open the door and there on the sofa is Josie, clad in a semi-transparent pink nightgown that is riding up her thighs. A hint of cleavage nestles against the lace V-neck. Draped around her shoulders is a dressing gown, but not like the cosy, all-encompassing towelling dressing gowns that Mike and I own. This is half the size and made of thin cotton. On her feet are slippers with huge dog faces staring out, the type a five-year-old would wear. Combined with her racy nightwear, she looks quite a sight.

"Josie," I breathe, shocked.

Mike is sitting next to her on the couch, seemingly not at all perturbed that it's almost two o'clock in the morning.

"What on Earth are you doing here?"

Josie self-consciously pulls her nightgown further down her thigh and hocks the V-neck up. A mishmash of blue veins shine through the bright white of her legs and chest. I'm transfixed, noticing again how thin Josie is. I glance down at my own comfortable tartan pyjamas, highlighting the soft swell of my belly and sturdy thighs. While I could do with losing some weight, I'm certainly not fat, but Josie makes me feel like a big lump.

"I heard Poppy screaming through the walls," Josie says in her usual soft tones. "I was worried and just wanted to check she's OK."

My anger boils over. "Absolutely no need to do that and especially not at this time." I glance pointedly at the mantelpiece clock. "It's just a child crying over a bad dream, if you must know. Mike and I were quite able to cope with that, as her parents. What on Earth did you think was happening?"

My mind races. *Did Josie think that Mike and I were harming or neglecting our little girl? Are we just a phone call away from social services?*

Josie's cheeks flush. She opens her mouth but Mike is quicker.

"Clara!" he snaps, frowning. "Josie is just trying to help."

"We don't need her help," I hiss, furious that my husband is taking Josie's side.

"I'm sorry." Josie's voice is quieter than ever. "I didn't mean to cause any upset."

Count to ten. Count to ten. I take a deep breath. I want to scream at both of them but that would make things even worse.

"Children often cry and have tantrums. But I guess if you don't have your own kids you wouldn't know," I snap.

Hitting her where it hurts. Good.

Josie's face is still. But her hand clenches the sofa cushion, her knuckles prominent against her skin.

"I'm very sorry," she says slowly. "I just wanted to be a good neighbour."

"Please don't apologise!" Mike bursts out. "I'm happy to have a neighbour look out for us." He ignores my grimace.

A faint dimple appears in Josie's cheek.

"I'm just glad everything is OK," she says. "It must have been an absolutely dreadful nightmare."

She stands up, again self-consciously pulling her nightie down. It still rides high above her knee.

"I'll be going. You guys need your sleep."

"As do you." Mike has his charming smile on as he bounds up to show her to the door.

"Oh, I'm an insomniac," Josie says, walking to the door. "I barely sleep at all." I follow them.

"Thanks again," Mike repeats. "And you must really meet Poppy properly."

Josie smiles. "I would absolutely love to."

She stares at me. Then raising her hand, she is gone.

Steve's voice pops into my head.

"She's bad news," I murmur.

Mike double-locks the door and turns to me. "What?"

"Nothing," I murmur sullenly. "Why are you taking her side? You're my husband."

To my embarrassment, I realise I sound about seven years old. I hear the petulant whine in my voice.

Mike scowls and I brace myself, wondering if we're going to have another argument. But then his face relaxes and he touches my arm.

"Don't be silly. I'm definitely not," he says soothingly. "But her heart's in the right place. Something bad could have been happening and I'm glad we've got a neighbour looking out for us."

We climb the stairs in silence. Poppy is spreadeagled across our bed. "I'll move her to her room," Mike murmurs.

"Don't worry," I say stiffly. His positive words about Josie reverberate around my head and I'm breathless with rage. "I'll just go and sleep in Poppy's bed. You can stay here with her."

"OK, sure."

I bridle that he isn't protesting. "I can't believe what she was wearing. It wasn't appropriate to come dressed like that, half naked. Trying to look sexy. For your benefit, no doubt." I glare at him.

"I can't believe you're still talking about her," Mike says wearily. "I didn't even notice." His eyes slide away from me.

"Yeah right!" I snort.

Mike frowns, his body stiffening. "What are you trying to say here? Just leave it, all right? We've had a stressful time and I don't need this. She's a kind neighbour — that's it. OK?"

"Keep your voice down," I whisper. We both glance warily at Poppy as she wriggles in her sleep.

"We need to be careful. I don't trust her. You know, I didn't get the chance to tell you, but I bumped into her husband today. They're divorcing, seems really bitter. She's been saying it's—"

Mike threw up his hands. "We've no idea what's really going on behind closed doors and I don't want to know, to be honest. I still can't believe you're accusing me of getting off on what she was wearing."

"Because . . ." I retort. But the door closes in my face.

I shuffle unhappily to Poppy's room. I slip into the single bed, turning uncomfortably. There's no space to stretch my legs, but at least Poppy isn't here to make it an even tighter squeeze.

Mike is only on the other side of the hall, but the distance between us feels as wide as a canyon.

CHAPTER 11

Ding-dong.

I've grown to hate the sound of the doorbell.

"Hello." Keith the electrician is standing on the doorstep.

I forgot he was coming. Little wonder, given the chaos of the early hours. I woke consumed by regret and went to Mike, head and heart pounding, hoping to make up. He barely acknowledged my apology and dressed in silence.

I felt sick. Now we'd had two bad arguments within a couple of days in our dream home. *Our dream home.* We should be happy and grateful and pulling together even more. Josie hovers on the frontier of my mind, like an unwelcome house guest.

I told Fiona at the nursery what happened.

Fiona gave Poppy a cuddle. "How stressful for you," she said sympathetically.

"Honestly, I think it's another sign of what we talked about. Poppy's unsettled by the move. And come to think of it, a few children in this group are showing signs of sleep regression. We'll chat with her today and try to calm her down."

Fiona is wonderful, I think as I face Keith on my doorstep.

"Do you happen to have a timer switch?" Keith asks.

"What's one of those?" I ask blankly.

"An automatic timer, so you can choose to have the lights go off at certain times and then come on again," explains Keith. "People often use them to save electricity, or when they go on holiday."

I flick on the light switch in the garage and Keith pounces instantly at something on the wall.

"Ah ha. Here we go!" He points triumphantly to a switch with a small clockface sticking out of the wall.

"Oh, good." I'm pleased that we've found the problem but also unsettled.

"But Mike and I weren't even aware of this switch. As far as I know we haven't touched it," I worry.

"You'll have pressed it by mistake. Look — not far from the main garage light switch."

I find that hard to believe. While the switches are close together, it's the main one that's nearest the door. It seems unlikely that I'd unwittingly reach past that to turn on the other one.

"Yeah but . . ." I trail off. No need to jump down yet another rabbit hole. Not when they seem to appear everywhere I turn.

"These kinds of things happen more often than you realise," says Keith. "The boss will email over an invoice."

* * *

I hesitate. In one hand I clutch my phone, while the other hovers uncertainly over the screen. I'm unsure whether to text Mike. I want to tell him about Keith's visit but also to apologise. It's bothered me all day that Mike left for work with our rift still unmended.

The doorbell rings.

I want to leap up and kick the door. *Leave me alone.* I start tapping away. *Hi Mike, just wanted to give you an update after the electrician. All sorted.*

I pause. No more ringing. Hopefully whoever was there has gone.

It's due to a light switch timer in our garage.
Ding-dong.

I groan. *It had better not be . . . yes, it is.*

Josie is in a chiffon dress that hangs almost to her ankles. She's holding a bunch of tulips and proffers them wordlessly.

"Thanks." I take them, heart sinking. *Now I'll have to ask her in.*

"An apology for last night," Josie says formally.

"You didn't have to, but thanks again," I say weakly. My heart hardens. Why have I said thank you to Josie twice? I need to start asserting myself. Mike calls me a "people pleaser". He means it kindly, but he has a point.

"Can I come in, if you have the time?" Josie fills a pause that is becoming more loaded with every second.

"Yep." I lead her into the living room.

"It's as I said last night," Josie begins, "I was alarmed to hear her in such distress."

"Well, next time you'll know she's just having a dream," I reply curtly. *So don't come round, half dressed, showing off your body to my husband.*

"It reminded me of things that have happened here before," Josie says. She lowers her voice to a soft pitch, and I wonder if I've heard correctly.

But as *What? Who? Where? Why?* race through my head, Josie changes the subject. "There's something else too. I've really struggled to get over my infertility and not having children. Then the final straw was Steve leaving."

She looks away and I feel a surprising spark of pity for her.

"I had five IVF treatments. They were so hard. All the hormones they pump into you, the low mood, the headaches and hot flushes. Then all the hopes, before they came crashing down. It took a huge toll." Josie's face is paler than ever. She stares ahead.

"We were only successful once. The last round, we had two embryos placed and they both made it. Twins. We couldn't believe it. We booked a private scan at seven weeks."

Josie swallows. "The heartbeats were too slow. But it wasn't necessarily bad, the sonographer said. It could have been because their hearts had only just started beating. It could have gone either way. I think you know the answer."

She takes out her phone. "I still have the video of it. The clinic sent it to me as part of the package."

She hits play. Two tiny tadpole-like creatures float on the screen, a small beating circle inside each of them. They glide slowly, like otherworldly animals.

I feel sick. They're going to die, these tiny, innocent creatures, and they don't know it. Those pumping dots will stop for ever and they'll disintegrate. I picture my scan of Poppy wriggling and somersaulting on the screen and feel so grateful. I hope I don't have to go through anything like Josie has.

Impulsively, I wrap an arm around her. Josie holds herself still, then quickly pulls away.

We stand up together. "I am so sorry," I say sincerely, pushing Josie's abrupt gesture from my mind. *No need to be offended, the poor woman is struggling.* Maybe Mike and Layla are right. Perhaps I shouldn't have judged Josie so hastily.

"Come and babysit for Poppy," I say without thinking. "She would love to meet you."

Josie pauses and smiles slowly.

"I'd love to," she says. "Just give me a date."

We settle on a date in the next few weeks and I close the door. *It reminds Josie of things that have happened here before.* I want to shake myself. Why did I allow myself to get waylaid with Josie's personal life? I'm none the wiser and unease fills me. Was Josie alluding to my house? Her own house? The street? Or something else entirely?

Then I remember Steve's words and how different they were from Josie's version of events. Can I even trust her to tell the truth? Steve versus Josie — I know which version I believe.

* * *

"I'm sorry." I bend my head and stare at my glass of wine. "Please can we just forget it. I messed up."

"Of course," says Mike. He stands up and rubs my arm. "I'm sorry too. Last night was horrible. We were stressed and we took it out on each other. And Josie's timing was bad. But as I said, at least her heart's in the right place."

The image of Josie's white shimmering body, with its flashes of blue veins, floats in front of me. It hangs between us. I want to mention it but what to say? *Did you enjoy looking at her? Do you think she dressed like that for you?*

"And I'm so pleased you agreed to a babysitting night. When do you want to go out?" he adds, his smile stretching from ear to ear.

"In the next few weeks," I mumble. Then changing tack: "What do you think about the lights? I don't think we would have pressed the light control rather than the garage light."

"Let's have a look." Mike bounds up. I'm glad he's in good spirits. We go to the garage and I flick on the light and point out the light control switch.

Mike laughs and reaches over. "We'll have been pressing it by accident," he says. "They're not far away. Anyway, the problem's solved, so let's forget it."

He marches out of the garage, leaving me alone.

"If you say so," I declare to an empty room.

CHAPTER 12

"Right! All sorted." Tony's cheery face peers down from the loft opening.

"Oh, great!" I stop the automatic tapping of my foot as I stand on the landing below.

"Two of the traps are empty, so the mice have taken the poison. I'll replace it, but I'm sure this has solved the problem."

Tony's face disappears again as he clumps around the loft.

"Mike!" I shout. "All sorted!"

"What?" Mike calls up from downstairs. I can hear strains of *Peppa Pig* wafting up from the TV.

I raise my voice. "It *is* mice that have been rampaging around up there."

Mike comes to the bottom of the stairs. "Was that ever in doubt?" He smiles.

"I was worried it was rats," I retort. The thumps I heard in the loft echo through my mind, making me feel uneasy. "Anyway, some of the poison from the traps has gone, so hopefully that's got rid of them."

"Well, at least that's something else to tick off that rather long list of ours," Mike answers, glancing at his watch. "You'd better get a move on for that party Poppy's going to."

"Oh gosh, yes! Can you sort out Tony's payment?"

* * *

Poppy lets out a squeal of excitement as I guide her into the soft play centre where Lila, her friend from nursery, is celebrating her third birthday. I dislike both soft play and children's birthday parties, but I feel it's important for Poppy to attend. Especially as this is her first party since we moved.

The sound of a child sobbing their heart out cuts through the chaotic screams of delight. A swarm of children are clambering all over the equipment and filing down the slides, like an army of ants dividing and conquering. A ball hits me in the stomach.

"Ouch!"

I wish I could press fast forward on the next hour and a half. I head to the section reserved for Lila's party.

A gaggle of parents huddle around a coffee trolley. I feel a sense of dread. Although confident and authoritative in my job, I sometimes find it difficult to introduce myself to strangers. All these parents know each other and seem to form an invisible barrier to newcomers. I loathe having to myself in, making pointless small talk.

"Hello! You must be Poppy's mum!" Lila's mother appears in front of me, beaming. "Lila is so excited Poppy has joined the nursery."

At that moment, a mini-me I presume is Lila runs at Poppy, shrieking. The little girl is dressed as Elsa from *Frozen* — a firm favourite of Poppy's. Poppy utters a war cry in return and the pair charge off to climb the structure.

"I'm Libby. Let me introduce you to some people." Libby marches off as I reluctantly trail in her wake.

"This is Lucy, Molly's mum, and this is Poppy's mum, Clara. Oh, Tommy's mum has just arrived! 'Scuse me for a moment!"

She dashes off.

Lucy smiles distractedly. I'm embarrassed, feeling sure Lucy would rather be chatting with the other mums.

"Molly loves Poppy," Lucy gushes.

I smile gratefully. "That's great to hear. We only recently moved here, and she was very settled in her old nursery, so I'm happy it's going well."

"Where are you from? And whereabouts have you moved to?" Lucy asks.

"We were in South London and we're now living near Twickenham Green. Lunn Road, in case you know it."

Lucy scrunches her face up. "That really rings a bell," she frowns. She places her coffee cup down. "Now, who . . . oh yes, of course! Someone I used to work with lives there. You don't happen to know Josie Sanders?"

I gasp. "She's the woman next door."

"What a coincidence," Lucy replies with a small squeal.

"How do you know each other?" I ask, leaning forward.

Lucy looks a little awkward. "We used to work together," she replies. There's a pause and she adds, "We're both in PR and I work at a local agency. Josie worked there as well until around six months ago."

"Oh." I'm surprised. That's not what Josie told me. Without thinking I blurt out, "But Josie still works there. She's off on long-term sick leave."

Lucy looks uncomfortable. Realising my blunder, I backtrack. "I mean, maybe I've got it wrong."

Lucy fidgets. "Well, actually, she was . . . *asked to leave* is probably the polite way to put it."

Fired.

I'm on tenterhooks, desperate to know what happened.

"Sorry, I'm being very nosey, but what happened?" I ask. "Don't worry, I won't say anything. I barely know her," I add hastily as Lucy frowns.

"Look, I don't really know the ins and outs," Lucy says slowly. "But she was behind with her work, missing deadlines, annoying clients, writing press releases full of errors. I mean, I know she was struggling . . ." She tails off.

"We all knew she was going through IVF and it wasn't successful. It must have been so hard for her. I think that really interfered with her work, which is understandable. But . . ."

Molly appears from the structure, running at Lucy and headbutting her in the pelvis.

It reminds me of Poppy and I scan the play structure anxiously. Almost instantly I can see Poppy marching across the wobbly bridge, bossily leading a crew from the nursery.

". . . but she seemed obsessed with our colleague Sara's little girl. I think Sara complained, and that didn't help."

Lucy's voice is so low I can barely hear her above the screams of the children.

"Sorry, I didn't hear you properly." I raise my voice.

Molly headbutts Lucy again. "I need a wee, Mummy!"

Lucy is off, dragging Molly to the toilet.

Obsessed with Sara's daughter. Lucy's words reverberate around my head. I'm jolted back to reality as Poppy appears, moaning, "I wet myself."

I sigh when I see the wet patch spreading down Poppy's leggings. She is potty-trained but still has the odd accident. I forget about Josie as the smell of dirty nappies wafts from the toilet door.

CHAPTER 13

"My want my birthday party at soft play!" Poppy shouts as she skips from the car to the front door, grasping her party bag in one hand and holding a squashed slice of birthday cake in the other. Crumbs decorate her cheeks.

"Of course we'll have it there," I say automatically, fumbling for my door key. Poppy had a great time, so I'm pleased that we went. The mums seemed quite nice too. I chatted to a few of them while the children sat and had their party meal. Still, I cannot stop thinking about what Lucy told me about Josie. I burst into the house, desperate to give Mike an update.

Mike is slumped on the sofa, eyes focused on the football match on the TV. His beloved Tottenham are playing. "Yes!" He shoots a fist out as his team scores. "Two-nil! Awesome!"

"Enjoying some child-free time, then?" I ask drily.

"Yep," says Mike sheepishly. "Party good?"

Poppy climbs onto his knee. "Daddy, Daddy! I went on big, big slide and chocolate cake and Lila was dressed as Elsa!"

Mike gives her a hug. "Sounds super," he says, one eye on the screen.

I collapse next to him on the sofa. "I heard some very interesting information. I met a mum, Lucy, who used to work with Josie — coincidence, hey? I say used to work, because it seems Josie was sacked. But Josie told me that she'd been signed off work for stress."

I pause dramatically. Mike, eyes firmly fixed on the screen, shrugs. "Right."

"And Lucy said something about Josie becoming obsessed with a colleague's little girl. Reading between the lines, it sounds like that might have contributed to her being fired." Unease chews the pit of my stomach when I think about the nameless little girl. I picture Josie getting her claws into Poppy, watching her, gaining entry into her life, taking her . . . I give myself a metaphorical slap. *Don't be ridiculous.*

Poppy drops her party bag on the floor. A notebook, mini crayons, a plastic frog and sweets spill out. She leaps from Mike's lap to grab them.

I wait for Mike's reaction. He continues to stare at the screen. I seize the remote, frustrated, and slam the pause button.

"Oi!" Mike slams his fist on the sofa. "Why the hell did you do that? Turn it back on!"

"You're not listening to me," I snap. "It's another indication that Josie isn't right in the head. She lied about being off sick from work when really, she was sacked and developed an obsession with a colleague's daughter."

Mike shakes his head impatiently. "I'm not really interested in gossip from some mum," he says scathingly. "So what if she was fired? I'm sorry for her but it doesn't affect our lives."

"It does affect us because she lives next door and is a liar. Fine if she's keeping a distance from us but she's not. She's coming round, wanting to be part of our lives. She's very interested in Poppy, and I'm starting to see that in a sinister light."

Mike sighs. "What's happened to you since we moved here? Clara, come on! This is your dream home, or so you keep telling me. But I've never known you to be so on edge, so paranoid."

He pauses, a panicked look on his face as he remembers Poppy is in the room. But Poppy is oblivious as she scribbles determinedly on the little notebook.

"You've got to stop this." He reaches out for the remote control. I slam it into his open palm.

"Her own husband said she was bad news, as I was trying to tell you the other day," I retort. "I don't believe a word that comes out of her mouth, and she certainly won't be babysitting Poppy."

I stomp out to the kitchen. *Why doesn't Mike take this more seriously?* I'm frustrated and sad. We've argued more in the few weeks we've been in our new house than in the last few years. My thoughts turn back to Josie. She's never actually met Poppy. Well, I'm going to do my best to keep it that way.

I lean forward to pull open the freezer door, then pause. It's slightly ajar. I throw it open and water drips from the shelves. I pull open the three trays in quick succession. Chicken thighs, steak, a slab of beef, mince and salmon are defrosted and soft. Small portions of cooked meals for Poppy have water droplets clinging to their covers.

I screw up my face and wail. *The final straw.*

I grab the packages of meat and Poppy's frozen meals and hurl them onto the floor.

"What's wrong?" Mike appears at the door, Poppy clinging onto his hand.

I gesture. "What do you think?" I look at Mike meaningfully. "Some idiot left the freezer open."

Mike bridles. "I haven't been anywhere near the freezer. I don't appreciate you accusing me."

"I never said it was you." I throw a bag of frozen peas on the floor. The water from the defrosted food is spreading across the tiles.

Poppy watches agog, eyes wide and mouth open.

"Darling, you won't be in trouble at all, but did you open the freezer at all, maybe to get one of these?" I wave a sodden mess of an ice lolly.

"No, Mummy," says Poppy earnestly. "You and Daddy give me my lollies."

"OK! Must have been a ghost," I mutter, leaning back on my heels.

"Oh, give over!" Mike's mouth is a thin line.

"I was joking." I give a rictus of a smile. "Or maybe not. The lights switching on and off. Poppy's night terrors. The noises in the loft that don't sound like mice."

I'm counting them on my fingers.

"Careful." Mike glances warningly at Poppy, but she's bending down, prodding soggy sausages with her fingers.

Mike's eyes are hard as he surveys me. Then he pulls me to him. "Come on, Clara, what on earth is wrong? You're not acting rationally. Since we've moved into this house, you seem anxious and unhappy, but you wanted it so much."

He strokes my hair. "We've got to put those issues behind us. And forget about Josie. Just because she's our neighbour, it doesn't mean that you have to speak to her. Look, I think she seems nice, but she obviously bothers you. So cut her out."

I'm shocked to realise that tears are streaking down my cheeks. "I'm so sorry. I don't know what's wrong with me," I say. But relief at Mike's words has made my chest and shoulders sag. "Josie and the weird things in this house have really got under my skin."

Mike gently runs his thumb across my cheek, wiping away tears. "Leave the freezer to me," he says briskly. "I'll clean it and get rid of all the stuff in it." He gives a sheepish smile. "I know I was cross with you, but thinking about it, it probably was me. I got an ice lolly out for Poppy yesterday. I bet I didn't close the door properly."

For the second time, a wave of relief envelopes me. "So, hopefully it's not a ghost." I manage to raise a smile.

Poppy leaps up, bored with prodding limp, wet food.

"Mummy, let's play with my toys." She leads me firmly by the hand to the family room, which is in a chaotic state. Poppy's toys are scattered over the floor. Perspex storage boxes are upturned. Jigsaw puzzle pieces are trailed across the floor and lumps of dried-out plasticine are dumped in various places.

I sigh. I'll have to get this cleared up tonight. I wish the house had a dedicated playroom, but then I give myself a shake. There's always a compromise, and the house ticks all the other boxes. *Apart from the next-door neighbour.*

I bend down over Poppy's favourite baby doll and its buggy. Out of the corner of my eye, I glimpse Poppy's mini magnetic letter board. I'd rather play with that, to be honest, as I've played "babies" hundreds of times. I like the idea of teaching Poppy about letters and words. I catch myself, shudder and smile. I don't want to be one of *those* parents. Poppy's only two and a half!

Nevertheless, I wander over to the board, intent on luring Poppy over. A jumble of letters is already attached to it. I squint to see which ones.

ididit

I frown as I survey the letters. It looks familiar. I move closer.

ididit

I parse the letters. *I did it.*

My heart races and I feel sick. Even though I know there is no way that Poppy could possibly have written this, I call her over, trying to sound calm.

"That's clever, isn't it?" I point. "Did you stick the letters there, Poppy?"

Poppy gives a little squawk, looking longingly at the doll she has left. "I don't know!"

Well, of course she doesn't. She's two. And cannot read or write in any shape or form. *There is no way she has done this.*

"Mike," I shout urgently. "Come here!"

"Hang on. I'm just wiping the freezer shelves. Can you wait a minute?" Mike calls back.

"No, you need to come now." My voice raises a notch as I pace, all the time my eyes fixed on *ididit*.

Poppy moves a chubby hand towards the magnetic board, but I grab it. "No, darling. I just want Daddy to see it and then you can play with it."

Mike utters a loud, theatrical sigh. "OK. What now?"

He comes into the family room, wiping his hands on a tea towel.

I stab my finger at Poppy's board. "Just look at that!"

Mike crinkles his eyes up. "What?"

"Look at what it says." I know I'm sounding increasingly hysterical, but I don't care.

"Random letters pushed together." Mike shrugs, irritated. "I don't understand what you're getting at."

Are you thick? I berate myself for my harsh words about my beloved husband but I can't understand how he's failing to see the obvious.

I jab my finger again. "I did it. I did it. I did it," I say manically. "Can't you see?"

Mike frowns. "Now you point out I do," he says slowly. "Wow, did Poppy honestly spell those words out? That's unbelievable!"

I shoot him a withering look. "Of course she didn't. She's two! But someone else obviously did."

Mike takes a deep breath. "Now hang on, that's some jump. She's obviously put together a jumble of letters and it's a big coincidence."

"Big, all right," I say, restlessly pacing. "I'm sorry. I think there's something up with this house."

"I just think you're looking for trouble now. You're looking for things to be wrong, to fit your narrative that this place is bad news."

Mike's face reddens again. "You seriously think someone has found an ingenious way of sneaking into our house, just to play around with a few magnetic letters?" He's incredulous. "Josie perhaps? A ghost?" His voice is dripping with sarcasm.

I remember the creaking sounds in the loft. In my heart of hearts, I'd never really believed that mice were responsible. "Something's not right." My voice is trembling.

"*I did it* — did what?" Mike snaps.

"Meddled with our lights or left the freezer door open," I say instantly.

I glance at the shared wall, as though Josie might leap through it.

"Me play with my letters," says Poppy, jumping forward eagerly and abandoning her doll face down.

Mike swipes roughly at the board and the letters scatter.

"Come on, love, let's do some spellings."

He glances at me. "You finish sorting the freezer," he says sharply, before ruffling Poppy's hair and picking up the letter P. "This is P, for Poppy!"

I lean forward and touch his shoulder. "I'm sorry, I've probably gone over the top. But my nerves are totally on edge. Of course I don't think someone can be coming in." I bark a hollow laugh. "But I don't understand how proper words were formulated on Poppy's board."

"And O is after P," Mike continues, ignoring me. He flinches at my touch.

I feel helpless. I hesitate and then walk to the freezer. *I did it, I did it, I did it* beats in line with my steps.

* * *

I know what I'm doing is strange. Well, more than strange. Wildly inappropriate and creepy. Not to mention illegal. But when has something being illegal stopped me? It feels like an addiction. I have to keep doing it, keep going in, to get my fix. I think about it all the time: what I'm going to do, how I'm going to do it. I wonder about their reactions. I don't see those, of course, but I wish I did. In my head, Clara loses it. She's a nervy sort who lets her imagination run away from her. Mike is steadier, more robust. I just do little things. But they all add up, don't they? It was so easy to slip open the freezer and stick a few letters on Poppy's magnetic board. I keep thinking of their daughter, twisting between desire and envy. If my life hadn't gone so dramatically wrong, I could have had my own child. I could have had a loving childhood like she does. But beyond the new people living here, I'm drawn to this house like a moth to a lightbulb. Despite everything, I want to be in it, immerse myself in it. I dream of a different life when I'm in it, a sharp contrast to what really happened. A house to die for. I smile at my flash of dark humour. I'll keep taking my opportunities, little things here and there, slow and steady. But I'm getting a little impatient. It might be time to take things up a level.

CHAPTER 14

I lie uncomfortably, my limbs tense and tight. I'm sure I heard a creak up in the loft, but now there's silence. I grab my phone from the bedside table to see the time. Three in the morning. I really need to get to sleep. But *I did it* keeps reverberating around my head. After I'd finished with the freezer, I made up with Mike, but I feel I'm treading on eggshells around him. I'm careful to hide my growing anxiety and distress, for fear of another argument. But resentment is beginning to simmer. *I should be able to speak to him about my feelings. How can he think those letters were a coincidence?*

Then I start to doubt myself. How can someone be coming into our house, without us knowing? How would they get in? Josie flashes into my mind. Did she by any chance have a key? Perhaps Helen gave her one, as Mike did to Layla, in case of an emergency.

Layla has a key.

I give myself a mental shake. I'm being ridiculous. Layla is one of my best friends. A solid, dependable person and someone I can count on.

What's that? I'm sure I heard another creak in the loft. *No, I'm imagining it.* Yet, still, I cannot settle. The silence is heavy, wrapping itself around me. Then *tap, tap, tap* . . . like the sound of footsteps moving across the ceiling. My heart beats so fast it pounds in my ears. I want to wake Mike but feel unable to move. One final loud creak and then silence.

Mike grunts in his sleep and I lay a hand on him, desperate to tell him that something is in the loft and that it isn't a rodent. But the thought of breaking our fragile truce stops me. Perhaps it's best to keep quiet for now. I make a decision. If I can pluck up the courage, I will go into the loft and see for myself.

A familiar sound interrupts the oppressive stillness. I sigh and head for Poppy's room. At least this sounds like a normal sleepy cry and nothing like her recent night terrors. *Be grateful for small mercies.*

* * *

Mike appears at my bedside with a steaming cup of coffee. Poppy is at his side, carefully holding a plate of buttered toast.

I stretch. "Ooh, this is a treat. Thanks so much." I smile gratefully at Mike. I slept really badly and it was kind of him to give me a lie-in. My heart feels a little less sore as he plants a kiss on my head and gives me the coffee.

"Me buttered the toast me-self," Poppy proclaims proudly.

"I thought we could explore a bit today. Fancy Kew Gardens?" he asks.

I sip my coffee and smile. "Perfect."

The tension has thawed and Mike radiates warmth again. *Thank God.* I really need to forget about Josie and the weird things happening in this house for now. Poppy snuggles up to me.

There goes the doorbell. Again. It cuts through my relaxed, lazy mood and I sigh with frustration.

"Who is that at this time in the morning?"

"Well, it is almost nine thirty," smiles Mike. "Not like the crack of dawn. I'll go down."

"Me too, Daddy," Poppy shuffles down from the bed and slips after him.

I snuggle back against the pillow and take a satisfying sip of my coffee. *We're going to have a lovely day getting to know the area, and I'm not going to let my concerns spoil it.*

The sound of a woman's voice rises from the hall. I freeze. Josie. *Not her again.* My first reaction is to hide under the covers. Then the new things I learned about Josie the day before flash into my head. I jump up and grab my dressing gown. I don't want Josie meeting Poppy without me there.

I dash down the stairs and land in the hall with a thud. Josie is crouched on the floor, holding a tray of fairy cakes covered in pink icing and adorned with Smarties and chocolate buttons. Poppy has grabbed a cake in each pudgy hand and is crowing with delight.

Josie smiles at me. "Just something simple I made that I thought Poppy would like."

I can feel myself shooting daggers. I try to stretch my mouth into a smile, but nothing happens.

"That is so kind of you, thanks so much," Mike rushes in, looking embarrassed. He glares at me. "What do you say, Poppy?"

"Thank yooo!" sings Poppy, and stuffs one of the cakes into her mouth. I lean forward and prise the second cake out of her hand.

"One's enough for now," I say, feeling like a wicked stepmother.

Poppy momentarily sticks her bottom lip out but is soon distracted by Josie, who coos, "It's so lovely to meet you at long last."

Poppy reaches over and tugs at Josie's flaxen hair with her pudgy fingers. "Me love your hair. It's white," she marvels.

"Is it natural?" I bark, aware that my own dark wiry hair needs a good brush.

Josie smiles tenderly at Poppy. "It's unusual, isn't it? You're right, you don't normally get hair so blonde it's almost white!"

Then addressing me, she adds: "Yes, one hundred per cent natural. Lucky, aren't I!" She gives her hair a flick and it swishes immaculately.

"I show you my baby dolls," Poppy says, stroking Josie's hair. I clench my fists as my daughter stares entranced at our neighbour. Taking Josie's hand, she merrily leads her to the family room, splodges of pink icing and a lone Smartie trailing in her wake.

Mike moves over to me. "I know you don't like her but for Christ's sake can't you hide it? It's awkward," he hisses. "And it's kind of her to make those cakes for Poppy."

"It's not that I don't like her," I snap back, sotto voce. "I don't trust her."

Mike gives an exaggerated shrug and stalks off in the direction of the kitchen. I scurry after him. I don't want Poppy on her own with Josie.

"Coffee?" asks Mike genially.

"Yes, please. Thank you," says Josie, flashing that dimple of hers.

Josie and Poppy are huddled over one of Poppy's dolls. Josie is pretending to feed it milk from a toy bottle and Poppy is delighted. Josie is engrossed in Poppy's baby doll. She tenderly strokes her, sings to her and earnestly sticks the toy dummy in her mouth.

I make a mental note: I must play with Poppy more.

Mike hands Josie her coffee and makes excuses to retire to his computer in the study. I roll my eyes. *Great. I'm stuck with her on my own.* I pointedly look at my watch and wonder when I can hint we need her to go so we can have our day at Kew Gardens.

Poppy places the baby carefully in its cot. "Sleepy time," she sings. Josie raises her eyes to me. "It's so lovely to see such happiness in this house now. She's such a contented little girl."

"Oh, thanks." I'm slightly mollified. Then I frown.

"What do you mean, *now*? Do you mean it was sad or something happened before we moved here?"

Josie drops her eyes down to the doll and strokes its head. She clutches her hands until the knuckles are white and then stares straight into my eyes. I force myself to look away. *She's hamming it up.*

"Something very bad happened here," Josie mutters.

"Let's change her nappy, Josie!" interrupts Poppy, pulling down the doll's Babygro.

Josie joins in with gusto.

I stay very still, and my heart thumps harder. A chill sweeps through me as I weigh up Josie's words.

Death? Rape? Murder? Abduction? Arson? The possibilities swirl around my mind, out of control.

Josie looks at me.

"You don't know, do you?" It's a statement, not a question. "I shouldn't have mentioned anything. It just slipped out. I can't help thinking of it when I'm here — and when I'm not here, in fact."

"Josie, Josie." Poppy tugs at her hand impatiently and Josie bends her head over the doll again.

My mouth is dry. I want to press Josie on this. Then I remember Steve contradicting Josie's description of their split, and Josie's apparent lies about her job. Lucy's words ring in my ears: *She seemed obsessed with Sara's little girl.*

I keep my counsel. Josie raises her head from the doll and stares at me. Waiting eagerly for me to ask what happened, no doubt. "It reminds me of things that have happened here before."

Talk about a drip feed. She just wants a reaction. I resolve not to give Josie the satisfaction.

"Oh dear, that sounds tough," I say blandly. "Best I don't ask anymore!"

I pause. "I bumped into one of your former work colleagues, Lucy, at a party that Poppy went to yesterday." I make sure to emphasise *former*.

"Josie, baby did a poop!" shouts Poppy with a wild giggle. "We need to change her nappy again."

I survey Josie's face for any hint of unease or surprise. But her expression remains the same: peaceful and calm.

"Come on then, let's change it again," she says jovially to Poppy, and the two bend over the doll in concentration.

I think that Josie isn't going to respond to me, but eventually she glances up. "Oh yes, Lucy. We didn't get on particularly well," she says with a smile.

I'm about to ask what really led to Josie leaving her job but, again, think better of it. Josie ruffles Poppy's hair.

"Two blondes together," she murmurs.

Poppy grabs a handful of Josie's hair. "Me love your hair."

I jump up, holding my hands behind my back to stop myself from grabbing Poppy and pulling her away from Josie.

"Right, Josie, we've got a trip planned to Kew Gardens today. So, I'm sorry, but we'd best get a move on."

Josie nods and gets to her feet. "Well, it's been fabulous meeting you, Poppy, and I can't wait to see you again."

Poppy grabs Josie's hands. "Don't go. Play with my dolly with me."

"Ah, I'm so sorry but your mummy has plans today for you and Daddy and I don't want to get in the way. I'll come again very soon."

I feel like someone has placed a rock in my stomach. "Come on, Poppy, love. We need to get going. We're going to have an exciting day!" I babble, trying not to jog to the front door.

Poppy grips Josie's hand as they head to the hallway. Mike bobs his head around the living room door.

"Thanks for coming round. It looks like you've made a little friend." He smiles at Josie, ruffling Poppy's hair.

I'm battling with my anger that Mike is being so amenable to Josie when he knows my feelings about her, when Poppy's face crumples.

With an effort bordering on the superhuman, I manage to keep my composure. The same cannot be said for Poppy. "Me want you to stay," she shrieks, tears rolling down her flushed cheeks. "Please, please." She flings herself at Josie.

I grab Poppy and pull her from behind. "Come on, darling, we're going to have a great day. You can have an ice cream and we'll find a playground." I'm struggling to keep my voice calm.

Poppy hits me with a bunched fist.

Mike moves over to Josie quickly. "Come over again soon . . ." He starts to close the door.

Josie stands on the doorstep. "Oh, I will. And Poppy, I can't wait to see you again. I'll bring you a little something for your doll. And as I said to Clara, I'm so glad that this house is happy again."

Mike seems not to have noticed Josie's final sentence and turns instantly to Poppy.

"Poppy!" he scolds. "Do not hit your mother."

I take my phone from my pocket, fighting the urge to type "Lunn Road Twickenham deaths" into Google.

Josie lies. And Josie wants me to be upset and unsettled, I'm sure of it. *I'm not going to give her the satisfaction.*

The doorbell sounds again.

An electric shock courses through me. I've never felt so close to the edge as I am now. My self-control evaporates.

"What now?" I scream. Though she's no longer in our home, I can't escape Josie. I feel those marble-blue eyes boring into my soul. I want to poke my fingers through them.

Poppy stops crying and gives a sharp intake of breath. "Josie?" she says hopefully.

I march to the door and fling it open, my mouth a snarl. Layla stands there, sturdy boots on and clutching two takeaway coffee cups.

She looks alarmed. "Oh gosh, have I come at a bad time?" she asks.

I hastily rearrange my face. "Just had Josie the next-door neighbour round and she is utterly trying," I sigh, eyes darting around. I half expect Josie to leap out from the bushes separating our drives.

"Oh no." Layla pulls a sympathetic face. "I hope I'm not interrupting. I just thought I'd pop over and see if you fancied a quick walk and a coffee with me? Got you a flat white." She holds out one of the cups.

I'm torn. I've had enough of people surprising me and want my day out at Kew Gardens with my family. But on the other hand, I want to offload to someone about Josie. Specifically, to someone who isn't Mike. Even though my mind is on fire I don't want to say anything to him for fear of breaking our fragile bond.

Poppy's tears have stopped at the sight of Layla. She propels herself out of Mike's arms. "Layla!" she shrieks.

Mike grins at Layla and turns to me. "Go for a walk and a nice coffee with Layla. You need to decompress," he urges.

"Are you sure? What about our day out?" I ask.

"We'll go when you get back," says Mike, smiling at me encouragingly.

I hesitate, then seize the coffee. "Thank you," I murmur gratefully, kissing him.

We pass Josie's house. I glance at the windows and am relieved to see no ghostly face peering at us.

Josie wants to lead me a merry dance. *Well, just let her try.* Finally, I can feel the spring returning to my step.

CHAPTER 15

I put some lipstick on and survey my face in the mirror. A flash of guilt runs through me. I don't want Mike to think I take him for granted. I grab my brush and rigorously pull it though my hair, grimacing at the dark, wiry curls. Silky, smooth-as-butter blonde hair comes to mind.

Josie hasn't visited since Saturday. I saw her in her drive yesterday, after collecting Poppy from nursery. Hauling Poppy along, I sprinted to the front door and slammed it shut.

I'm really looking forward to tonight. Layla, upon hearing my woes on our walk at the weekend, has offered to babysit. I've booked a tiny Italian restaurant tucked away by the river, recommended by Mabel. Then hopefully we'll have a nightcap in the pub on the way home.

Ker-chunk. There is a grinding sound coming from downstairs, and then the front door handle rattles. I fly down the stairs. Poppy, for once, has gone to sleep quickly and I cannot risk her being disturbed.

My heart pounds as the handle pumps up and down.

"Who is it?" I ask stridently.

"Me, Layla." Layla sounds cross.

Of course. My heart rate slows as I open the door.

Layla stomps in. "I thought I'd use my key to let myself in so as not to wake Poppy by ringing the doorbell."

"We actually got the locks changed yesterday." I fight my frustration that Layla has once again tried to let herself in without checking with me first. *She was being thoughtful*, I tell myself.

Layla pounds her feet on the mat aggressively as Mike appears.

"You changed the locks," she says accusingly to Mike, dispensing with pleasantries.

"Yeah, we did. I think you feel more comfortable now, don't you, Clara?" Mike places a hand on my shoulder. I resent his slightly patronising tone. *Poor old Clara and her overactive imagination.*

Mike moves over to the hall table. "Here's a new key for you." He passes it to Layla, who pockets it.

I bite down on my lip. My mind screams, *I don't want anyone apart from Mike or me to have a key. Not even my best friend.*

***

"You look as relaxed as I've seen you since we moved." Mike holds my hand as we sit in a corner of *La Vicina*, the candle on our table casting flickering shadows on the beams above. "And you look lovely too." He smiles at me.

I squeeze his fingers, with a little flash of pleasure. I've managed to tame my brunette curls, and a dash of mascara and eyeshadow have emphasised my large, chocolate-brown eyes. *Yes, I've scrubbed up well.* I may not have Josie's ethereal look and blonde locks, but I tell myself firmly that I'm just as striking.

"Thank you. And you don't look too bad yourself." I admire Mike's boyish, clean-cut good looks. His shiny, thick dark hair and hazel eyes.

A waitress arrives with our starters: calamari for me, and king prawns for Mike.

I take a bite of a squid ring. "Ah! Delicious!"

Mike dips his buttery fingers in the bowl of hot water provided.

I wonder whether I should tell him about Josie's dark hints about our house's past. I open my mouth to speak but then find myself gulping from my wine glass instead. *We've had enough problems. No point souring the evening.* And I don't want to give Josie the satisfaction.

* * *

We settle the bill. Mike goes to freshen up and I wait for him at the table. I put on my coat. From the corner of my eye I see a woman leave the restaurant. She has a sheet of gleaming dark hair. A red-haired man has his arm clamped round her. I frown. That smooth, shining mane rings a bell. I shrug. *How many women must there be who have hair like that?*

The woman turns to face her partner and I gasp. *Helen.* The couple head out of the door. I have so many unanswered questions. *Why did you leave the wall scribbled with pen and the cooker top broken, and then insist you hadn't? Did Josie bother you? Did she show interest in your children? Did you have lights going on and off, apparently of their own accord? Did you hear noises in the loft? Did something happen in the house before?*

I jump up and run out of the restaurant. "Helen!" I shout. The woman looks straight at me as she climbs into a taxi. The angular bone structure, prominent nose. Yes, that's Helen all right. Her eyes widen and I see a spark of recognition in them. But she turns her head quickly and slams the door shut.

The car drives off. I fling a hand out in frustration as Mike emerges from the door. He looks annoyed. "What are you doing here? I thought you were going to wait for me at the table."

"I saw Helen and her husband in the restaurant and they drove off in a taxi. They're meant to have moved to the Midlands. Why are they still here?" My composure has deserted me as quickly as it returned.

Mike frowns. "I don't think we should jump to conclusions. Maybe they've come back for a visit."

"So soon after they moved from the area and in the middle of the week?" I shake my head. "She recognised me, I'm sure of it. She didn't want to speak to me. I think they're hiding something from us."

My mind is off the leash now and zigzagging unpredictably. Helen attributed their departure to a new job. But what if there was no new job, and they still lived in Twickenham? What drove them out of their house? I visualise Josie's face at the window. *Ididit, ididit. I did it.* My main course of spaghetti carbonara is a dead weight in my stomach.

"She probably feels embarrassed about the way they left the house, that we called them up on the damage and they denied it. She's undoubtedly annoyed they had to capitulate in the end and pay us for it," argues Mike, now making no attempt to hide his irritation.

The sighting of Helen has changed the atmosphere. We hold hands stiffly, marching past various pubs and abandoning the after-dinner drink we'd planned.

I turn the key quietly and we creep down the hall to the living room. Layla is snuggled on the sofa, huddled over her phone. She glances up, surprised.

"You're back quite early. I thought you'd be later," she says, putting down her phone with a flourish.

"We had a lovely time at the restaurant but thought we should call it a day. After all, it is a work night," says Mike, giving Layla a smile that doesn't reach his eyes.

I notice this and am keen to change the subject. "Was everything OK? I hope Poppy didn't disturb you."

"She was a little star," says Layla promptly. "She woke briefly, about an hour ago, and I was about to go up and settle her when she went back to sleep on her own."

Her phone beeps. Layla grins. "Matt again," she says dreamily. "He's been messaging me all evening, and we're going out tomorrow night."

"That's great," I say. I really hope this one works out for Layla.

"Looks like you've got a good 'un this time," Mike responds easily, flinging himself down on the sofa.

"Tea, anyone?" It feels only polite to offer after Layla did us a big favour, but I'm tired and hope that Layla refuses it and heads home.

But Layla is in the mood to talk, especially about Matt. "Yes, please. I'd love a cuppa before I go home," she says. Mike accepts the offer too and I head off to the kitchen. Switching on the lights, I see a small puddle on the floor. Layla must have split some water. I reach for some paper towel to mop it up when there's a splash of water on the top of my head, and then another. I look up at the ceiling and see a large damp patch, surrounded by a few smaller ones, from which water is dripping. There's a bang and the kitchen lights go out.

I gasp. "What the hell?"

With a sinking feeling I remember the bathroom is above the kitchen and dash down the hall and up the stairs. The hall carpet is sodden as I run into the bathroom. The bath is overflowing and water runs over the tiled floor, covering my feet.

I look around the room wildly as I give the bath tap handles a violet twist. What will the damage be to the house? How much will it cost?

"There's been a flood in the bathroom!" I shock Mike and Layla into silence. "Water's gone everywhere — all over the bathroom, into the hall and through the kitchen ceiling. That'll be why the lights have gone out."

Mike jumps up as if a rocket is underneath him and dashes up the stairs.

Without pausing for thought, I turn on my friend.

"What on earth has happened, Layla?" My voice is aggressive and angry.

Layla is white, her mouth agape. "I don't understand," she mutters, disbelief etched on her face. "I didn't turn the bath on. I didn't go near it."

93

The two of us follow Mike up the stairs like zombies. Mike grabs a towel off the radiator, I think to try and mop up the water on the floor. But he throws it across the room at the window. He picks up another towel and hurls it and then the last one on the rail he slams into the bath, into which it sinks.

"Fucking bloody hell!" he roars.

I watch him with alarm. "You'll wake Poppy. Please, Mike . . ."

"I don't care," he shouts, picking up a shower gel bottle and throwing it, water droplets spurting up and splashing my leg as it hits the floor.

"I've bloody had enough of this place. It's cursed." Apoplectic with rage, his face is flushed scarlet and his eyes bulge. My frenzy at the flood has been displaced with worry about Mike. I've never seen him so angry.

I place a hand on his shoulder but he shrugs it off. Turning to face Layla he demands: "How on earth did you miss this, Layla? Too busy on the phone to your new bloke?"

Layla's eyes pool with tears. "I'm so, so sorry." Her voice cracks. "I have no idea how this happened. I don't understand it."

Mike's meltdown means that I have to be the calm one and take control.

"The taps weren't on when we left," I say, thinking quickly. "I gave Poppy her bath as usual and we took out the plug — in fact, she took it out, she loves to do that."

"It must have been Poppy," mumbles Layla, dabbing at her eyes. "There's no other explanation. As I said, she woke up briefly a little while ago. She must have turned the taps on then."

Mike picks up a shampoo bottle. I put my hand on his arm warningly. He lowers it slowly onto the side of the bath.

"How would a two-year-old manage this?" Mike's rage has turned to despondency. "She has a stair gate."

I dart to Poppy's room to check the gate. It's just as we left it.

"It's closed," I report to Mike and Layla when I return to the bathroom. "But Poppy has been desperately trying to climb over that gate, and almost achieved it just yesterday."

"OK, well, I guess that must have happened," says Mike slowly.

"I should have gone up to her when I heard her cry out," says Layla, wringing her hands.

"It's not your fault," Mike sighs. "I'm sorry I snapped at you. It felt like the last straw, after the rough time we've had since moving here."

"Me too," I say quickly, shamefaced at my earlier sharpness.

"It's OK." Layla hangs her head. "Let me at least help you guys try and clear this water up."

"Thank you," I say gratefully. Running on adrenaline, my mind races as I try to work out how to mitigate the damage as much as possible.

"We need towels, as many as possible." I survey the soaking towels Mike flung in the water. *I wish he hasn't done that.*

"There are towels in the linen cupboard in the spare room. Layla, please can you get them. Let's open the bathroom window wide. Mike, can you peel the carpet back in the hall, to let the floorboards dry out. We have a dehumidifier in the utility room, remember we used it for the dampness in our flat? Let me go and get that now. Mike, I'll ring an electrician, to sort out the lights in the kitchen tomorrow."

As I turn to go downstairs, I peer into Poppy's room. She's sprawled across the bed, breathing deeply and peacefully.

We work as quickly and efficiently as possible. After an hour, I review our progress. There is still water on the floor, and the bathroom is filled with a musty smell, but we've done as much as we can for now.

"Come on, let's call it a day," I say.

"We'll have to replace the carpet," says Mike glumly as we pass the rolled-up, sodden hall carpet, the floorboards still wet under our fleet despite scrubbing them with towels.

"We'll deal with it tomorrow," I say. I can't believe how calm I am. It's usually me that crumbles. Now that the roles have reversed, I've been forced to step up and take the lead.

"I'm so sorry," Layla says again as she shuffles into her coat.

I hug her. "Don't worry. How were you to know? And thanks again for babysitting and helping to clear up. Are you sure I can't call you an Uber?"

"No, I need a walk. I want to clear my head."

Layla opens the door.

"Please be careful, and text when you get home," I say.

No sooner have I closed the door than Mike says, "I'm sorry, but she shouldn't have missed Poppy turning those taps on. She must have made a noise, climbing over the stair gate and back and going to the bathroom. Like I said, too engrossed with her new bloke to notice." He curls his lip disdainfully. "Pathetic. I don't want her coming again to babysit. She's not mature enough."

I sigh. I too feel a spark of anger against Layla, tempered by genuine love for my friend.

"Accidents happen," I say, flinching at my glibness.

Mike puts his arm around me. "I'm sorry for my outburst before," he says shamefacedly. "I don't know what came over me. It feels like just another thing with this flipping house."

"I know." I give his arm a squeeze. I manage a reassuring smile. "I know I've wound you up too with my ranting and raving! We'll just have to make sure Poppy never does that again."

"She wouldn't have managed that if we'd been here," Mike mutters. I agree silently.

Mike gives me a bear hug. "You were amazing tonight, thank you," he says. I cling to him, my happiness at our renewed closeness briefly overshadowing the latest crisis.

"Well, for once I was calm and collected, just about!" I smile at him again. "Better that than totally losing my rag."

Later in bed, I run over the events in my head. *Is Poppy really capable of climbing over the stair gate, putting the plug in the bath, turning the taps on and then climbing back? And if she is, surely it would have been a struggle and Layla would have been alerted.* I file the incident along with the lights switching off, the words on Poppy's board and the noises in the loft.

But if it wasn't Poppy, then who was it? Layla's face looms in my mind, but I banish it quickly. *Of course not.* She's one of my most loyal friends and we've been through ups and downs together since university.

I've bloody had enough of this place. It's cursed. Mike's voice, trembling with rage and despair, fills my mind. I cling to him. *What if it is?*

* * *

I didn't actually intend to turn on their taps. Honestly. But the opportunity came my way and I couldn't resist. If those taps couldn't flood the whole house out and wreck it, they were at least guaranteed to give Clara another nasty shock. Job done.

CHAPTER 16

I wake with a start, heart pounding. I wonder why I feel so agitated and peer at the ceiling fearfully. *Please, no more noises.* Then the events of the previous night barge into my mind. I groan and squeeze my eyes shut. That sodden carpet. Those wet floorboards. That mess in the bathroom.

I don't think I can feel worse than I currently do, but then I sense that familiar gripe in my lower stomach and tears squeeze through my eyelids. I pad across the room to the damp floor of the hall, the musty smell permeating my nostrils. Soaking wet, freezing cold towels greet my feet as I squelch across the floor. The skirting boards around the bathroom are discoloured and the paint is starting to peel. The dehumidifier whirrs in the corner.

Grimly, I sit on the toilet and my suspicions are confirmed. The thought of the pregnancy tests lined up in the bathroom cupboard are the final straw and I burst into tears.

I had set such high hopes that this month I would conceive — silly, really. My sensible self knows it can take months, and at thirty-five I'm still young. The disappointment is sharper because of the flooding in the bathroom, and the other stresses our new house has caused.

I make my way slowly back to bed and curl up in the foetal position, tears streaking down my cheeks. I don't try to stop them. The day's tasks stretch in front of me, endless. Arrange for a new carpet. Call an electrician. Call the insurance company. Clean. Dry. Repair. Repair. Clean. Dry. Not to mention handling Poppy's daily needs. I bury my head under the duvet.

Arms snake around me. "What's up?" Mike's voice is sleepy, his breath in my ear.

"What do you think?" I cuddle into him. "Sorry, I don't mean to be snappy. I'm dreading everything we'll have to do today to sort out the flooding. And I just found out that there's no baby this time. Oh Mike, I had such a good feeling. It's kind of tipped me over the edge." I bite into my pillow to stop a sob.

Mike pulls me to him and I gratefully bury my face in his chest, scrunching my eyes shut. I want to stay like this for ever. I can't face the day.

"We've tried once, just once, Clara," he says into my hair, in between kisses. "Everyone knows it's really rare for it to happen immediately. We'll keep trying and it'll happen, I know it. We've had Poppy and we'll have another."

I know he's right, but I feel so empty and despondent.

"I'm taking today off sick," Mike announces. "We're going to sort this out together."

Relief floods through me as he busily taps on his phone. "Let me just email my boss," Mike murmurs, concentrating. "Then I'm going to check our home insurance documents, just to see if we're covered for the damage."

"OK, well, I'll ring the electrician who came round before." I grab my phone and grimace. "Ah, maybe it's a little early. I'll text him instead."

My words are punctured by a sleepy cry from Poppy. We jump up and head to her room together. I just hope that Poppy admits that it was her. I would a million times rather that it was my daughter than an alternative. *Whatever that might be.*

Mike winces as we step over the sodden floorboards to Poppy's room.

Poppy is sitting up in bed, her curls wild, looking adorable. I slip into bed with her to cuddle her and Mike sits on the side of it.

"Darling," I say gently. "I need you to tell me something. I promise you won't be in trouble. Did you climb over your stair gate last night and turn on the bath taps?"

I hold my breath. Poppy rubs sleepy dust from one eye with a curled-up fist. "Milk!" she shouts.

I sigh and try to cover my frustration as Mike leans forward and places Poppy on his knee.

"We'll get you your milk, but we just need to know — did you get out of your room, by getting over your staircase, and go into the bathroom and turn the bath taps on?" he asks gently, speaking slowly.

Poppy looks at us wide-eyed. "Me can't get out," she says loudly. "Me not go to bathroom. Milk!"

My chest is heavy. But Mike shakes his head slightly. "I didn't think she'd admit it. She probably can't even remember, half asleep or something," he mutters, placing Poppy back on the bed as he rises to get her milk.

I take a breath. "I believe her. I don't think she's capable of climbing over the stair gate, putting the plug in the bath, and turning the taps on, and then climbing back." As I list the tasks, it becomes even more incredible to me that Poppy would be able to do this. "And all without Layla noticing."

Irritation crosses Mike's face. "Well, who else could it be?" he retorts. "Someone came into our house, turned the taps on and fled, or Layla herself?"

Despite his words, I'm sure I spot a flash of doubt in his eyes. He looks away quickly.

* * *

I lay my head on the table. It's only 10 a.m. but it feels as though we've been at it for hours — making calls, leaving messages, sending emails. The insurance company won't pay out as we're deemed responsible for leaving the bath taps on. Keith the electrician is due in the afternoon to inspect the damage. Meanwhile, Mike has gone to Kingston to hire a more powerful dehumidifier.

To cap it all, I really need to get to my laptop and start work. I'm walking to the kitchen door when the doorbell echoes through the house. That sound was once so innocuous but now feels anything but. I flatten myself against the side of the kitchen wall and peek around the door.

I can see a small, slight, blurry silhouette through the coloured glass of the front door. I'm sure it's Josie. *Go away. I can't face you.*

The figure stays there, immobile. My heart pounds, rage and unease swirling through me. *Fuck off.* I clench my fists, on the verge of marching to the front door to send Josie on her way.

Hang on. Wouldn't that be the mature reaction, rather than hiding behind the door?

I'm preparing to confront Josie when a hand appears through the letterbox.

I stare for a second, transfixed. The flap falls back with a thud and I storm across the hall, flinging open the door. Nobody there.

I sprint to Josie's drive only to find it empty, the front door closed. I wonder whether to knock on her door but decide against it. I don't want to engage with Josie at the best of times. Certainly not today.

I'd like nothing better than for Josie to leave my family alone. *Why is she so bloody weird?* I run up the stairs to my office, grimacing at the still-damp floorboards. Then I tread on something small and hard.

"Ouch!" I lift my foot up quickly and uncover a silver metal object. Frowning, I pick it up. I'm sure it wasn't there before. I turn the smooth shape over in my hand, noting the way it tapers to a spiral point. *What is it? It looks a bit like a . . . no, it can't be.* The flooding has played havoc with my nerves and I'm imagining things.

Nonetheless, it feels very important to know what it is. I reach into my pocket for my phone and use my image recognition app. The results are through instantly. A row of images, with the same word included in the captions.

Bullet.

I scream and drop the smooth object like a hot coal, watching it clatter on the exposed wooden boards. I run to the bathroom, hands shaking as I slide the lock across the door. *Is there someone with a gun in the house? What do I do?* Despite my terror, I'm so grateful that Poppy is at nursery. I clutch my phone, type in 999, then pause. I place my ear against the door, wondering if I'll hear the familiar creaks from the loft. But all I can hear is the whirr of the dehumidifier.

My hand hovers over the call button. There is a bullet in my house. That means someone with a gun could be in it, as it wasn't there before. I'm sure of it. But then doubts start to creep in. Maybe the app is wrong. Maybe the "bullet" was there previously and was uncovered when Mike rolled the carpet back. Though even if that were true, why was it there in the first place?

Something very bad happened here. Josie's soft tones fill my ears. I shiver. I inch towards the door and unlock it, peeking out. Nothing.

I tiptoe to each room, sliding my head round the door. Once satisfied, I creep down the stairs, holding my breath. An inspection of every room on the ground floor shows that I'm the only person in the house. *Now.* Noises in the loft are one thing. But an actual bullet in the house. I sit on the window seat, frozen with fear, desperate for Mike to come home.

* * *

Mike climbs from his car and I jump up, ready to dive out of the front door, when a familiar, slight figure appears by his side. Josie's wearing a shift dress that clings to her figure and reaches only to mid-thigh, showing off her legs. She's wearing thin nylon tights. It's February and I feel cold just looking at her.

Josie looks as though she's asking a question. Then Mike talks animatedly and at some length, no doubt informing her of the flooded bath. Josie stares at him intently. She tucks silky hair behind one ear and tilts her face, so she's looking straight at Mike. Her gaze is rapt and her eyes don't leave his face.

A vein thumps in my forehead as Mike ends his monologue. Josie leans forward and places her hand on his shoulder.

She leans forward until her mouth is close to his face, speaking earnestly. Her hand remains there. Mike is smiling and focused on Josie. Josie stops speaking and neither of them move. Then Mike breaks the spell by heading off to the boot of the car. I see him lug the big, unwieldly box holding the dehumidifier out.

He turns to Josie and says something. "Goodbye," I presume. He beams at her and turns to the house. Josie stands still, watching Mike go. The key in the lock turns and Mike slams the door. Josie's still standing there. She looks at the living room window, and her eyes lock onto mine. We stare at each other. Her friendly smile disappears. She turns slowly and retraces her steps down the drive.

Anger and distrust fight each other but I need to forget about that little interaction for now, as my finding must take precedence. I rush out to the hall.

"Hi, Clara. I've got the dehumidifier; it's a big old beast," Mike says cheerily, his face falling as he looks at me. "What's the matter? Oh no, has the water caused some other damage?"

I grab him. I want to bury my head in his shoulders, to block out everything.

"It's worse than that. Mike, I found a bullet on the upstairs landing. I swear it wasn't there before. I think we're being targeted by someone, someone with a gun." I struggle to catch my breath. "We're in danger. We need to call the police."

I whimper, sounding like an infant, but I don't care. Mike abruptly lets go of the dehumidifier and it falls like a rock.

"Show me." Despite my fear, I note that for once he isn't trying to deny my worries. Mike's eyes are wide and I can see anxiety clouding them. He follows me in silence up the stairs.

"There." I gesture to the area of the floor where I dropped the bullet. Mike's eyebrows rise and then it hits me. There's nothing there. Just an expanse of sodden wooden boards.

"Where the . . . ?" I scan the landing, even grabbing the rolled-up carpet and shaking it violently.

"I know I dropped it there, I know it," I cry. "Someone must have been in and taken it away. They might still be in the house."

The scepticism that is quickly replacing the concern on Mike's face tells me how crazy I must sound.

"I'm not mad!" I shriek. "I'm not." Fumbling with my phone, I show Mike the image search results. "See, this is what the app suggested." *Surely he will see "bullet" and realise that our lives are in danger?*

But after briefly scanning the images, Mike drops his head in his hands. "I don't know, but I'm not sure the app has got this right. I mean, why would there be a *bullet* here?" His voice softens. "And how can it just have vanished? Look, Clara, I know how stressful this house has been. God, I feel it too, and the flooding is the last straw. I think perhaps you're seeing things . . ." He pauses. "Which maybe aren't there or you're . . ."

"What the hell are you trying to say?" I butt in, enraged. "Are you suggesting that the bullet is a figment of my imagination? It was here. I know it was." I point frantically at the corner of the floor where I know I dropped it. "I didn't just imagine it." I gesticulate at my phone. "I don't feel safe. I'm going to call the police."

"About what?" The gentleness of Mike's voice is being replaced by a more abrasive quality. "There's nothing here."

I fling my phone on the floor with frustration. He's right. But I know there was a bullet in this house, and it popped up out of nowhere.

I look hard at Mike. He should have my back and yet he doesn't believe me. How did that bullet get onto the landing? He's the one who spent so much time up here last night, pulling back the carpet.

"You were up here for ages last night. Maybe it slipped out from under the carpet as you rolled it. Or maybe you planted it."

I clamp a hand over my mouth. I can't believe what I'm saying.

Mike's eyes widen in shock and his mouth becomes so thin it almost disappears.

"What's wrong with you?" he asks furiously. "You think your husband left a bullet on the landing? What the hell would my motive be?" He steps towards me, fists clenched. I take an involuntary step back and then he's running down the stairs, shouting. He slams the front door and I hear a vicious revving of the car engine.

I slump to the floor, my anger slowly replaced by remorse. *What have I done?* I feel let down that Mike doesn't believe me, but of course that doesn't mean he planted it himself. My cheeks burn with shame. My kind, wonderful husband. How could I possibly accuse him of that?

But where the hell is it? I look carefully around again and check the bedrooms, including the beds. I search the living room once more. Nothing. *I'm such an idiot.* I curse myself for not putting the object in my pocket.

I wonder uneasily when Mike will be back. I'll try and make it up to him for my outburst. Opening the box, I drag out the dehumidifier and struggle with it up the stairs. As I plug it in, I reconsider the incident with Helen. If it even was Helen. Maybe that was why "Helen" blanked me when I shouted her name.

At the time, I was certain. But Mike's scepticism has made me doubt myself and deep down, I know what I'm doing is irrational.

I wonder if Helen left this house because she felt like me. Eyes everywhere. Unexplained events. Worst of all, that sinister presence just the other side of the wall. I wish I had a way of contacting Helen or her husband, so I could ask them why they left.

Back to more important matters. I need to make up with Mike. I grab my coat and head out to buy him a bottle of decent red wine and some chocolates. When I get back, though, there's still no sign of him. On the floor by the front door is a blank white envelope. With a shudder, I recall the hand snaking through the letterbox earlier in the day.

A sense of dread overwhelms me. I open the envelope slowly. Usually, I rip them open impatiently. Several newspaper cuttings spill from the envelope and float to the floor. I gather them and begin to read.

UNIVERSITY PROFESSOR FOUND DEAD WITH WIFE AND DAUGHTER.

Beneath the headline is a picture of a house with a large rowan tree and bay windows. Police officers patrol the outside of the property, which has been cordoned off.

That's our house. I collapse on the sofa. *Something very bad happened here.* Josie's voice echoes through my mind again. The page shakes in my hand as I squint to see the date. Ten years ago.

A history professor from prestigious Petersham University in London has been found dead in his house with his wife and daughter.

Professor Jonathan Maynard, 45, his wife Anna, 45, and their daughter, Jasmine, 11, were found dead in their house in Twickenham at 2.15 a.m. on Tuesday.

But their other daughter, Lily, 13, was found alive and unhurt in the house.

Officers from Middlesex Police said there was no third-party involvement.

A gun was recovered at the property that was licensed and registered to Jonathan Maynard.

Neighbours heard gunshots fire out in the early hours of Tuesday morning, accompanied by screaming, and called the police.

Professor Jonathan Maynard worked at Petersham University for 10 years. He was an eminent military historian, specialising in weapons of war, and had written a number of books. Anna Maynard was a nurse who worked at Twickenham Hospital.

In a statement, the university wrote: "We are shocked and horrified by this news. Jonathan Maynard made a wonderful contribution to life at Petersham University, where he was respected by staff and students alike. We hope the family's privacy can be respected at this extremely sad time."

Mrs Maynard's family released their own statement: "We are utterly heartbroken and stunned by this news. Anna was a loving daughter, sister and mother. Jasmine was on the cusp of a wonderful school career. For the sake of Lily, our niece and granddaughter, we ask that our privacy is respected."

Middlesex Police said that the deaths had been reported to the coroner.

I retch, struggling not to vomit. Which rooms did they die in? The memory of the bullet is seared in my brain, along with an image of a gun.

I had been so focused on the photo of the house — my house — that I'd neglected the other image in the article. I pick up the cutting and there is the family of four. They're laughing and linking arms, on top of a hill.

The sun is shining, layers of light covering the people in the photo. The man with the beaming smile must be the father — Professor Jonathan Maynard. I hold the cutting closer to my face. His eyes are brooding, but you wouldn't notice if you just clocked his beaming smile.

His wife, Anna, has wavy hair. She's smiling but her teeth aren't visible. Jasmine looks like her mother.

Lily has a shock of curls and huge eyes. *She looks like an older version of Poppy.* I push the thought away. I cannot bear to compare my beloved daughter with this girl and her tragic history.

Jasmine's arms are around her parents but Lily has her arms folded across her chest.

There is another clipping. Almost unconsciously, I pick it up. It is dated a few days after the previous one. I scan and read.

Anna Maynard, 45, and her daughter Jasmine, 11, were shot dead in a murder-suicide by their husband and father Professor Jonathan Maynard.

Their daughter Lily, 13, was unharmed and was found by police "hiding in a wardrobe", according to sources.

Neighbours called the police after they heard screams and a series of gunshots.

Josie Sanders, a neighbour, said: "I grew close to the children, especially Lily, and I am heartbroken about this. I cannot imagine how Lily feels."

She added: "I used to hear Jonathan shouting through the wall. I believe that his daughters, particularly Lily, were scared of him."

Anna's brother, Andrew, said: "We have lost the most wonderful sister, daughter and mother, and our amazing, talented, wonderfully funny niece, Jasmine. We are now focused on Lily. We need to help her overcome the terrible trauma she has experienced and would ask that our requests for privacy are respected."

Accompanying it is a picture of the family on a speedboat on holiday. Throwaway smiles and hair flying behind them.

Were Jonathan and his wife in the bedroom I share with Mike when he fired the gun? Did blood spatter the walls and ceiling and carpet?

I picture Jasmine in Poppy's pink room. Although maybe it wasn't painted pink then. An innocent girl, killed. There would have been worse on the wall than the huge, scribbled mess we found when moving in.

I think of the room we've earmarked for our second child. Who did that one belong to? I love to spend time in it, imagining a tiny baby in a cot in the corner, sleeping peacefully.

Was it Lily in there, cowering in the closet that is right now filled with our bedding?

I hear the key turning in the front door and frantically weigh up whether to show Mike the newspaper clippings.

Now isn't a good time. I shove them under the sofa. I've never kept secrets from him until now. Another wedge between us. I take a deep breath as Mike enters the living room. In my mind's eye the walls are splattered with blood.

* * *

Now they know what happened in that house. Good. The secret is out. I'm amazed that it took so long. Most people research houses before they move in. Surely if they had, they wouldn't have touched it with a barge pole. Then again, the people before them hadn't known about the history either. How can they continue to live there still knowing what happened? Dream home? More like a house of horrors. And they can't wind back the clock now. What's done can't be undone. They're seeing the house for what it really is. There's more to come too, believe me. Watch this space.

CHAPTER 17

I pick up the newspaper clippings. My hands shake as I stare at them. I know what I have to do.

It's the following morning. I've barely slept, and I can't stop thinking about that family. Especially Jasmine and Lily. When I finally fell asleep, in my dream Poppy morphed into Lily, hiding for her life in the closet.

I was desperate to research the murders on the internet, to go through all the past newspaper articles that night, but I didn't want Mike suspecting anything. And I needed to focus on making everything right with him. He accepted my apology and the wine, even having a glass. But now there's a glass door between us. Transparent, but no matter how hard I try to break through, I can't. We speak kindly and politely to each other, but between us hangs so many words unspoken.

Tears spring to my eyes and I scrub them away fiercely with my fingers. *I can't think about this now.* I have questions that need answers quickly. Number one: did Josie post those clippings? *Of course she did.*

I slam the front door and march over to Josie's house. I hesitate before I ring the doorbell. I've never been to her home before and despite myself, I'm curious. I want to look around, to see if there are any more clues about this strange woman who has come to dominate my thoughts.

I press the buzzer firmly and a few seconds later Josie appears at the door. She's dressed in her usual floating gear. This time a creased pink skirt that stretches to her ankles, and a silky blue top. *Not like the tight-fitting, thigh-skimming dress you wore when Mike saw you yesterday.*

I get straight to the point. "I need to talk to you about these." I wave the cuttings in Josie's face.

Josie's eyes widen. "You'd better come in," she says. I follow her. The hall is similar to the one in my own house, with the same original parquet flooring. Josie leads me into the living room. The dark navy walls contrast pleasingly with the white plantation shutters in the bay window. I sit on the sofa and hand the news stories to Josie.

"They were posted through our door yesterday." I strive to keep my tone even. "As you can imagine, they gave me a real shock."

Josie scans them and sighs. "I can imagine. Look, I never put these through your door." She stares at me directly, unwavering. My retort of "Yeah right" dies on my lips. Against my better judgement, I'm starting to wonder whether it might have been someone else. *Another neighbour out to get us?*

"It'll be someone local — everyone here knows all about the house and its history," says Josie. "And actually . . . look, I wasn't going to mention this as I didn't want to freak you out, but Helen also received anonymous newspaper cuttings."

"But why would someone do this, and to both of us?" I wonder.

"I suppose they want you to know the history. Why, I don't know. Maybe they're trying to warn you."

"What about the people who lived in the house before Helen?"

"They bought the house after the murders. They knew all about it but I'm not sure how bothered they were. They were retired and weren't around much as they spent half their time in Spain. They're the ones that carried out the extension."

Not bothered? I find that hard to believe. I wait to see what Josie has to say next.

"I was surprised that you had no idea about it." Josie sounds offhand, as though she's trying to play down the matter. "I tried to drop a few hints — clumsily, I do realise — to see whether you did know anything, but I could see you had no inkling."

I'm an idiot. Why did I not do a quick google of the house before we put an offer in, especially after learning that Helen and her family were leaving after only a year?

"I'm surprised you don't remember it," says Josie. "It was all over the papers and TV."

Ten years ago, I'd been living in Singapore, working for a business publication there. I'd had the time of my life and lived in the moment. I certainly wasn't spending much time reading UK news online.

"I had no idea," I say. "I was living abroad at the time. I hadn't met Mike. But he was in Edinburgh then. It happened in London, you know. Maybe he just didn't . . ." My voice trails off.

"Maybe it's not so odd you don't know." Josie's voice has climbed a few decibels, clear and confident. "For people in Twickenham it was huge, but then it would be. It's right on our doorstep. And as I said, Helen and her husband didn't know either."

I open my mouth to speak but the words don't come. I take a breath and try again. "I'm struggling," I say at last. *Keep it simple.* "I'm scared in my home. Please can you tell me what you know?"

I stare at the floor. I don't want to meet Josie's gaze. I would prefer simply to listen to what she has to say.

"I understand." Josie's voice is back to its quiet timbre and I suppress a frustrated sigh.

"When I moved to this house, they were already living here," Josie begins, a faraway look in her eyes. "I became friendly with the girls. Especially Lily. She used to pop over, or I'd see them hurtling down the road on their bikes. I didn't get to know Anna very well. She kept herself to herself, but she was happy for me to be friendly with Lily. As for him . . ."

In a flash, Josie's dreamy expression gives way to contempt.

"I didn't know him well. He was aloof. The odd 'hello' as he marched to his car, if I was lucky. The Big I Am. Off to his important, clever job."

Another dramatic pause.

"But my God! Based on what I heard, I didn't like him one bit."

Apart from the time that Josie grabbed my arm in my kitchen, it's the most emotion I've ever seen her show.

"I could hear him constantly, through the wall. Shouting at them. Berating them. It seemed mainly to be directed towards Lily, although I could sometimes hear Anna and Jasmine get it in the neck. Whatever Lily did was never good enough. And he was especially down on her about her education."

I imagine a menacing man with dark hair, bushy brows and angry eyes pacing the house. Tormenting his daughters. *In OUR kitchen. Sleeping in OUR bedroom.*

I pull myself back to the present. "Why?"

"Lily said her father expected perfection, and she just — Look, I thought she was wonderful, but she wasn't academic. When they . . ."

Josie stops for a second and tilts her head at the wall, as though Anna and Jonathan are still on the other side of it. Sitting in the living room. The living room that now belongs to me and Mike.

"When they discovered I'd studied English literature at university, they asked me to give Lily private tuition. She had a tutor for all the other subjects too. He was desperate for her to pass the Eleven Plus and go to grammar school. He was furious when she failed."

Josie takes a breath. "Jasmine was outstandingly bright and that put even more pressure on Lily."

My stomach churns. I wish more than anything that I was back in my cosy Tooting flat. Driven by a dreadful urge I cannot resist, I demand more details.

"But why did he murder Jasmine and not Lily?"

"Lily managed to escape. She hid in the wardrobe of her room."

Yes. Of course. I remember the newspaper article.

All the bedrooms have built-in wardrobes. Which had Lily been in? I squeeze my eyes shut.

"As for why he killed Jasmine . . . Well, that's a mystery." Josie looks skywards for a moment. "There has never been a solid reason why he murdered his wife and daughter and then blew his brains out."

I wince at the harsh language.

"Did you hear anything?" Again, I cannot suppress that awful urge. *Why do I even want to know?*

"Yes. I was in bed, but I suffer from insomnia. Steve was away for work. I just remember the *bang, bang, bang* and I almost jumped out of my skin. It sounded like it was in our house. I tried to tell myself it couldn't have been what I thought. A gun in suburban London? Really?"

Josie looks at me, as though expecting a cue to continue. None is forthcoming but on she goes.

"But then I heard screams. At least three or four. I still hear them at random times of the day. I'll be showering or going shopping and they go off in my head, taking me right back to that dreadful day."

Josie shudders. There's darkness in her eyes. I'm briefly sympathetic. What a thing to live through.

"It says in the newspaper reports that neighbours rang the police."

"Yes. That was me. I also called an ambulance. Mabel did too. I think we rang at the same time, or seconds apart. I ran outside and so did Mabel. Looking back, it was probably a silly thing to do when there was a gun around. Luckily the police and ambulance arrived within minutes."

Josie pauses and stares at her hands. She twists the fabric of her dress.

"Jonathan, Anna and Jasmine — their bodies came out in blankets. Then Lily came out. Two police officers were practically carrying her. Her face was slack. I wasn't even sure she was conscious. Then I saw she was shaking from head to toe. At least she was alive. I never expected her to be."

"What happened next?" The words are out before I can stop them.

"The coroner ruled that it was a murder-suicide. Jonathan shot them. As you'll have seen from the articles, he was a licensed gun holder. I knew that."

Josie's tone is scornful.

"Not from him, of course. Lily used to tell me about it. He was hugely interested in target shooting. I wouldn't be surprised if he used it as a way of exercising control. Lily was both scared and fascinated by it. It seems he liked to flaunt his gun to her."

"What happened to Lily?"

"She's currently in a psychiatric hospital — been in and out of them for years, more in than out. She was diagnosed with serious mental disorders, psychosis I think, and possibly other things. It's all down to what that man did. It's ruined her life and totally changed her."

"Do you keep in touch?"

"Yes. I should spend more time with her really. I've been caught up with my own issues. And also, her mental health problems are very severe. I don't often recognise her as the Lily I knew."

Her voice fades.

"If I'm honest, that puts me off seeing her, which I know is cowardly and I need to put my own feelings aside after everything she's been through.

"But we email and I do visit her, even though it's not as often as I should. When she's not in hospital, she stays with her uncle in Richmond. But she's been in hospital for a long stretch this time."

I see a large, framed photo on the bottom shelf of an alcove. Josie and a familiar-looking girl with curly hair are arm in arm. I jump up to examine it. The girl from the paper. *Lily.* She stares out of the photo, a peaceful smile on her face, which is half resting on Josie's shoulder.

Josie joins me at the alcove.

"It's nice, isn't it?" she remarks. "A lovely memory. Steve took it in our garden. We'd decided to finish tutoring early that day, so we sat in the garden with an ice cream instead. Lily was thrilled."

Looking around the room, I notice there are no other photos on display. Perhaps there were some of Josie and Steve that have since been removed. But it seems odd to have one of Lily, her former next-door neighbour of a decade ago, and no one else.

"I was very close to Lily." It's as though Josie can read my mind. "I'm not close to my own family. My mum walked out when I was a child."

"I'm so sorry," I say, and mean it. Abandoned by her mother. Unable to have children. Murder next door. Divorce. *What a life.* Perhaps I need to cut Josie a little more slack, much as I fundamentally dislike and distrust her.

Josie nods at the photo. "Poppy reminds me a little of Lily, and not only in looks, but in personality . . ."

"Well, thank you for your time." Hearing my daughter's name, I'm brought back sharply from my trance. I jump up, grasping the news cuttings firmly. The fragile connection between us shatters.

I walk to my house, and as I enter the porch and turn the key in the dark grey door, I picture three bodies being carried in the opposite direction. Wrapped in blankets. Horribly still.

I resolve to repaint the door. Green? Blue? Hell, paint it bright pink. Something, anything, to keep those memories at arm's length. I stop in the hall. *Who am I kidding?* I know it will take more than a fresh coat of paint to erase what happened. I look around me. Shadows seem to lurk in every corner. Shadows of the past. *Why does the air feel so heavy?* Instinctively, I seize my coat and rush out of the door.

CHAPTER 18

"Mummy! Daddy! Mummy! Help! Help! Help!"

Poppy is hysterical, her loud voice slicing through the walls. I'm out of bed in an instant. Mike is unmoved. *How can he sleep through her screams?* Sometimes I wonder if he does it on purpose. I battle my rising irritation as I rush to Poppy's room. Poppy is sitting upright, her arm rigid and pointing at the door.

"Who is she?" she moans. Although her eyes are wide open and staring, the pupils huge in the light cast by her elephant night light, I think she's half asleep.

"There's no one here, darling, just me." I try to be as calm as possible.

"There is, person here, there, there!" Poppy's arm bobs up and down. In between her exclamations she wails, reaching a crescendo of screaming before fading into whimpers. Her cries eventually awaken Mike and he joins me, rubbing one eye and yawning.

"Oh no, this again," he groans. "I thought we were past it."

"Yes, it's a shame," I say politely. We're being so courteous with each other, all stilted pleasantries, before descending into silence. A silence that used to be companionable and easy, but which is now loaded and heavy with unspoken words.

When I returned from Josie's house yesterday, I decided — reluctantly — not to tell Mike the story of the house. The last thing I want is to make him angrier and risk the rift between us growing even wider.

"I think she's half asleep," I volunteer at last. "She's saying she's seen someone, like before."

Mike shrugs. "Bad nightmare?"

Suddenly my neck tingles and unwelcome thoughts fill my mind. Who is this person? Could it be to do with the murder? Had this been Jasmine's room, and was she . . . she . . . I feel embarrassed even forming the thoughts in my head, but could she still be here, haunting it?

I shake my head. I don't believe in ghosts. Even as a child, I laughed when my best friend claimed her house was haunted and that an old lady used to wander around. When I stayed the night there, I was never scared.

Mike approaches Poppy as though facing a tiger. "It's Daddy," he croons. "Just Daddy and Mummy are with you."

Poppy slowly lowers her arm and her face slackens. "Daddy," she murmurs. Mike takes her in his arms and she cuddles up to him.

"Big girl in door, coming for me," she mutters into Mike's T-shirt.

"Shhh. It's just a dream," Mike whispers. "She's not there now."

"She not nice, Daddy. She has girl's hair, but no face." Poppy starts to sob again.

I freeze. *Those words again.* I glance at Mike, to see what his reaction is. But Mike is busying himself with climbing into bed with Poppy, and smoothing the duvet over them.

"Go," he mouths to me. "We'll be OK."

On the one hand, I'm sad Poppy has, as usual, turned to Mike. On the other, it means I can go back to bed.

I nod formally and pad back to our room, where I grab my phone and google "church blessing house ghosts" before I fall asleep, clutching my phone to my cheek.

* * *

Mike has a later start in the morning, as he has a meeting away from the office, so he offers to take Poppy to nursery. I jump on this with alacrity. Poppy is subdued when she wakes. I hope she's forgotten about her nightmares, but Poppy informs me: "Big, bad girl in my room last night. And Mummy, she has no face."

I feel that Lily, Anna and Jasmine are in the kitchen with me as I fall to my knees and grip Poppy's hands. "Mummy and Daddy will look after you. There is no bad girl. But Poppy, what do you mean 'she has no face'?"

"Me see her hair but not see her face," Poppy says earnestly. "And she's going to get me."

I hug her, shuddering at the caricature image Poppy's words have drummed up in my mind — a woman with gouged-out features. *Surely this is just a particularly horrible dream that Poppy is having?*

I'm relieved when Mike scoops her up and takes her to nursery.

"Thank you," I say. We're like two tomcats circling one other.

I make myself a strong coffee and sit at my computer, my work email unopened and my job forgotten. I tap in "Maynard Twickenham" and hundreds of links come up. A wave of anger washes over me. I can't believe that Mike — and Layla too, in fact — has missed this. I was living in Singapore, so I have an excuse. OK, Mike was in Scotland, but this was front-page news. *How the hell did it pass him by?*

Maybe it didn't. He just didn't join the dots that it's our house, I concede reluctantly, not really in the mood to be charitable to him.

I click on link after link. Jonathan had loved to shoot for sport. He was an eminent history professor, one of the leading authorities on military history. He had written three books on the subject. One article included a link to buy these works.

His students and staff waxed lyrical about him. *Such a great guy. A brain the size of Britain. He always had time for his students. He was so patient and understanding.* He had not, it seemed, taken the same approach towards his children.

Josie's name appears regularly in the articles, offering her views about this tragic family. Jonathan "was obsessed with his gun". Lily "did not live up to his expectations", whereas Jasmine was "a chip off the old block".

The journalist also spoke to one of Jasmine's teachers, who described an "outstanding" student. "Every subject, she excelled at. I'm devastated that she has had her potential ripped away from her."

I'm drawn to the photos of them. The same ones have been used repeatedly, leading me to believe there aren't many of the family together, besides the image of the four of them on a speedboat on holiday. Lily stares earnestly at the camera while her sister beams, carefree. Lily's eyes are solemn and give nothing away.

Anna's brother Andrew gave a brief interview. He said Anna's family had worried something was wrong with the marriage because of the way Anna had acted around her husband.

She would never criticise him. Indeed, whenever her family tried to raise the subject of their marriage, she would either change the subject or lapse into silence.

I note that Andrew never referred to Jonathan by his name. Always "he" or "him". During Anna's marriage she had been anxious, unsettled, serious, quiet. The opposite to the relaxed, bubbly sister he had known before she met *her husband*.

"I tried to ask but didn't like to push it. If only I had, it might not have ended in tragedy." Andrew's quote stands out in bold in the newspaper article.

A notification pops up that I've received a new email from my boss, Jake. I ignore it in my obsessive search for more information.

As I scroll through yet more articles, a familiar name jumps out at me. Belinda Jackson. I screw up my face — I know that name. Then it strikes me. Of course! Mabel's daughter, the one who couldn't wait to get away from me when we met.

I click on the article. It details the neighbours' reaction to the murder-suicide. Josie makes an appearance, of course.

I skim-read. Same old stuff. Someone called Miriam Adams, sixty years old, makes a standard comment about the horror of it all and about how the neighbourhood will never be the same again. I have no idea who she is, or even if she still lives in the street.

Then "Belinda Jackson" is interviewed. I learn that Belinda, who was twenty-three at the time, was living next door to the Maynard family. She had moved back home after gaining a first-class degree to complete an MA in history.

By coincidence, she had studied at Petersham University, where Jonathan Maynard himself had lectured. Reading on, I discover he had even taught her. Ms Jackson had babysat several times for the family. She expressed "utter shock" at what had happened. "Jonathan taught me for my MA," she says.

He was so knowledgeable. I loved his seminars, they really fired me with passion. What's more, him being next door was wonderful. He was always available if I had a quick query or wanted to discuss a point in one of my assignments.

I never noticed any problems within the family. The girls seemed settled and well behaved. I especially loved chatting to Jasmine about history. Even at that age, she was interested in the subject, especially her dad's specialist subject — military history, particularly combat weapons. It seemed funny for a young girl to know so much about guns, but Jasmine did. She used to say she was going to become a history professor and I had no doubt she would have done so.

Belinda certainly had an emotional reaction to what happened, I think. From her words, she appeared to have been close to *that monster*, as I label him in my mind. My thoughts turn to Mabel. Maybe it's time to pay her a visit.

Another work email notification pops up on my screen, and I hesitate. What am I hoping to achieve? It's all in the past, after all. Does it really matter what Mabel says? I steel myself anew. This is about my home. My new family home. *Mike's home too.*

I had hoped this would be my — *our* — forever home and what I now know threatens to ruin our lives, perhaps beyond repair. I'm compelled to discover as much as I can and, somehow, to find a way to move on. Lock the door and throw away the key, if possible.

Picking up my bag and keys, I head over to Mabel's.

I knock on the door and admire Mabel's sparkling doorstep and pin-neat drive, with not a leaf out of place. No answer. As I consider whether to knock again or go home, the door sweeps open and Mabel stands there, dressed in an elegant plum jumper and black jeans. She does not look very pleased.

"Oh sorry, am I disturbing you?" I ask, flustered, giving myself a mental shake. Why does Mabel reduce me to a nervy shadow of myself?

"Well, I wasn't expecting anyone and I am in fact busy," says Mabel, in her customary cool tone. "But no matter. You'd better come in."

Feeling like a naughty schoolgirl, I follow her. I'm invited to sit on a blue velvet sofa that looks as though it has arrived from a furniture showroom that very morning. I wonder what Mabel has been so "busy" doing.

"I . . . I . . ." I stutter. Then I pause, take a deep breath and begin. "I found out about what happened to the Maynards at our house. Unbelievably, Mike and I had no clue."

"Nor did the ones who lived there before you," interjects Mabel drily. "Goodness, don't young people these days watch or read the news?"

I blush. "I found out through a newspaper clipping about the murder, posted anonymously through our door."

"Well, it certainly wasn't me," Mabel snaps. *I didn't imply it was*, I think.

Though Mabel has never been especially friendly towards me, she has never been as prickly as this. Bordering on rude, in fact. I'm curious.

"Oh, I certainly didn't think it was you," I say quickly. "Actually, I thought . . ." I wonder whether to say anything, but discretion can only get me so far. In for a penny, in for a pound. "I thought it was Josie."

Mabel raises her arched eyebrows. I can see she has either dyed them or drawn them in, noting their darkness in contrast to her steel grey bob.

"Hmmm."

I wait, agog.

"Yes, I'm not too surprised. I would think it was a possibility."

"Why?" My question is like a bullet fired from a gun and I lean forward eagerly. "She told me it wasn't her."

Instantly Mabel seems to regret showing such candour. Her eyelids half close, her mouth tightens. Then she stares at me. What does Mabel know? What is she prepared to reveal?

"Josie was close to Lily, the elder daughter, and very upset over what happened." I can see Mabel is choosing her words with great care. "She did not like Jonathan. That much was obvious."

Mabel sighs and shakes her head.

"Josie seems very unstable, poor woman. It's hardly surprising. I don't think her home life was very happy both before and after she met her husband. Steve, was it? Sorry, I didn't know him well. I don't know her well either, but I think a few of us on the street are aware her marriage is in difficulty." She pauses and taps her foot, with a glance at her watch.

"Did you know the Maynards?" I press on.

"A little," Mabel sighs. "It was a total shock. Jonathan was charming, I must say. I found him so helpful, and a very attentive neighbour. Ken thought so too — my husband," she adds quickly. "He passed away, sadly. A year ago."

She pushes like a tractor over my timid condolences.

"Anna was quiet but seemed very pleasant."

I decide it's time to cut to the chase. "I read that Jonathan taught Belinda for her MA."

It sounds clumsy and I cringe as Mabel frowns, in full headmistress mode.

"Yes, and he was a wonderful lecturer," Mabel says at last. "Belinda adored him and the whole thing affected her terribly. She used to babysit for the children. Jasmine seemed a delight, but I know my daughter found Lily quite difficult. From my own experience, Lily did seem — how shall I put this? — challenging."

"Why?" I lean forward and then, aware I shouldn't seem overly excited, stiffen my shoulders and clasp my hands in my lap.

"Well, once I was watering my plants in the front garden and Lily came racing out of the front door, screaming. 'I hate you, you fu—' Well, I'm not going to repeat what she said, but it was most unpleasant. Screaming and swearing at her parents."

Mabel folds her hands primly. "Not that it's any excuse for the terrible thing he was supposed to have done," she adds quickly.

Supposed to have done?

There's a knock on the door. Mabel climbs to her feet. "My daughter," she says, smoothing her skirt. "We're going into Richmond."

I feel my heart sink and my curiosity rise as I wonder how Belinda will act towards me this time. I stand up too. "Let me get out of your hair," I say. "Thank you for speaking to me."

Mabel pauses and stares at me earnestly. "My dear, I do hope this isn't too shocking to you and doesn't drive you away from the house. I hope you can make happy memories there.

It's a wonderful street and area, and I hope you can overcome its history."

A chink in Mabel's frosty demeanour. I'm touched and can feel tears prick the back of my eyes. "Thank you so much," I say, genuinely grateful. "Do you think it drove Helen and her family away?"

The shutters are back over Mabel's face. "As I mentioned before, she told me she left because they were relocating for her husband's job," she says evenly, going to the door and flinging it open.

Belinda is on the doorstep. She smiles at her mother, but I notice her expression harden when she sees me.

"You've met Clara, haven't you, dear?" Mabel booms. "Clara's had a bit of a shock. She found out about the Maynards." Mabel shudders.

"Someone put a newspaper story about it through her door." Mabel arches an eyebrow. "I wonder who that might have been."

"Oh." Belinda hesitates. "I'm sorry. That must have been a shock."

At least she's engaging with me, I reflect. More than she did last time.

"I still can't believe it, I really can't. But Jona . . . he's a disgusting human being." Belinda is practically hissing with anger. She stares unseeing beyond Mabel and me and into the hall.

Mabel looks stunned, but quickly recovers her poise. "Calm down, darling," she says briskly. "And I must say, I thought he was a delightful man. I'm still shocked by what he did."

Belinda's face darkens and she turns away from us.

I take my cue. "I'd better be off, then."

"Bye, dear," says Mabel. She touches my hand. "I do hope you can move beyond this."

Belinda mutters something unintelligible. She's withdrawn into herself completely and is no longer acknowledging me.

What is it with people around here?

I stomp back to my house, irritated. Belinda was marginally less strange than last time, but still very peculiar. And why was Mabel sticking up for Jonathan? A convicted murderer, no less.

I slam my door shut and slump to the floor, my stomach churning. Though Mabel was pleasant enough, I've returned none the wiser. It was a waste of time going over there.

One last thing. I rummage in my pocket for the crumpled news clippings and takes pictures of them on my mobile phone camera. I WhatsApp them to Layla: *Ring any bells?*

Layla texts back within a minute. *Oh my God!!!! I knew I recognised that house. Oh God, Clara. I'm so sorry, that must be horrible for you to discover x*

CHAPTER 19

"Me not want to go to bed. That persman comes and watches me," Poppy pouts. Usually when Poppy says "persman" to mean "person", I find it adorable. Not tonight.

Poppy is refusing to lie under the covers, despite my best efforts. Feeling a little ashamed, I offer my daughter two chocolate buttons — the most naked of bribes.

Every nerve is taut. "*I want my evening!*" I scream inwardly. I hear a key in the lock and exhale with relief. Thank God! Mike is back, and he'll help me. Poppy responds better to her father, after all.

"Clara!" Mike says in a loud whisper. I tear down the stairs. Poppy is alone in her room, cross-legged and mutinous.

"Thank goodness you're here!" I embrace Mike, momentarily forgetting the coolness between us. "Poppy's being a nightmare."

"Leave it to me." Mike shrugs off his coat and pounds upstairs. I heave a sigh of relief and collapse on the sofa. I'm just putting my feet up when the doorbell rings.

I march over to it, knowing who it is before opening it. Josie is pale and visibly distressed. Her eyes are wide, her appearance unkempt.

"I need your help," she gasps.

"Yes?" I know I should be ushering my neighbour in with kind words. Instead, I stand in the entrance, arms folded and legs apart. *You are not coming into my house.*

"My dad is dying. I need to get to the nursing home to see him but I've got a flat tyre." Josie's words fall over each other. "I'm crap at that kind of thing. Would either of you be able to help?"

Before I can reply Mike has reappeared. *Like an eager puppy*, I think bitterly. "Don't worry! I'll give you a lift." He scoops up the car keys from the hall table.

"Oh, thank you!" Josie clasps her hands together, her eyes boring into Mike.

I'm seething. Mike knows how I feel about that woman next door and yet he's bending over backwards to help her. Where has this "dying dad" come from, anyway? Surely Josie would have mentioned something before now?

"Wait, you're leaving just like that?" I'm floundering, aware of how unreasonable I must sound. The woman's father is dying and Mike is doing a good deed. On the face of it, there's no conceivable reason why he shouldn't lend a hand.

Mike looks pained. "Josie's dad is dying," he enunciates. He might as well have added: *And what part of that don't you understand?*

"Oh, I don't want to cause you any problems," says Josie quickly, looking up under her eyelashes at Mike.

I want to tear into him, to scream in his face, to grab him.

"Well, how long will you be gone?" I say, hating myself for sounding whiny but unable to help it. My violent dislike of Josie has overcome my rational mind.

"I'm only staying a few hours," says Josie.

Mike gives me a quick peck on the cheek. "I'll stay in touch," he says, turning to head out of the door.

I glare at Josie, and quick as a flash she winks. Winking! How dare she! I stare in shock but then the grave look is back on Josie's face. "Thank you," she says quietly, following Mike out. Maybe I imagined it. *Perhaps it was just a blink?*

I watch them walk to Mike's car. "You said you weren't even close to your family," I mutter.

The house is noiseless. Thankfully, Poppy's asleep, though a part of me wishes she would wake and break the silence. It feels thick and heavy, wrapping itself around me, like a gag over my mouth and nose.

I know I should get over it. I need to cook myself a meal. I want to pour myself a glass of wine. Instead, I pace the house. I pick up a cushion that Poppy flung to the floor earlier. I clock the flowers on the dining room table wilting in their vase and hurl them in the bin.

Then I spot a pile of Poppy's toys by the TV in the corner. Dolls of various sizes in varying stages of undress, random jigsaw puzzle pieces, Peppa Pig figures and cuddly toys lie in an untidy heap. I cluck disapprovingly.

I know she's only two, but what a mess!

Marching over to restore some order, I spot Poppy's magnetic board in the heap. Letters have been arranged deliberately in order.

My stomach lurches. I suppress an urge to scream. The last thing I want to do is to scrutinise the letters more closely. Yet I know I must.

The letters are placed so haphazardly that it does look like Poppy has pushed them together at random with her chunky hands. A closer look tells a different story.

stillhere

With a shaking hand, I move the letters to place the gap in the right place. *Still here.*

My heart is galloping so hard I wonder briefly if I might have a heart attack.

Poppy. I dash upstairs and into Poppy's room. My daughter is sleeping peacefully. But I feel glued to the spot. Someone could be in the house. I need to protect Poppy. I admit it to myself: yes, I'm terrified. I should call the police.

I stare at my empty hands. *Damn.* I left my phone downstairs. Should I rush down to get it? Or grab Poppy and lock the two of us in the bathroom?

Thud. Thud. Thud. Someone at the front door.

I freeze. I hope against hope that it will be Mike but know in my heart that it won't be. Why on Earth would he knock when he has a key of his own? Some people forget their keys regularly. Mike is not one of them.

I inch down the stairs. I can see a dark shape through the richly coloured glass in the front door. "Who is it?" I hiss, my breath quick and shallow.

"It's me," murmurs a low voice. "Layla."

Flames of anger flick at my fear. I take the chain from the door. "You frightened the life out of me," I say tersely.

Layla's eyes widen. "I'm so sorry. I really didn't mean to scare you. I would have used my key, but I know you don't like that either," she adds meaningfully. "I hope I didn't wake Poppy?" Her eyes rise up the stairs.

I shake my head. For all my annoyance, I'm mightily relieved to have someone with me.

"Come in."

A blast of cold air follows Layla into the house as she stomps her boots on the mat. She's bending to take them off when I grab her shoulder and propel her to the family room.

"Look." I point to Poppy's magnetic board.

Layla is silent as she digests the words.

"Who do you think did this?" she asks at last.

I shake my head. "I was at the point of calling the police when you turned up. I was convinced there was an intruder in the house. But now I've calmed down, I just don't know."

"My first thought was *her*." I cock my head at the wall we share with Josie. "But unless she has powers to step through walls, I can't see how. Also, she's not at home this evening."

An image of Mike and Josie together flashes into my mind. I pick the board up and shove it into a kitchen drawer, pushing it shut hard. *There. I won't look at it again.* Hopefully Poppy will forget about it — at least temporarily.

Layla gives a quick nod of approval.

I continue, "I feel an idiot saying this, but I'm starting to wonder if these incidents have something to do with the Maynards. Something still in the atmosphere from the violent way they died."

"Ghosts?" Layla volunteers.

"Yes," I mutter, embarrassed. "I've never believed in them in my life. I used to laugh at my friends' terror doing Ouija boards when we were teens. But I'm not sure what else explains what is happening in this house."

I think about the bullet twinkling on the landing. The way it disappeared without a trace.

Layla stiffens slightly. "I came round because I've got something to tell you. The house seemed really familiar to me when we went knocking on the neighbours' doors. I went home and I couldn't stop thinking about how I recognised it. The drive, the front door, that big tree you have at the front . . . I googled the address and the history came up, and then I remembered the news story. It was all over the telly and the newspapers at the time."

"Why didn't you tell me?" I cry. "If you'd have told me, we'd never have put an offer in." Acid rises in my throat and I wish I had a Rennie to hand.

"Because you were so excited. You said you'd found your dream home!" Layla's tone is beseeching. "I felt like I couldn't burst your bubble. I hoped you'd never find out, and that if you did, it would be years later and that you'd be so happy here that you'd disregard it."

"You lied," I snap. I feel betrayed.

"No, Clara, I withheld the truth," Layla says. "I did it with the best of intentions, although I now realise I probably made the wrong choice."

She bites her lip so hard she leaves vivid red marks. She's obviously remorseful, but my anger and resentment are still sharp. How could my best friend withhold such important information? If only Layla had told me, then Mike and I would have been spared the nightmare of this house, and of Josie.

Layla is waiting for me to calm down, to tell her I understand. I clamp my mouth shut.

"If you'd only have said, Mike and I wouldn't be in this situation," I say instead. "It's affecting everything — my head, my marriage. *How could you?*"

Layla's corkscrew bronze curls and hazel eyes look unfamiliar to me.

"I'm so sorry, I really am," Layla babbles, tears springing into her eyes. She dashes to the hall and digs around in her rucksack, producing a generous bunch of tulips and a bottle of wine.

"To say sorry," she says. "I feel really responsible for the flooded bath. I admit I should have paid more attention, but I just didn't know that Poppy was capable of getting over her stair gate."

She pauses. "And I'm truly sorry for not saying anything about the house. I just didn't know what to do. I went over and over it in my head and decided at long last that it was best to leave it. That was obviously a big mistake."

Layla's voice trembles. She's waiting for my forgiveness. I take the gifts.

"Thank you," I say quietly. It's hard to get the words out. With an effort, I try to push Layla's actions from my mind, for now. Despite my anger, I don't want Layla to go yet, leaving me on my own with my whirling thoughts about Josie and Mike, and with those words glinting on the magnetic board.

Leading my friend silently to the living room, I install myself on the window seat. The shutter slats are slightly open so I can see when Mike returns.

"I'm shocked about the murders that took place in this house."

I see a flash of relief cross Layla's face that the subject has been changed.

"I found out in such a creepy way. Someone anonymously posted those newspaper articles through the door."

"Who would do that?" Layla cocks her head to the shared wall with Josie's house.

"She's adamant that she didn't," I say. "All I can think about is that family living in our home. Actually, their home. It doesn't feel like our house anymore, now I know the history."

I can see them in my mind's eye. The professor and Jasmine bent earnestly over a book. Lily sullen in a corner. I blink twice and shudder, the image shattering. It almost felt real. *Still here.* Maybe they are. *Stop it, stop it, stop it.*

I'm so consumed by my thoughts I nearly forget Layla is with me. But Layla's eyes are trained on me throughout.

"I see them everywhere. I don't know how I can come to terms with living here." I take a breath. "It was meant to be our dream home, but now it's a nightmare. Sorry, I know that's a cliché. With that and everything else that's happened, I just think maybe we should cut our losses. Put the house up for sale and leave."

I stare at my phone, willing a message from Mike to appear, when Layla breaks the silence.

"Does Mike know?"

"I haven't told him yet."

"I do think you need to tell him about the history, and then you can make a decision together."

If you'd told me the history, we wouldn't have bought it in the first place.

CHAPTER 20

Layla has just left. With a pang of guilt, I realise I didn't ask her a single question about herself, or the man she's dating. Unusually, Layla didn't volunteer the information. She seemed more than happy to chew over what was happening to me. *It must be bad.*

I glance at the clock. Nearly ten. Still no word from Mike. What the hell can he be up to? He could have at least given me an idea of when he'd be home. I open WhatsApp again to see when Mike last checked it. An hour and a half ago. What is he doing? Waiting for Josie, presumably. More than enough time, surely, to send a quick message.

I peer out of the window and gasp. Mike's car is parked on our drive! I wonder how I failed to hear the engine.

Right, that's it. I've had enough.

Blinded by a shot of white-hot rage, I push my feet into my trainers and grabs my keys. I glance upstairs. Silence. Surely Poppy will be OK for the five minutes that it will take to go to Josie's house and demand that my husband come back home.

There's a scraping at the front door and my heart pounds. But I realise it's simply the key in the lock as Mike opens the door and steps in the hallway, stumbling slightly. His face is flushed.

I'm ready to give Mike both barrels. Why did he rush off like that? Why couldn't he have messaged me? Why the hell did he have to go to that bloody woman's house? But a little voice whispers that it's not a good idea to unleash my rage straightaway.

"So, how was it?"

I try to keep my voice calm, but a hard note creeps in. Mike shrugs off his coat and heads upstairs to our bedroom. I follow in his wake.

"Fine. I dropped her at the nursing home and she spent some time with her dad. But it's so hard for her." Mike sighs with empathy and I dig my fingernails into a pillow.

He sinks onto our bed.

"Her dad is seriously ill with dementia and has days left — if that. She's never been close to him, though. She hadn't seen him for years. But when she heard he was on end-of-life care, she wanted to see him. Her mum just walked out of her life when she was five."

Sob story. I clamp my mouth shut to stop a hasty retort that will instantly put Mike's back up.

Mike continues, full of sympathy. "Her stepmum and half-sister were at the care home too. Josie says they were awful to her. She's had no contact with them for years, either. The stepmum never wanted her and when she and Josie's dad had her sister, that was it. Josie was completely pushed out."

He drones on and I can't find any sympathy for my next-door neighbour. Maybe that makes me cruel, but I don't care.

"Where have you been? I saw your car parked outside."

Mike looks down at his phone and sighs deeply. I can smell whisky on his breath.

"I just feel really bad for her, about her situation with her family and her husband, and she was so distressed after seeing her dad. He didn't seem to know who she was. She asked if I wanted to come in for a quick drink at hers, as a thank you for the lift."

Mike sighs again, breathing more whisky fumes into my face. "I'd rather have come back here, of course." He buries his face in his pillow.

Don't say anything. Wait until tomorrow.

I purse my lips to suppress a scream. Anger and disappointment wash over me. I never thought I had to worry about Mike's loyalty. He's never shown any interest in anyone else since we've been together.

My mother is always telling me how lucky I am that he's so devoted to me. But now I'm not so sure. There's no doubt in my mind that Josie has set her sights on Mike, and I feel let down by the way he's reacting to it. I can't believe he accepted Josie's offer of a drink.

On the other hand, perhaps I should give my husband the benefit of the doubt. He's a genuinely decent man — that much is certain. He would have felt sorry for Josie.

Naive comes to mind. That doesn't mean he's disloyal, though.

But I want to get as far away as possible from the woman next door and this house's past. Now is the time to tell Mike about the Maynards. I close my eyes briefly.

Mike is unlikely to respond well. But we can put the house on the market straightaway. Maybe move back into London, get a bigger flat. I've seen some great maisonettes online, almost as large as houses.

"There's something I need to tell you."

"I know."

My eyes snap open. "What?" *He can't.*

"Josie told me about the history of this house," he says, calmly. "About the murders."

"Why the hell did she tell you?" I can no longer keep my fury in check. "I wanted to tell you."

"She assumed I knew." Mike says calmly. "She was shocked I didn't and was very apologetic for bringing it up."

"I didn't tell you because I wanted to wait for the right time. I was worried about your reaction, after all the bad stuff that's happened here. I know how angry you were with the way Helen and Jim left the house."

I'm still seething, but at this stage it's just wasted energy. Either way, the truth is out. Now I need to get my point across.

"It's really upset and shaken me, as I'm sure it has you. I think the best thing is to get the house up for sale and get the hell out." Relief washes over me at the thought of leaving. I reach over to clasp Mike's hand. We can get back on track and never see Josie again. And Josie will be unable to get her claws into Mike.

But Mike withdraws his hand. "We can't put the house up for sale. We've only just moved in. People will wonder why we want to move so soon and it'll put them off. Besides, we won't have made any money." His mind is made up. "No, Clara. We'll have to stay, at least for a while."

"But doesn't it make you feel sick to live in a place where a man shot his family? I mean, I see them everywhere. Shadows all over this house."

"I'm not thrilled, obviously. It's just another bloody thing wrong with this place."

Mike slaps his forehead suddenly.

"I should have thought to do a bit more digging when the price seemed so reasonable, for prime Twickenham. But Josie told me the owners after the Maynards changed the house a lot. They added the big family and kitchen extension and created a fourth bedroom.

"So, we have to focus on the fact that it's different to when they lived here. We have to think with our heads here and be clinical about it, Clara. If we really find it impossible to cope with what we know happened here, we can sell in a few years. But we're going to have to stay put for now."

My mouth is dry and my heart feels like lead. My eyes dart around our bedroom, with its beautiful bay window and picture rail. The soft light of the bedside lamp emphasises the generous size of the room. It made my heart sing when I moved in. Now, more than anything, I want to be back in our old, cramped bedroom in Tooting.

There's so much I want to say to him. That our marriage has hit the rocks since we moved here. That Josie appears to be interested in my husband and that I'm hurt at how he's stuck up for her. That he chose to help Josie this evening rather than be with his family. And the cherry on top, that he decided to go back to hers, late at night, for a drink.

Was it just a drink?

Tears prick the backs of my eyes. Just a week ago it wouldn't have crossed my mind that it could have been anything else. But now I can't say with absolute certainty that I believe nothing happened between them.

Bang.

Mike and I stare at the ceiling. There's another bang, and then another. My heart races.

"There's something in the loft again," I whisper.

Mike's eyes have widened and his body has stiffened. *Good.* Maybe he recognises that there might be something up there more ominous than a mouse.

"I think you were right the first time," he mutters. "Maybe it's rats and not mice. We'll get that pest guy out again to take a look."

Right. A rat that sounds as if it weighs at least five stone.

I need to talk to him, to tell him that this house and its history are destroying us, and that Josie is threatening our marriage.

"Mike—" my voice is low — "we need to talk. I'm really trying to be calm here, but I feel betrayed, if I'm honest."

Too late. Mike has fallen asleep. Indignation rises in me like indigestion.

There's another creak above our heads. Despite my frustration and sadness, I snuggle up to Mike.

What is up there?

I know I need to get up that ladder and take a look around in the morning, but I'm fearful at what I might find. Rats' droppings would actually be a relief.

Mike's breathing becomes heavier. I suspect that he's had more than a single whiskey at Josie's.

His phone beeps and lights up with a text. Never in our relationship have I ever felt the need to look at Mike's phone. But this time, I lean over him and grab it.

I appreciate your help so much. It really helped to have you take me there and back, and not a faceless taxi driver. And I loved having a drink with you at mine. You're welcome to come over any time. Big kisses to Poppy. I'm so glad you like the idea of me taking her to the zoo for the day. It will give you and Clara the chance to do house stuff. Josie xx

I drop the phone. The breath has been knocked from me, as though I've been punched in the stomach. An image of a gun floats in my mind, the gun that Jonathan used against his family.

I imagine it in my hands, its smoothness lying against my palm. I hear the shot ringing out. I imagine the bullet tearing through Josie's skull.

I shiver. I hate this woman who appears to want to destroy my family. But I'm a peaceable person, not a potential murderer. This house's macabre history is eating away at me.

But you are not taking my daughter on a day trip away from me.

A high-pitched wail breaks the spell. "Mummy! Help me!"

* * *

I hate my dad. I'm happy to tell anybody that and I never feel the need to apologise for it. He was not in any sense a father to me and deserved everything he got. But of course, things are never black and white. I still get flashbacks of him being nice to me. Few and far between, but they are there. Helping me to ride a bike for the first time, him pushing my bike hard and me laughing, my hair streaming behind me as I try to balance. And then another time, I saw a tiny teddy in the local shop. "Aw, it's so itty-bitty," I cried out, and I was desperate for it but didn't have enough pocket money. I cried when he bought it for me. Not just for the teddy, but because he had been kind to me, like my friends' daddies. The children who were the apples of their fathers' eyes. The apple of my father's eye was my sister, of course. But in those two moments I could pretend he cared for me as he did for her. Two rays of sunlight in the otherwise endless blackness. Of course, there was my mother. But she was useless. She let me down at every opportunity. I trained myself to harden my heart against her. There was no point fixating on it, or I'd find myself drowning. I blocked her out of my mind. And my sister. He always loved her so much more than me. Every single thing she did surpassed me. I don't want to think about her.

It's not Clara's fault, or her family's. So why am I fixated on them? It's probably simple. I want what they have, but it's something that eludes my grasp. I'm more likely to win the lottery than have a happy family set-up. That eats into me and I'm more than happy to throw a few grenades into the works. Like my little message to her on her daughter's board. But I'm only stating the truth. I'm still here.

CHAPTER 21

Poppy is quiet in the back of the car. I hope that it's simply because she's exhausted after last night, which followed the same pattern as before. Screaming and crying about a "big girl with no face" in her room. Even Mike woke up from what I suspect was a drunken sleep, and eventually we managed to calm her. She slept in our bed for the rest of the night. When Mike tried to move Poppy back to her bedroom, she cried again and clung to him.

My hands shake as I navigate the roads to Poppy's nursery. My mind is pulled this way and that and I'm at my wit's end. *Concentrate.* Mike was subdued this morning. I know that Poppy's repeated night terrors upset him, but was it more than that? It would be no surprise if the knowledge that the house was the scene of a murder was playing on his mind.

I hope it was also because he regretted going to Josie's for a drink, and for prioritising the needs of a neighbour above those of his family.

And yet . . . I cannot rid myself of the thought that Mike's reticence was because something happened between him and Josie. Josie's text flashes into my mind. Maybe Mike wants to be with her now. *Josie, not me.*

My palms sweat and I suddenly feel so nauseous I wonder if I'll vomit. The feeling passes but my stomach aches.

I'm prone to catastrophising. I know I need to rein in my feelings and be sensible. I have to speak to Mike about Josie, but I need to pick the right time.

I'm distracted by the large stone building in the distance, with its simple but beautiful steeple. The local Catholic church. I was brought up a Roman Catholic. I did communion and confirmation — my saint's name is Bernadette. Mum is a devout Catholic, although Dad is, I now realise, an atheist. Mum took me to church determinedly every Sunday and I also did Sunday school.

I haven't been to church for years. I stare at the building in the rear-view mirror.

Poppy gazes out of the window. She looks dazed and is chewing her lip. Usually, she's full of chatter and peppering me with questions: *Why? But why? Why, Mummy?*

My anxiety growing again, I wonder about Poppy's unsettled nights. Maybe they're caused by a girl long gone, a studious, brilliantly clever girl who used to live in the house.

A girl who lost her life in the most horrific way and wasn't ready to go. A girl still raging against the dying of the light. A pinprick of sweat drops into my eye as a searing pain in my stomach makes me gasp. My IBS playing up again, no doubt. It always does when I'm stressed.

The image of the church is in my mind as I carry Poppy into the nursery and explain to Fiona that, yet again, my daughter has suffered night terrors.

Fiona leans over Poppy. "Poor old Poppy, haven't you had a time of it?" she says cheerily. "Don't you worry, we'll look after you. Maybe a little nap this afternoon, hey, as you must be exhausted."

Poppy sticks her bottom lip out and clings to Fiona's legs.

"I'm worried about her behaviour," I confide. "She's really subdued and it's not normal for her. I don't know what she's seeing at night."

I feel sick to my stomach. I resist an urge to cling to Fiona like Poppy is doing and pour it all out to that comforting face.

Fiona straightens herself and touches me gently on the shoulder. "Please try not to worry," she says earnestly. "So many children have night terrors. We'll really keep an eye on her today and she'll be as right as rain when you pick her up, I promise."

I want Fiona's firm, calm hand on my shoulder for ever. "Thank you," I say with relief, Fiona's confident words creating a cocoon around me.

But it might not be as simple as that. The memory of poor, doomed Jasmine fills my head. Another wave of nausea hits me.

I recall again the church I saw on the way to nursery and make up my mind. I'm heading there now, and sharpish.

I pull into the church car park. The priest will probably not be there, but maybe there will be someone who can help me.

I can't believe my luck when I spy a man in a white gown with a rectangular cloth over his shoulders, bent over a candle. He turns around and I have a jolt of surprise at how young he appears — probably in his mid-forties, rather than the elderly, wise-looking figure I'd anticipated. He has a thick head of dark, curly hair and wide, dark brown eyes. "Um, are you the priest?" I ask, feeling immediately foolish. *Of course he is.*

It's so long since I've been in church that I'm unsure of myself. My mother's reproachful tone reaches me all the way from my parents' home in Surrey.

"Yes." He smiles at me. "Can I help you?"

"Do you do house blessings?" I say clumsily. "Something bad happened in our house."

* * *

I pull into my drive. Well, that had been easy enough. Father David does indeed do house blessings and has promised to be with us this afternoon. Hopefully he will cleanse the house and get rid of *them*.

I reach for my phone to text Mike and stop. Once upon a time it was something I did so easily without a thought. But now I'm unsure what to say, my finger hovering over the letters. I put the phone back in my pocket and slam the car door shut.

Father David is coming over at two o'clock. I just need to survive until then. I tell myself that he will cleanse the house and remove all trace of the Maynards. If only he could do the same with Josie.

Once more I picture a smooth, silver gun in my hand. I shake my head in horror. What is wrong with me? What am I, a Bond villain?

This house and its history are driving me mad. The pain in the centre of my belly spikes again and I grimace.

At two o'clock sharp, the doorbell rings. Father David has arrived as promised. He smiles at me and his eyes look so kindly I want to weep, feeling less alone.

Father David clasps me by the hand. "Let me talk you through it," he says as he steps in. In his hand is a vial.

"I'll walk through each room, scattering holy water," he explains. "And I'll pray for you all. I'm very confident that peace will be restored to your lives again. You're not the first person who has asked for my help, and it's always worked before."

I nod, full of gratitude. My forehead burns, and I press my hand against it. This house is making me ill.

"What do I do?" I ask awkwardly. "Shall I come with you, or would you like to go round on your own?"

"Come with me," says Father David. "It will help reassure you."

I wonder whether to offer tea or coffee. But I decide it would seem a little incongruous, so I keep quiet and follow him meekly around the house. Father David sprinkles holy water and mutters prayers including the Lord's Prayer and the Hail Mary.

I repeat, "Hail Mary, full of Grace . . ."

I recall Mum's gentle expression, with her half-moon spectacles and curly hair. I know I must invite her to stay with us and tell her everything. I've been putting it off because I don't want to worry her, but it's not just that. If I admit to my own mother that there are serious problems with this house, I'm also admitting it — definitively — to myself.

The priest's voice is soothing and I feel lulled into a rhythmic step and a calm frame of mind.

We enter Poppy's room and Father David pauses. "I feel this is where a lot of the problems are," he says quietly. "I think that something bad happened here."

I nod, torn between relief and fear.

"This is where my daughter sleeps. She has night terrors and says that a woman comes into her room."

Father David nods. "I'm going to spend time giving extra healing here."

A drop of holy water hits me as he sprays his vial through the air.

"My feeling is that this was Jasmine, the younger daughter's bedroom. She was shot in her bed," I explain.

I feel sick just thinking about the sinister history in Poppy's ice-cream-pink room.

Father David nods and continues his prayers. My forehead is burning, but my hands are clammy. Pain courses through my stomach again and I have to force myself not to cry out.

Father David is diligent, I note with relief. Although I hope he'll leave soon. I'm meant to be working, but all I want to do is curl up in bed with a hot water bottle on my stomach.

The priest raises his eyes when he sees the naked floorboards in the hall, the tidemarks up the walls in the bathroom and the dehumidifier blasting out.

"My toddler turned the taps on in the bath and flooded the bathroom," I explain weakly.

Father David nods slightly, and for a split second I think I can read doubt in his eyes. *Does he think it's something to do with the Maynards' bad spirits?*

Surely not. Surely I've imagined it. Even if one believed in ghosts, it was a stretch to think they would turn the taps on in the bathroom.

Still here.

I shake my head silently from side to side. *Go away.*

Half an hour later, Father David is in the hall pulling on his shoes. "I understand your concern, I could sense the house's history. I feel — and this is a personal view and not the church's — that spirits have been trapped here and that has generated the negative energy that you have been feeling. I am confident, though, that the blessing will have done its work. I can sense a lightness now. When I first entered your house, the atmosphere was crushing to me."

He finishes tying his shoelaces. "But if you have any more problems, do let me know and I can come back," he says earnestly.

I hold my breath after I close the door and hold my hands out as if I can physically touch the air around me. Is there a difference in the atmosphere? I desperately want to feel it. The house seems the same as ever to me. But if the priest says he has exorcised the spirits, I have to believe him.

Another wave of sickness overwhelms me and I jump up the stairs two at a time, making the toilet with a second to spare. My vomit hits the water violently and splashes up the sides of the bowl.

Rummaging in the bathroom cabinet, I find the thermometer and stick it in my ear. 39.2 Celsius. So, I am ill. This is not IBS caused by stress.

The griping in my stomach moves to my lower right-hand side. I curl up in a ball on the floor. The tiles cool my hot cheek. *I'll get up in a minute*, I tell myself. *I'll just lie here for a bit.* It must be a stomach bug, probably caught from Poppy's nursery. Since Poppy started nursery, Mike and I have caught so many bugs. Viruses seem to spread like wildfire in those places.

"Hello!" Mike's voice echoes as he closes the door. I'm surprised. I hadn't expected him back so soon, although I'm unsure what the time is. The pain in my side is growing more intense. I twist on the floor in an attempt to relieve it.

"I'm here, in the bathroom!" My voice is weak and I raise it as I hear Mike pounding about, oblivious to my shout. The pain in my stomach stabs through me and I gasp as I hear Mike thud up the stairs.

He opens the bathroom door, a look of shock on his face as he sees me.

"God, are you OK?"

Mike crouches beside me, his hand on my face. "You're boiling."

"You're back early," I mutter. "Oh, Mike, I feel dreadful." I cry out as the pain reaches a crescendo.

"My meeting finished early so I came home," Mike replies, his eyes full of concern. "What's going on? You seem really ill."

"I thought I had IBS, but I've got a temperature. I've been sick and the pain in my stomach is horrendous," I say, clutching my right side.

Mike kneels down. "Is your pain here?"

He presses his hand against me and I screech. "Oh God, yes! Don't do that again, that was agony."

"Clara, I think you might have appendicitis," says Mike gently, concern etched on his face. "It's characterised by right-hand pain, which you have. And I seem to recall a temperature. I had appendicitis when I was twelve," he adds. "I'm sure I told you."

"Oh yes." Bile rises in my throat and I retch. "It's probably too late to get a doctor's appointment, so shall we call 111?"

Mike shakes his head. "They'll only tell us to go to hospital. So, let's cut out the middleman and I'll take you myself now to A&E."

I struggle to sit up. "What about Poppy? One of us needs to get her from nursery. I'll get an Uber to hospital. It might not even be appendicitis, anyway."

Another stab of pain. I lie down again on the cool tiles of the bathroom.

Mike grabs his phone. "I'm going to make a call or two. Leave it to me."

He hurries out and I groan, trying but failing to find a comfortable position.

But despite the agonising pain, I'm happy that Mike is my lovely, caring husband again. His kindness and concern envelop me in a hug, such a contrast to his indifference last night. Although, I still can't comprehend how he took Josie's side over mine, how he went to hers for a cosy nightcap.

Mike re-enters the room. "Right. Plan of action," he says calmly. "I rang Layla and she's away in Wales on a work trip. So, I tried Josie. She's available and will pick Poppy up from nursery and look after her for as long as it takes. I called the nursery to tell them."

I feel as if I will vomit again, but not due to the appendicitis. *Josie in my house, with my child, her head bent over her, cuddling her and getting her ready for bed.*

"No, no, no," I sound hysterical. I need to try and modulate it, to stop any disruption of the fragile peace between me and Mike. "I'm not comfortable with that. We barely know her, and Poppy has only met her once. I don't want her in our house without me."

I gasp as the burrowing pain in my abdomen ramps up.

Mike leans down and touches my cheek. "Look at you. You're in agony and we need to get you to hospital. Clara, I'm your husband and you need urgent medical help. Josie can help us and we need to take her up on the offer, regardless of how well we know her. Although, I do actually feel I've got to know her a bit. She's a good person."

A good person? That is the final straw for me and I slump forward. I can't cope anymore. If someone could send me into oblivion, take away all this emotional and physical stress, I would willingly take them up on the offer.

"Fine," I mutter in a monotone.

Mike half carries me, stumbling to the car. He straps me in tenderly, as if I were a child.

"We'll sort this out," he says, clutching my hand. I hope he means more than just the current pain I'm feeling.

I squeeze his hand back, and then Mike is driving carefully, but as swiftly as possible. "You poor thing, I remember the pain."

"We don't know that it is appendicitis," I point out, but there's no doubt the pain is more severe and constant. My heart pounds and a tear rolls down my cheek. While the pain is horrific, I'm also a bit of a hypochondriac and my mind zipwires around other even more serious explanations. What if it's turned into peritonitis, which is life-threatening? Or what if it's not appendicitis at all but something even more sinister? Will the hospital give me a battery of tests? Blood tests. Ultrasounds. Scans. *God*, I think. *I hate hospitals.*

It's the last straw. The last straw. The words whirl around my mind. I focus on the sentence to try to take my mind off the pain. *This house has been hell and this is the last straw.*

I glance at Mike, as, his face tense, he drives through a traffic light just before it turns from amber to red. A wave of comfort accompanies a spasm of pain. Despite everything, he does love me. Maybe he will agree to move house after all.

Another punch to the stomach. I feel like I've taken a blow from a heavyweight boxer. Now I'm squirming and moaning, pushing all other thoughts from my mind. Snapshots flood my semi-conscious state: Josie and Mike, giant animals in the loft, Poppy, Layla's boots, the bullet, the gun. The muzzle pointed at Josie's temple. I moan again and this time the pain is too much. Blackout.

CHAPTER 22

I lift up my hospital gown to examine the scar. A livid line of stiches runs across the bottom right of my abdomen. I run my finger along it, wincing slightly. The painkillers are working well, though, and this slight pain is nothing compared to how I felt before the operation.

Mike was right: it had indeed been appendicitis. After blood tests and an ultrasound, I was rushed into surgery and sank thankfully into the relief of nothingness under general anaesthetic.

The operation took place late last night and I feel woozy and tired this morning. Mike stayed with me until my surgery, and then he went home. He's coming back to see me later this morning, after dropping Poppy off at nursery.

I glance around the ward. I'm in a women's general ward. One woman is intoning loudly on the phone about her ovarian cyst. Another is absorbed in a book, and another is padding back from a shower. There is a nurse dealing with someone else at the end of the ward. Her eyes are sympathetic but tired. I snuggle under my thin blanket and despite the dull ache, despite being away from my family, for a brief moment, I relish being in this ward. I'm comforted by the people all around me and the kind nurses and doctors who have helped me.

A woman presses her button for attention and the noise shatters my peace. *Poppy with Josie.* My bay suddenly feels claustrophobic. Someone in the bay next to me shouts out for assistance. The voice vibrates through me. I just want to be back with Poppy, and for Josie to be as far away as possible.

Right on cue, my phone beeps. It's Mike, forwarding a video. In it is Poppy, cradling her swaddled doll and crooning. "Ah, lovely," says Josie's voice, with a little chuckle. She's obviously filming Poppy on her phone. "And you have a little message, don't you, sweetie?"

My hand grips the phone tighter. I want to hurl it at the floor. *Do not call my child sweetie.*

Poppy carefully puts her doll down and stares at the screen. "Miss you, Mummy. Get well soon and come home."

My anger subsides briefly. Suddenly I cannot wait to be home, to cuddle and kiss my daughter. And for Josie to disappear next door where she belongs. The doctors have told me I'll be discharged at the end of the day or first thing tomorrow, depending on how I feel.

Mike sends me another text. *Thought you'd like this video. Poppy is really missing you. She's been such a good girl. Have taken her to nursery and am on the way over. Can I pick anything up for you? xx*

In a previous message, Mike mentioned that Josie had returned next door as soon as he got home to be reunited with Poppy. I cannot help but wonder. Would he lie? What if Josie and Mike had enjoyed another cosy nightcap together? They could have stayed up chatting into the night and grown closer.

What if Mike had invited her to stay the night? What if she had actually ended up in our bed? Josie's silky blonde mane on my pillow, a vivid contrast to Mike's dark hair. Their bodies moving together and . . . *stop it, stop it, stop it.*

I kick my legs agitatedly and my scar throbs. I almost welcome the interruption to the thoughts in my head, which are even more painful than my surgery.

My mind is flying. I need to calm down, I tell myself sternly. *My husband loves me.* Look at his concern yesterday, the way he hadn't wanted to leave my side. And he's coming over as soon as he can this morning.

Which reminds me of more mundane matters. I still haven't replied to his text. *Can you bring me a diet coke and a newspaper?* xx

* * *

"How are you feeling?" Mike pulls the curtains around the bed and takes my hand. "You gave me quite a scare. I called your mum and dad this morning. Your mum is concerned. She wants to come and visit as soon as she can to look after you."

"Yeah, I've already heard from her," I smile. "She texted me earlier."

"So how are you feeling physically?"

"Just a bit sore and bruised. The painkillers are helping. I just really want to go home. I hope tonight, but if not tomorrow."

"Tonight seems a little soon," says Mike, eyes widening. "You've just been through surgery. You still don't look that well to me."

"Let's see what they say." I'm impatient to change the subject.

Mike settles back in his chair. "I can stay with you all day," he says. "I've got time off work. And Josie has offered to collect Poppy from nursery and stay the evening to look after her if need be."

I swallow. I love that Mike wants to stay and look after me. Hopefully it's a sign we're putting things right again. Yet I hate knowing that Josie is in our house. With Poppy. Without me.

"We can ask Layla to look after Poppy," I say quickly. "She's texted to say that she's back from her work trip today. Although I'm not sure what time."

Mike says gently, "You know, Josie was wonderful with Poppy. Poppy loved having her there."

I want to slap him. He knows how much I dislike Josie, especially after that night he took her to see her dying father. His words are a kick in the teeth.

I can tell by his expression that he has an inkling of what I'm thinking.

"I know you're not keen on her, and I'm sorry you were upset by me taking her to see her dad and having a drink with her. But I felt sorry for her and I think she's a nice person and that's it."

His voice becomes fierce.

"You're my wife and I love you. And I'm sorry about the issues we've had since we've moved here. We'll get it sorted, I promise."

My heart sings. I want to cry with relief. But still, "Josie was wonderful with Poppy" stings.

"I'm so happy you think that," I say, fighting back tears. "But I think that house is sinister. I think the history is going to affect us for ever and stop us being really happy there. I think we should sell the bloody thing as soon as we can."

Mike looks down. "Let's just see what happens," he says finally. "I don't want you to be unhappy, but I think we need to give it a chance. See if it gets better."

Perhaps Mike is right, I say to myself reluctantly. I tell him about Father David's blessing. I catch a look of alarm on Mike's face and he seems ready to voice his concern, before thinking better of it and settling for a neutral response.

"There you go. We need to give the house a chance, then. Maybe Father David really will manage to get rid of the ill feeling there."

I know Mike, an atheist, doesn't believe in Father David's blessing any more than he believes in the tooth fairy. But, I wonder, is he yet at the stage where he can link the unsettling events of today to the horrors of the past?

A fizzing pain rips through my shoulder. Doctors warned me I could experience pain in my shoulder tip after the laparoscopy.

Maybe Father David really can make the house a happy place to live again. If only he could fix the problem next door.

CHAPTER 23

Mike pulls up in front of our house, and I'm pleased to be home. Maybe Father David's blessing has worked. Maybe there will be no more creaks in the loft. No more letters on Poppy's board. No more unexplained flooding. No more anything.

I'm instantly worried, however, to see the house in total darkness. Josie messaged Mike to say she'd collected Poppy from nursery, but it's 7 p.m. now. They should have been home some time ago.

"They're not in!" I shout, pulling off my seatbelt, ignoring the pain in my side as I violently wrench the car door open and jump out. "Where are they? They should have been back for ages."

Mike frowns and shakes his head. "Calm down. Maybe she took Poppy to hers instead."

I dash next door, feeling as though there's a weight attached to my stomach. Josie's house is in darkness too.

"Where are they?" I drop my bag of painkillers and wail.

"For goodness' sake!" Mike stomps up behind me. "You're being ridiculous. Maybe they're held up somewhere. I'll give Josie a call."

He prods his finger hard against his phone and I can hear the tinny ringing sound. I hold my breath. *Pick up, pick up, pick up.* I drum my hand against my thigh.

"*I'm sorry I can't take your call, please leave a message and . . .*"

"She's taken her." I don't recognise my own voice. It's wild and guttural. Images of Josie hustling Poppy on a train, strapping her into her car or marching her onto a plane fill my mind. *She wanted her and now she's got her.*

"Clara!" Mike grasps my shoulder. "You're really worrying me. I knew they shouldn't have let you leave the hospital so soon. You're ill and you're not acting right. Please calm down."

He tries to stroke me but his short, sharp touch belies his frustration. He glances at his watch. "The nursery will be closed now. Luckily, I've got Fiona's mobile. I'll give her a call.

"Hi Fiona, Poppy's dad Mike here. I hope you don't mind me calling you . . ."

I hold my breath. There are black spots floating in front of my eyes and I wonder if I'll pass out. I almost welcome it. Sweet oblivion and then maybe Mike will somehow sort it all out and Poppy will be there when I open my eyes.

"Ah right, OK. Yes, she did let us know. I just wanted to check. OK, thanks. Bye."

Mike looks at me with trepidation. "Josie picked Poppy up at five — as she said in her message," he says steadily. I can't believe he's so calm.

"We need to call the police." My breath is short and sharp. My wound throbs in time with my heartbeat. "Our neighbour has abducted our daughter."

Fear flashes over Mike's face — but not for the reasons that so unnerve me. "Clara, you're being totally irrational. I think I'd better take you back to hospital. That operation has done something to you."

I pick up my bulging bag of painkillers and throw it across Josie's drive. Why can't Mike understand the danger that Poppy is in? We might have lost our daughter for ever to that witch next door.

"I'm going to check our house just in case they're there," I pant. "If not, I'm calling the police."

And then I'm stumbling towards our house, wincing as I burst through the door.

"Poppy!" I shriek into the darkness. "Poppy!"

I'm frantically running through the rooms, the glare of the lights making me blink as I snap them on.

Silence. Mike watches me helplessly in the hallway. A vein starts to throb in his temple. He dials Josie's phone again and I hear it go straight to voicemail.

"She's taken our daughter!" I scream. The pain in my stomach and my terror combine and I fall to the floor.

There is a flash of lights as a car pulls into the drive.

Mike dashes to the door.

"Josie!" Relief fills his voice.

I scramble to my feet and seconds later I'm at the car wrenching a passenger door open.

"Poppy." My eyes drink in my daughter's curls, chubby cheeks and wide smile, which abruptly disappears as I pull her out of the car seat.

"Where the heck have you been?" I scream at Josie, as she slowly emerges from the car.

Poppy's face crumples. "Stop it, Mummy!" she shrieks.

Surprise sweeps across Josie's face. "I took her to the cinema," she says. "I thought it would be nice for her to see the latest Disney film."

She hesitates. "Sorry, I should have let you know. But I didn't want to bother you both in hospital and I thought that you'd be back much later."

Poppy wriggles violently. "Let me go," she roars. "Me want Josie."

"I tried to call you," says Mike stridently, his voice almost lost in Poppy's screams. I'm glad to hear that he sounds annoyed.

"I'm sorry," says Josie, though she doesn't sound especially apologetic. "I had my phone on silent."

Poppy thumps me right on my stitches. My arms fall as pain rips through me and Poppy dashes over to Josie, burying her face in her stomach.

The relief I feel that Poppy is safe is overwhelmed by jealousy and rage. Poppy clings to Josie as Josie strokes her hair.

"Let's all calm down," says Mike, his steady tone belied by the anger in his eyes as he glares at me.

CHAPTER 24

Mike pulls open the door and I walk in gingerly. The anger has dissipated and now I just feel a fool. Mike is cross with me. Worse still, I can see contempt in his eyes. I know I overreacted but what Josie has done still doesn't sit right with me. Who whisks a toddler off to the cinema without informing the parents first? Especially when one of them has been in hospital.

Josie half walks and half shuffles in, Poppy still clinging to her. She sniffs, and then detaching herself, takes my hand.

I stroke her hair tenderly. "I'm so sorry if I scared you, darling," I murmur, "I was just worried about where you were."

Poppy gives a little smile and clambers onto the sofa with Josie. The two blond heads are together, one flaxen and one a dark golden colour.

Mike walks into the room with a bottle of Chablis and a bouquet of beautiful mixed tulips for Josie.

When did you last buy me flowers? I think petulantly. A small, drooping bunch of daffodils from the local supermarket a good few months ago, I seem to recall.

Josie beams at him and buries her head in the flowers, sniffing appreciatively.

"Thank you." I watch Josie gaze at my husband, that disarming dimple in her cheek. *Disarming to some, maybe.* Mike's eyes crinkle as he stares back at her.

"I can't thank you enough," Mike says.

"Poppy, go and give your mummy a cuddle. She's been really poorly in hospital," he adds gently.

I hold my breath. Poppy freezes at first, and then she's in my arms. I bury my head in her strawberry-shampoo-scented hair, holding her tighter. "I'm so happy to be home, darling," I mutter. "I'll take you to bed and read some nice stories to you."

Poppy extricates herself. "Don't want to go to bed." She folds her arms and sticks her bottom lip out.

"How about I get you to bed?" suggests Josie. "We can have cuddles and counting like last night and I can read *The Gruffalo* to you in funny voices."

"Yes!" Poppy is all smiles.

Mike moves over and puts an arm round me. "Let her go with Josie," he says quietly. "Don't take it personally. She's probably upset you went away. She won't understand you needed to and sees it as a rejection of her."

I take a breath. My stitches throb and my legs are weak. I want to lie down. Mike is right.

"OK." I try to sound light-hearted and keep the hurt out of my voice.

Poppy jumps up. "Come on, Josie," she urges, pulling at her hand. "Night-night, Mummy, Daddy." She waves breezily at us. Josie's eyes light up and she smiles tenderly, that dimple back in her cheek.

Poppy's offhand farewell is like a dagger through my heart. Another woman, someone I don't like and trust even less, is lying cuddled up to my daughter in bed, reading to her and kissing her good night.

I jump up. With these thoughts tormenting me, I cannot keep still. I stalk to the kitchen and family room. Poppy's dolls have been arranged in a circle. Various accessories surround them: a pretend potty, nappies, nappy cream, talcum powder pots.

In the middle of the circle is Poppy's dreaded magnetic board. My heart pounds. It was meant to be firmly shut away in the kitchen drawer. *Who found it and got it out?* With a sinking heart I realise that letters are neatly lined up on it.

watching you

I spin around automatically as my brain scrambles to make sense of it. There is just Mike behind me, staring at me quizzically. My eyes scan the room and I point at the board.

"Look." I gesture, my hand shaking.

Mike looks strained.

He sighs. "It's probably Josie playing with Poppy. I saw them playing for ages with the board. I really don't think it's anything to worry about."

Pieces of a jigsaw fit slowly into place. If Josie created this message on the board, albeit playing with Poppy, then was she behind the other messages? Was she the one who found it in the kitchen drawer? Or perhaps she already knew it was there somehow. A tingle runs down my back.

This woman is terrorising me in my own home.

I want to shoot up the stairs and shout and scream at her, put my hands around her neck and squeeze until those blue eyes pop out. I take some deep breaths and sit on the sofa as I tussle with my impulses.

Fortunately, my good sense wins the day. I know that if I runs upstairs, I'll upset Poppy and Mike will see me as the baddie. It won't take much — he's already angry with me over my hysteria earlier. As painful as it is, I need to wait for Josie to come down. I dig my nails into my palm, taking satisfaction in the pink scratch they make. Mike sits beside me.

"You need to calm down," he says gently. "I think some of this is, understandably, the trauma of the surgery. You're in pain and exhausted."

Don't gaslight me! I scream inside. My hand balls into a fist and I want to slam it against his head. I wait silently, tolerating Mike's arm around my shoulder, his hand on my knee.

There are light steps on the stairs and Josie bursts into the room. "Fast asleep," she says triumphantly, her grin directed at Mike.

I stand up and walk slowly and pointedly towards Josie.

"What's this?" I say harshly, pointing at the letters on Poppy's board.

Josie squints. "That's . . ." she begins.

I don't want to hear her explanation. "The thing is, I've been getting sinister messages on this board for a while. *Still here*, that mean anything?"

Josie looks puzzled. *Of course she does. She has that look honed to perfection.*

"I couldn't understand why I was getting nasty messages on this board, and from whom. I still don't completely understand, but I think you're behind it. Why are you watching me? How are you getting into our home?"

I take a step closer to Josie. "I also hid that board in a kitchen drawer. Did you find it and take it out? Routing round our kitchen, were you?"

"Clara!" Mike exclaims, moving towards me. I can feel his disgust and embarrassment seeping from every pore.

Josie is doing a good job of looking confused. "I don't understand what you mean about nasty messages," she says, shaking her head. "But yes, I wrote those words."

Her eyes meet mine, hard and icy. The dislike — hatred, even — is mutual.

I feel a quick shot of triumph. *Aha! I'm closing in on her.*

"Poppy loves that board and we were playing with it a lot. We set up her dolls as a pretend nursery class and Poppy made out that one of them was being naughty. I pretended to be the teacher telling the doll off. I wrote *watching you* — as in, 'I'm watching you, don't misbehave again.'"

What crap, I'm about to snort. But the words wither on my tongue. Mike is nodding away. "I totally get it. It's quite obvious." That was meant for me, despite the fact he is looking at and addressing Josie.

"How did you find the board?" I thunder.

Josie looks bewildered. "It was just here, in this room, among all the toys," she says softly.

Mike glares at me. "You're tired and unwell after the operation. Best we get you to bed," he says tightly.

I want to argue, to double down on my accusation. But I flounder. What, after all, do I know for certain? Josie has admitted that she wrote *watching you* as part of a game with Poppy. How can I argue with that?

Even though I don't believe Josie, I have no evidence to the contrary. Nor can I prove that Josie wrote the other messages, let alone that she's been entering the property independently.

Could Josie have really, truly, entered our house without alerting me or Mike? Not to mention Poppy. My doubt builds. It's simply not realistic. Even though I wouldn't trust Josie as far as I could throw her, it's difficult for me to pin all this on her. *Maybe it's the supernatural at play here, the family who lived here before.*

Unless those messages left on the board tie in with Josie dropping into see me. Dates and times of visits and the board messages buzz around in my mind as I tie myself in knots to line them up. I close my eyes briefly. I'm too tired to work it out. I need my painkillers and sleep.

"Come on," Mike takes my arm, but there's no warmth in his grip. "Let's get you to bed."

"I'm sorry I upset you," Josie says blandly. I used to think that Josie was timid — or, more likely, wanted to appear so. But recently her interactions with me have taken on a harder edge. She doesn't sound in the least apologetic. But then, I reflect bitterly, why should she? *Maybe it's not her after all.* My confused mind is pulling me in all directions.

"Thank you so much for everything," Mike says earnestly. The tightness in his face has gone as he looks at Josie. She smiles.

"Any time." Her voice oozes charm.

Josie grabs her flowers and wine, and heads to the front door.

"Call if you need anything," she says, pointedly addressing Mike.

The door closes.

"Did *you* find the board in the drawer and get it out?" I flounder on, knowing that this will only incite Mike's rage further, but I can't help myself. I need to know who took it out of its hiding place.

"No!" Mike raises his voice, his face turning red. "Stop going on about that bloody board. You probably got it out and forgot that you did, or Poppy did. Who cares?" He shakes his head violently.

I'm about to refute his accusations but think better of it. Doubts start to grow. Perhaps Poppy did have a rummage and find it.

"Can you get me my painkillers?" I ask weakly. I want to prevent this confrontation from going any further. I just want to pull the covers over my head and sleep.

In stony silence, Mike goes to collect them. He pours me a glass of water and hands it to me.

I gulp down my medication. "Mike, I . . ." I search for the words to make it right between us.

"I don't recognise you anymore, Clara." Mike turns away from me and plods up the stairs. "I don't know what's happened to the woman I married."

CHAPTER 25

Poppy clambers onto the bed. "Where's Josie?" she asks petulantly. My hand brushes against my bruised abdomen. My stitches feeling like tiny, warm bumps under my fingers.

My thoughts are blurry until at once everything rushes back: being discharged from the hospital, the words on Poppy's board, back in its usual position after I squirrelled it away, my accusations against Josie and Mike's anger and disappointment in me.

My heart thumps as I picture the look on Mike's face. After he flung his hurtful words at me, we got into bed and went to sleep in silence. I felt too drained to do anything but drift straight off to sleep. But now I consider his words coolly. It wasn't just what he said, but the way he said it. So cold, final and resigned. I feel sick, and Poppy's question hasn't helped.

"Josie's in her own home now," I say as calmly as possible. "But look, I'm back from hospital, and Mummy is so happy to be with you." I lean over to hug Poppy, but she flinches.

Mike intervenes. "Come on, Poppy, poor Mummy has been really unwell. Be kind to her."

I feel a swell of gratitude at his words, but Mike is avoiding my gaze, staring instead at Poppy.

"Me want Josie," insists Poppy. "Josie, Josie, Josie!" she wails, her voice high-pitched.

"I'm sure she'll be over soon, if you're good," Mike says, a warning note in his voice. "Now, let's go to your bedroom. I'm going to dress you."

He swings his legs over the bed and holds out his hand as I attempt to raise myself.

"No, you must stay in bed." His words are kind, but his voice is distant.

I sink back on my pillows. I'm glad I'm signed off work for at least a week, and more if I need it. I've no energy.

"Mike, I'm sorry about last night." I desperately want to bridge the gap between us, which started as a stream and now feels like an ocean. "Please just let me explain."

Mike shakes his head.

"We'll talk later." Curt and emotionless. "I need to get Poppy to nursery."

I feel dreadful.

"I'm working from home today to help look after you. We can speak when I'm back." He turns on his heel.

Tears spring to my eyes. What if I've blown it? I feel afraid for my marriage — not for the first time. The woman next door is hovering in the shadows, waiting to pounce.

I move slowly onto my side and close my eyes. Despite my anxiety, I'm drifting back to sleep when there's shuffling outside the bedroom door. "Go on," Mike whispers.

I hear a grunt then Poppy slides in. "Love you, Mummy, missed you," she intones dutifully, reaching up to kiss me on the cheek. She misses and hits the pillow. "Byyeee." She sidles out.

"Still want Josie," Poppy says in a stage whisper to Mike.

My chest is heavy, but then there is darkness.

* * *

I'm outside peering through a window of our house. It's pitch black and cold. Besides me is a pile of suitcases. The light inside glows. On the sofa are three bodies cuddled close together, and three heads. One flaxen, one golden blonde and one dark brown. They look towards the window. Mike, Josie and Poppy. Then they turn away and Mike stands up, and with a snap he shuts the blinds.

"You're not welcome here. We're a new family now, Clara," he says in that formal, robotic voice he's been using with me recently.

"Clara! Clara!" I wake with a start, grimacing at the shooting sensation in my side.

Mike is bending over me. "Clara!" At his words, my dream shatters like a vase crashing to the ground.

"Sorry. I'm so tired."

"Of course you are."

Polite, distant and cold.

"Here's your medication."

He hands over my tablets and a glass of water. I gulp them down.

"Mike, I'm really sorry," I say. "I know you're angry with me."

Contempt passes over Mike's face. "Josie did us a huge favour and you treat her like that." His voice is icy. "Yes, I'm angry and embarrassed. And worried about you. All this obsession with Poppy's board and her letters. I don't understand it."

I open my mouth and think better of it. There's no point saying anything. It will only make things worse.

"We're falling apart, aren't we?" Mike plucks at the duvet and stares out of the window. "I thought it was the house and its issues. But maybe that's just hastening our problems."

I feel sick. Mike is going to leave me, isn't he? He'll get together with Josie and I'll be on her own, minus the second baby I long for. All of a sudden, the dream from which I've just woken doesn't feel like a dream at all.

"Mike, I'm so sorry. You're right. I behaved very badly. But I just wasn't with it, to be honest. I felt so weak after the appendicitis."

I'm babbling now, searching in vain for excuses.

"Look, I want to make it up to Josie, to make it all OK. Why don't we have her over for dinner in the next few days? And we could ask Layla as well. Have a nice mishmash of friends." I know there's no realistic prospect of this happening. In fact, I can think of few things worse. But at this point I'll do whatever it takes to ensure my marriage survives.

Mike raises an eyebrow. "You've just had an operation. How are you well enough for a dinner party?"

"I don't know, but we'll manage it somehow." I force myself to sound enthusiastic. "If we aim for Sunday, that's four days away. And if push comes to shove, we can always do a takeaway. Please, I just want to fix things with you, with Josie."

My voice is dry as I spit out Josie's name. *That woman.* I couldn't care less about pacifying her. I just want my life with Mike to be as it was before we moved to this dreadful house. I want his cheerful grin to be directed at me, for his eyes to crinkle with their usual warmth and for his voice to regain its kind cadences. Not this formal, offhand tone he adopts when speaking to me.

I'll have to pretend to like Josie, to hide my real feelings towards her.

Mike's face softens.

"Well, if you're sure," he says hesitantly. "I think that would be a nice gesture."

I lean out of bed and cling to him. "Of course. I just want things to be OK with us, Mike. We were so happy and I want that back. I'll do anything." My voice is muffled as I bury my face in his jumper.

There's a pause then Mike slowly puts his arms around me.

"Look, I know it's been really stressful," he says slowly. "Things have gone wrong since we moved here, culminating in that flood, and now you've been ill. And the house's history is not ideal, to say the least."

I want to jump in and beg him again to consider moving. But I shut my mouth tightly. Now isn't the right time.

Mike gives me a pat on the back and pulls away.

"Look, I need to do some work now. I've got a Teams meeting. You rest, and shout if you need anything."

He moves to the door. "And thanks for the offer of the meal. Only if you're up to it though."

While his voice isn't at its usual warm pitch, at least some of the frostiness has disappeared. Just moments earlier, I'd thought Mike was on the point of leaving me. I can at least be happy with this halfway house.

Yet there is one scene I cannot erase from my mind: Mike and Josie together on the sofa, clutching their nightcaps and whispering cosily. Moving closer and closer to one another.

* * *

I've managed to raise myself from bed and walk downstairs, even though I'm still in my pyjamas. I don't yet feel up to getting dressed. I shuffle into the kitchen to make a cup of coffee. Mike is upstairs in the office, and even though I wouldn't have minded a cup brought to me in bed, I'm reluctant to disturb him at work.

Ding-dong.

I freeze, my muscles taut. *Josie.* I clench my jaw. *I can do this.* A polite smile, ask her to dinner, a few platitudes about how grateful I am. *Job done.* I stalk towards the front door, forcing the corners of my mouth to turn upwards.

But rather than Josie's blonde hair and petite frame, I'm confronted by a tall woman with red hair. Belinda. My limbs relax. Even though I'm not keen on Mabel's daughter either, she is the better option. Belinda is clutching a Le Creuset dish covered in silver foil, which she offers to me.

"From my mum," she says pleasantly, looking me in the eye. Belinda's manner is much more cordial than before. I can barely believe it's the same woman.

"Mike told her about you having appendicitis, so she wanted to make you a lasagne," she continues. "She said she knows how difficult it is being ill with such a young child. She once had appendicitis herself, so she knows what you've been through."

"Oh, that's kind." I take the dish. Belinda is making no move to go.

"Cup of tea or coffee?" I proffer weakly.

"Yes, please, a tea would be great." Belinda steps quickly into the house.

I place the lasagne carefully in the fridge.

"So, how are you feeling? It's horrible being ill, let alone with kids."

"I feel like I've been hit by a truck," I say, popping a teabag into a mug. "And it's hard with a lively toddler. Although she is in nursery full-time, so that helps. You have children too, don't you — I think your mum said you had two?"

"Yes, two girls. A little older than your daughter — five and seven." She drums her fingers on the counter. "Oh — milk and one sugar, please."

We retire to the family room.

Belinda sways ever so slightly on the spot, tapping her foot.

"It must be horrible for you, living here, knowing the history of the house," she volunteers eventually. "How are you finding it?"

"Horrendous," I say instantly, surprising myself at my candour. My stitches throb as I adjust myself on the sofa. "Everywhere I turn, I feel like they're here, watching me." I suppress a sob. "Since we moved into this house so much has gone wrong."

I glance around the huge family room and kitchen. It took my breath away when I saw it for the first time. Now I detest it. All I want is to put the house on the market, sell it and get the hell away. A cramped two-bedroom flat in Tooting would be bliss right now.

"I'm not surprised," says Belinda. She fusses with her mug. "You probably thought I was a bit strange when I first met you — not very friendly."

Not knowing the best way to reply, I opt once more for honesty. "Yes."

"My mum said you didn't know the history of the house. It made me extremely uncomfortable. It's no one's fault, obviously — the estate agent and Helen were hardly going to tell you — but it's such a horrible thing that happened, and I was pretty sure if you knew about it you wouldn't move there. I actually toyed with telling you myself and I suggested Mum did, but she was adamant that it was none of our business."

That's true, I think. It's very nice of Belinda to feel so much on my behalf, but I'm a total stranger to her.

I wonder how to phrase my thoughts. *Sod it. Just tell the truth.*

"That's very kind of you," I say. "But why do you feel so deeply about it? I know it's very unfortunate for my family, but you don't know us."

"I probably do feel too deeply," admits Belinda. "But it massively affected me. I was doing an MA at university and *he* was my tutor."

It's clear she doesn't even want to utter Jonathan Maynard's name. Her voice drips with contempt.

"I was living at home as well and had built up a good friendship with him. I really respected him academically. What happened knocked me for six. So I'm probably over-invested in it." Belinda's foot moves up and down, as though pumping up an imaginary airbed. "Also, Helen, like you, had no idea about the murder."

"I guess that's why she sold the house, then." I straighten my back. "Not for some mythical job."

"I'd think so," Belinda agrees. "When Helen found out about the murder, she said she couldn't live there — here, I mean — anymore. Said she had an overactive imagination and that it was consuming her."

"And how did she find out?"

Belinda pauses.

"A news clipping through the door. Like you."

Josie's pale face and nanny-goat blue eyes drift into my mind.

"It was me who sent the clippings to you both," Belinda reveals.

I'm stunned, despite Belinda's admission that she's over-invested in what happened.

"But why? It really freaked me out."

Anger rushes through me. If Belinda hadn't taken that step, then maybe I would never have found out. Which, on reflection, I would have preferred. *What you don't know can't hurt you.*

"That man destroyed enough lives." She doesn't hide her contempt. "I felt that the people living here — both Helen's family and yours — deserved to know what happened so they could decide for themselves whether to stay. I saw the impact on Helen, and when I realised you didn't know either, I was determined for you to know the full story too."

"OK." I'm agitated. "Why didn't you just tell me?"

Belinda hesitates. "I felt uncomfortable bringing it up, as I don't know you. And I thought with the clippings, you would have all the information to hand and know much more clearly what happened than if I had simply turned up trying to explain it."

"Why did you do it anonymously, though?" I push for more. "Surely you would realise that might scare me?"

Belinda rocks back and forth and tugs at her hair. "I'm sorry, I probably didn't think it through. I just wanted you to know and appreciate the severity of what happened. I didn't put my name to it as I thought you'd think I was weird."

It was a weird thing to do.

I eye Belinda uneasily. I want her to go now.

"It was probably silly, I do know that," Belinda hurries on. "But my emotions have been all over the place. My dad died about eighteen months ago from pancreatic cancer. It was a month between diagnosis and death."

A shadow passes across Belinda's face, as though recalling some best-forgotten event from long ago.

"I certainly wasn't close to him. God, not close at all. But it pulled the rug from under me. I probably haven't been acting completely rationally since then."

I feel a tug of sympathy. "Your poor mum too," I say softly.

"Yeah, she's a 'stiff upper lip' type of person. In all aspects of her life, including family," Belinda says cryptically. "But she was devastated. I've tried to help her out, as much as I can with a husband who's a hospital doctor and working unsociable hours."

I think of Josie. I need to ask Belinda about her but I don't wish to seem heartless by changing the subject too abruptly.

I make sympathetic noises and mean them. My own dad's face, with his affable smile and spectacles perched at the end of his nose, flashes into my mind. I would be distraught if I lost him, especially under the circumstances Belinda lost her own father.

"I hope you don't mind me asking," I say. "But what are your thoughts on Josie — you know, the woman who lives next door to me?"

Belinda frowns. "I haven't been in proper touch with her for years. But I remember her well from when the Maynards were here. Let's just say, she was close to Lily. Wherever Lily was, she'd be there."

I'm eager to hear more but Belinda stands up sharply.

"I'd best get out of your hair. I hope you feel better soon. Mum says she'll make you some more dishes."

"That's very kind of her indeed."

Belinda looks around the hall as we walk to the front door. "Just like *his* hall was," she says. "The parquet floor, I remember it well. And you've still got the same front door. I always liked the glass in it, the way the colours change with the light."

I make a mental note to change the door if we stay. I can't bring myself to change the original flooring but perhaps we could place a rug over it.

"Bye, then," Belinda says. "I'm sorry if I've upset you."

"It's OK — and thank you." I'm not sure what I'm thanking her for, but it seems an appropriate farewell somehow.

I close the door and watch from the living room window as Belinda walks away. She stops at the end of the drive and turns slowly round to face the house. She stares at it, a scowl on her face. I wait for her to move away . . . I start to count. *One, two, three, four . . . how long is this woman going to glare at my home?*

Belinda spits violently. I shrink back, repelled by the vicious action. Then Belinda turns on her heel, walking nonchalantly away as if nothing has happened.

Was Belinda's gesture meant for the house? The Maynards? Or for me?

CHAPTER 26

I knock on the door and wait. My stomach feels like a washing machine.

There is a long pause.

Just as I'm about to walk away, the door opens.

Josie's hair is pulled back roughly, highlighting her prominent cheekbones. I think about my own round cheeks. Polite people would call them rosy. Those who were more honest might say they were plump.

Josie says nothing. She stares into my eyes. To my frustration, I look away first. I'm uneasy at the change in Josie. Once so reserved and demure, she's now acting with open hostility.

"Hi, Josie." I fidget. I hate doing this so much. All I want to do is tell her to get lost. Instead, I need to be sweetness and light. *It's all for Mike*, I remind myself. It's for my marriage. I'll do what I have to.

"Come in," Josie replies, sounding as if it's the last thing she wants.

I hurry in. I'm feeling weak and want to collapse onto a seat. As I sink into the sofa in the living room, I notice a beautiful porcelain doll lying on the floor, wearing a pink knitted dress. Bright blue eyes gaze out. To my untrained eye, the doll seems to belong to a different era.

Josie follows my gaze.

"Vintage 1950s," she says proudly. "Isn't she divine? I saw her in a charity shop this morning, and I thought that Poppy would just love her. So, I bought it. I'll give it to Poppy when I pop round later."

The doll's tight ringlets are pale yellow, almost the same colour as Josie's hair. *When I pop round later.* The cheek of it. I want to explode. I take a deep breath.

I don't want Josie to give the doll to Poppy. It will only make her love Josie even more. The doll's eyes are fixed on me. I resist an urge to pick it up and slam it onto the floor, cracking its head and smashing those eyes.

"Do you want to come round on Sunday night for dinner?" I blurt out. I'd intended to build up to this moment with polite chit-chat. Without it, my invitation sounds jarred and clumsy.

"We've asked my old friend from university, Layla, too, and thought it would be nice to have a little do. And, of course, to thank you for everything you've done," I add through gritted teeth.

"Oh, how lovely, thank you." Josie's eyes soften and she smiles. "But are you sure you'll be well enough, after your operation?"

"I'm not one hundred per cent but should just about make it. Mike's going to cook. Probably won't be a late one though," I add quickly. I want that woman out of my house at the earliest possible moment.

I glimpse a familiar-looking van pulling into Josie's drive through the shutter slats in the window.

Josie's smile vanishes. "Steve," she says sourly.

Of course. I'm unsure what I should say.

"I'll be going." I jump up hastily. "Brilliant about Sunday."

Josie nods dourly. I wonder if she'll say more about Steve. Even though I want to leave, I find myself lingering, greedy for information. None is offered.

"I'll bring the doll on Sunday." Josie manages a quick smile.

"Ah, OK." *I'd rather you didn't.*

As I walk through the door, Steve steps out of his van, clutching official-looking papers. He smiles tightly at me. Then his mouth stretches into a grin.

"How's your little one, Poppy? What a character."

"She's great. You have a fan there!" I smile. A genuine smile, not like the rictus grins I offer to Josie.

Josie appears at the door, her face a death mask.

The happiness drains from Steve's face and he moves past me swiftly.

The door slams, but I pause. It is nosy — maybe the journalist in me — but I want to put an ear up against the door.

There's no need though. The voices are loud enough for anyone to hear.

Josie's voice has completely lost its usual quiet tone. It's high-pitched, piercing through the wall. Steve's voice is a low rumble until it becomes a roar.

"We have to sell this house!"

I perk up. This is potentially a good sign. If Josie is leaving, maybe I could put up with living here after all.

The screams grow louder. What if they open the door suddenly and catch me red-handed? I hobble off as fast as I can, to the safety of my own home.

My phone rings and Layla's name flashes up.

"Gosh, are you OK? You've given us all such a shock. I've told Lydia and the girls from uni. Poor you and poor Mike." I let Layla's voice wash over me, soothing me. Nevertheless, I've planted myself decisively by the window, staring out, waiting for Steve to reappear.

"All the girls send their love," Layla continues. "Can I do anything?"

"Yes. We're having a tiny dinner party on Sunday, and Josie is coming. Can you come too? Pretty please?"

I hear a sucking sound.

"You going to be OK for that?"

"Yes, yes." I'm impatient. "Mike'll cook and it won't be a late one."

"Of course I'll come. How are you feeling?"

"Physically, I'm a bit battered but getting over it." I remember that I need to take my painkillers. "Mentally — well, it would be great to chat."

There's too much to go into now and I realise that I haven't asked Layla about her life for a while. I pace the living room, my eyes not leaving the window.

"How's it going with, um, Matt?" I hope I've remembered his name correctly.

I hear a wistful sigh down the line.

"Well, I wasn't dumped for once! I actually went off him. We didn't have enough in common. He didn't like the cinema and had a face on him like a slapped arse when I suggested we walk by the river from Richmond to Twickenham. You know how I love to walk."

I wait for the next bit. I know Layla too well and have already guessed what I'm about to hear.

"And you'll never guess what: Max has been back in contact! I know we're getting divorced, but it's got my head spinning. I still feel something for him."

"Oh, Layla!" I'm frustrated. "He was awful to you. What happened to the other woman?"

I'm pacing round the living room when I see Steve out of the window, walking purposefully towards his van. Instinct takes over.

"I have to go," I say hurriedly. "Something's come up. I'll call you back."

I prod the phone, cutting off a faint squeal, and make for the door.

"Er, Steve." I approach slowly, my face flushed as I scramble for the right words. "Could I speak to you for a moment?"

Steve halts. "OK," he says at last, looking uncertain.

I exhale. "Would you like a coffee at mine? I won't keep you long."

"Why not." Steve follows, his feet scuffing against the drive tiles. "Actually, I'd really like a cig." He digs into his pockets, pulling out cigarette papers and filter tips.

"We'll go into the garden." I take him through the house and pull open the bi-fold doors of the family room. Luckily, the weather is mild. Daffodils are sprouting in a corner of the flower bed. I smile.

"How can I help?" Steve rolls his cigarette deftly.

"I've been having some issues with this house and your wife." I see no reason to tiptoe around the matter. "She seems very into Poppy, in a way that makes me uncomfortable. If I'm honest, she's having a really negative impact on my life."

I ponder whether to mention Josie's attachment to Mike, and the arrangement of letters on Poppy's board, but decide not to. The first might still be a sore point for Steve. The latter might make him think that I'm unhinged.

I eye Steve. He lights his roll-up and takes a deep drag. I inhale the smoke and smile. Most non-smokers hate the smell but I like it. It reminds me of my Gran, who smoked like a chimney but gave me plenty of cuddles and always had chocolates in her bag. The smoke envelopes me like a warm blanket, and Steve is a solid and reassuring presence.

At first Steve's face is impassive. After a while, it gives way to a wry smile. He rolls his eyes.

"Sounds like Josie." He takes another drag and closes them briefly. "She gets obsessed with other families, particularly their children. She just wants a family of her own. Pop psychology, innit?" He gives a dry laugh. "But there must be some truth in it, I guess."

"I can understand. She was abandoned by her parents and then to go through a miscarriage . . . especially miscarrying twins." I realise I might have sounded a little blunt. "I mean, I'm so sorry for you both."

"What?" Steve is shaking his head emphatically. "No, we certainly weren't expecting twins. Each round of IVF treatment failed. Josie never got pregnant. Obviously it would have been awful for her to have had a miscarriage, but at least it would have given some hope that there was a chance that IVF could work for us." He stares into the distance, his eyes suspiciously bright.

"Oh, I'm so sorry." I'm mortified. "I must have got the wrong end of the stick."

Josie lied.

The image of the ghostly embryos, floating serenely, fill my mind. It must have been a video Josie had discovered on the internet. When I met Steve for the first time, I sensed he was telling the truth. I feel the same way this time too.

I take a breath. The evidence is starting to pile up. Josie is, quite clearly, a dishonest woman. Why is Mike so inclined to believe her tall stories? I'll resist the temptation to talk to him about Steve, though. It will make relations between us even worse.

Knowledge is power. I hug it to myself. I'll use that to my advantage. But my stomach churns, nausea rising. *It wasn't just a little white lie.*

Poppy's little blonde head snuggled against Josie's fills my mind.

"Well, anyway, I best get off. I'm sorry you're struggling. It's not easy."

Without thinking, Steve throws his cigarette butt onto the patio and grinds it with his heel.

"Uh sorry." He scrambles to pick it up.

"Don't worry," I say quickly. I can deal with it later. I want to finish the conversation now.

As he turns to leave, Steve offers a parting shot. "I'd move if I were you. I was spooked living next door to the Maynards' house after Jonathan killed them. I wanted to sell up immediately, but Josie was adamant we stayed." He laughs mirthlessly. "She sure seems to love your house, and the people who live in it."

CHAPTER 27

"Sorry, Layla." I've called Layla back and cut through her greeting. "I saw Josie's husband outside and I needed to speak to him."

"Why are you still unhappy with her?" Layla's voice is filled with concern, but I can hear faint tapping; she's obviously working on her laptop, half an ear on the phone.

"Yeah, she's trying to steal my husband, my daughter and my life," I reply coolly.

There is silence, broken only by frantic tapping. "What? Oh dear! Poor you!"

Layla's not even attempting to mask the fact her mind is elsewhere. Despite myself, I smile. *Never change, Layla.*

"Please don't go back to Max, Layla. He was a bastard to you. An utter bastard."

The tapping stops.

"I know, I know. He's split with Celia, and I suppose I feel nostalgic. He was my husband, I loved him. I had so many happy times with him."

"And the bad times? And the fact that he left you for Celia?"

"It's just so depressing being on these dating apps. I either don't like the guys, or they're dating multiple women. I just want to be like you and our other friends, snug at home with my husband, and a baby, or at least hopes for a baby."

Layla's voice wobbles.

"I need a distraction, Clara. Any chance that Mike has a nice friend that he can invite to the dinner party?" She laughs wanly. "Sorry! I'm sure I've asked about his friends many times before."

I drag my thoughts away from Josie. *Callum.*

Mike's friend Callum split up with his long-term girlfriend five months ago. Like Mike, he's a shipping analyst. He and Mike met when they were in their first jobs as graduates. I wonder if Callum is bookish enough for Layla. She likes serious types, often those who work in IT.

"Leave it with me."

* * *

I swallow my tablets dutifully and decide to pop to the local shop. I'm sore and need to rest but already I'm bored and looking forward to getting back to work. Hopefully a good sign for my recovery.

I head slowly out of the door and wonder if I have the stamina to walk by the river to Richmond. The bracing air, serene waters and smell of fresh trees and soil as I stamp along the path will do me good.

I almost collide with Mabel, who is turning out of her drive, carefully holding a covered food storage container.

"Sorry!" I exclaim.

As usual, Mabel looks immaculate. Her hair is tightly coiled into a bun, her eyebrows are emphasised with make-up and her mouth is stained in blood-red lipstick. As usual, I marvel. *Can she really be in her seventies?*

"Ah, Clara! I was just coming to see you," Mabel says briskly, proffering her Tupperware. "I made an extra portion of chilli. I thought you and your family might like it.

"My dear, I'm so sorry to hear about your appendicitis. I can imagine how hard it is trying to pick yourself up with a lively daughter, a job and a house to run. Anything I can do to make it easier."

I take the container, enjoying the comforting, spicy smell. I'm touched. Just popping Mabel's lasagne in the microwave last night was wonderful. No standing sweating over a hob. And it meant that Mike could work later and not worry about stopping early to cook dinner for us.

My gratitude makes my eyes water. I want to show my thanks.

"Would you like to come over for dinner on Sunday?" I ask impulsively. "It's just a small gathering. Me and Mike, Mike's friend, my close friend Layla. Oh, and Josie next door."

"How nice!" Mabel says, her eyes lighting up. I realise she's lonely and feel a twinge of sadness. "I'd love to."

"And feel free to ask Belinda and Teddy." The words are out of my mouth before I can stop them.

What was I thinking? I don't want them over, especially following Belinda's admission that she sent the anonymous newspaper clippings.

"I'll ask them," Mabel says. "It might be difficult as Teddy works shifts at the hospital, but I can check. I hope it won't be too much for you, dear. How about I make dessert?"

My initial response is to hope Belinda and her husband don't come. But then I have a mischievous thought. Josie and Belinda, under the same roof. Now that would be interesting.

I exchange warm goodbyes with Mabel, who promises to bring some leftover fish pie the following day. I nip home briefly to put the chilli in the fridge and set off at a sedate pace towards the river.

As I approach its blue-grey expanse, the woody, slightly damp smell of the dense trees fills my nostrils. My shoulders and limbs relax as I march down to the path by the water.

I love this walk to Richmond. If we sell the house, perhaps we shouldn't hotfoot it back to London after all. Maybe we should buy a new house in this area instead.

I was really looking forward to taking Poppy on this walk and bringing her to a tiny cupcake café in Richmond that I've always noticed when I visit. I have a spasm of guilt that I haven't yet done so. The house has consumed me, in every sense.

My stride falters. My stitches ache and I feel worn out. There's no way I can make it all the way to Richmond. Instead, I rest on a log and watch the river, hoping its steady current will soothe my mind.

A tall woman with a gleaming mass of chestnut hair walks by. I frown. Why does she look so familiar? Then it hits me. *Helen.*

Forgetting my soreness and fatigue, I do my best to run after her.

"Helen!"

Helen whirls her head around abruptly. Recognising me, she accelerates. She comfortably outpaces my attempts at running.

"Helen! Helen! Helen!" I'm screaming now. A dog walker on the other side of the river stares. I don't care that I'm making an exhibition of myself. I need this woman to stop and provide answers.

Helen's pace slows gradually and she stops. She turns towards me, a resigned look on her face.

"Sorry," I puff as I approach, then give myself a shake. Why should I apologise? It's Helen who should say sorry for not being honest about why her family were selling up. Then again, will I really tell prospective buyers the truth if Mike and I look to move?

"I take it you're still living in Twickenham, then." I don't mask my anger. "Not the Midlands."

Helen stares at the ground. "Let's sit," she says in a small voice, gesturing to a nearby bench. I sink down gratefully, glancing at the inscription on the bench: *In loving memory of Anna and Jasmine. Taken far too soon. Forever in our hearts. At least you are together.*

Surely it can't be . . . I feel sick as I catch sight of the date of death next to their names. Yes. It is the Maynards. I want to bury my head in my hands. No matter what I do, I cannot escape that family. I wonder if Helen notices the significance of the bench, but she shows no sign, sitting stiffly and staring straight ahead.

I have an urge to pour everything out. But I force myself to wait for Helen to explain, closing my fists tightly in my pockets.

Helen sighs. "Yeah, I do live in Twickenham still. I could lie to you and say that the job in the Midlands fell through. The truth is, there was never a job there. We wanted to get out of that house, and obviously if I'd told you why, we'd never have sold it." She gives a nervous laugh.

"I take it the reason is the Maynards and the murder-suicide," I say.

Helen nods. "I didn't know about it when I moved in and nor did Jim. I mean, bloody hell, I feel totally naive." She pauses. "And I thought I'd never be able to sell it, that people would remember its history."

She glances up from under her eyelashes.

"That's why we set it at such a reasonable price. We had people round and they would be really enthusiastic, and then there would be silence. In every case they found out about the house's past."

The two of us look straight ahead. A heron perched on the riverbank studies its surroundings carefully and takes off, low over the river. Gulls swoop and shriek. A sudden wind causes the leafless branches to sway and buffets the gulls mid-flight. We sink further into our coats as Helen takes up the story again.

"We were so relieved when you made an offer. Our hearts were in our mouths waiting for the sale to go through. We were terrified you'd pull out like all the others had. That's why we did go and rent. That part wasn't actually a lie. We wanted to speed up the process as much as we could."

I kick myself again for not researching the house. A quick google and the Maynards' story would have been all over my screen.

"What happened to you in the house?" I ask.

Helen closes her eyes. "I saw someone. I was in Amy's room, just creeping out after I'd read her a bedtime story. I had one eye on her, to check she was falling asleep. But out of the corner of my other eye I saw a figure, dashing past the bedroom door. I couldn't see the face, but I think it was a woman. It was so quick, I can't really remember any details but I know I didn't imagine it."

Helen snaps her eyes open and it's as though she's been transported back to that time. Fear and disbelief cloud her slate-grey eyes.

"I was absolutely terrified. It was a while before I could gather the courage to go into the hall. There was no one there, but the attic ladder had been pulled down. It wasn't like that before — one hundred per cent. Jim and I hadn't been up there for weeks."

I'm reminded of watching horror films in my youth. The ones that made you too terrified even to stand up and turn off the television.

"So what happened then?"

"I shouted for Jim and he pounded up that ladder. But he couldn't see anything other than old furniture everywhere. It looked like it had been left untouched for years. There was no sign of anyone."

"My daughter Poppy says she sees someone in her room," I murmur.

Helen sits up straighter. "So it's not just me." She sounds both relieved and troubled.

"Jim goes on a lot of business trips and I couldn't bear to be in the house without him after seeing . . . that person. It made things really hard. Whenever he was away, I couldn't sleep a wink, and I ended up sleeping with my children in their beds. It wasn't sustainable."

"What do you think was behind those events?" I have a list of questions in my head that I want answers to.

Helen shrugs and raises her palms. "Well, I had no idea about the murders when this all happened, so I was flummoxed.

Then someone posted a newspaper clipping through the door about the Maynards. Anonymous, mind, which really scared me. When I read that, and then thought about the strange figure I saw, I thought — and I feel silly saying it — that the house was haunted. I have never, ever believed in the supernatural. But I can't see any other explanation."

I'm relieved that someone else has had the same experiences. Even if the implications are too much to bear.

"I've had stuff happening too," I tell Helen. "Sinister words being spelt out on my daughter's letter board. Lights going off for no reason. The bath taps left on." I've always told myself that the flooding was caused by Poppy. Deep down, though, I've never really believed it.

"I'm sorry." Helen hangs her head. "I really do feel guilty you're experiencing this, but we had to get out."

"Who do you think sent the clippings?"

"I have no idea. But that someone would do that really frightened me. As soon as I got that newspaper clipping, I knew it was to do with the woman I saw."

I weigh it up quickly. *Should I tell her?*

"I had the newspaper clippings through the door too. I now know it was Belinda."

Helen raises her face sharply.

"Do you remember her? Mabel's daughter, from number seven."

"Of course I remember her!" Helen is incredulous. "Why on earth would she do something like that?"

"I'm struggling to understand that too."

Rather than bitterness, I feel a degree of kinship with Helen. These have been some of the worst months of my life. At least there's someone else who understands how I feel.

"Belinda came to visit, out of the blue. Jonathan Maynard was her lecturer. She liked and respected him and feels horribly let down by what he did. She also didn't like it that neither your family nor mine knew what had happened. She felt we should know the truth."

Helen frowns, allowing this new information to sink in.

"In that case, I wish she'd just come and told me so, rather than send me the anonymous clippings. That made everything seem even more sinister."

Helen pauses regularly as she tells her tale. Even now, I think, this woman is finding it difficult to revisit that time.

"I thought she was a bit odd," Helen admits. "She seemed keen to avoid me whenever I saw her. But I bumped into her shortly after I had the newspaper clippings and she was so sympathetic. It was almost cloying.

"Another time, I noticed her at the bottom of the drive, peering out round the rowan tree. She stood there for ages. I was about to go outside and ask if she was OK, but she went in the end. That was before I got those newspaper cuttings. Maybe she was trying to pluck up the courage to tell me about the house."

Belinda spitting so viciously outside the house flashes into my mind.

Helen shrugs. "Well, anyway, that tipped it for me. I knew I could never be happy in the house knowing what happened in it. I could see the Maynards everywhere. And all the normal noises that houses make, the creaks and rattles, everything became ominous. The woman I saw was around every corner and door in my mind."

"That's exactly how I feel," I say. "I'm desperate to move. It's tearing me apart. But my husband doesn't agree. He wants to give it a go and see if things improve."

"Jim's got a bit of an overactive imagination like me," says Helen. "I didn't have to do much to persuade him. Plus he felt terrible leaving me in such a state when he went off on his work trips."

My anger at Helen has cooled. If we sell the house, Mike and I will have to lie about our reason for leaving too and cross our fingers that our buyers don't know its history. Or discover it.

"What did you think of Josie?" I ask suddenly.

"A pain. Strange, annoying, I just wanted her to stop coming round," Helen says. "Why, are you not keen either?"

"I absolutely *despise* her." I'm shocked at the hatred in my voice. I'm a peaceable person and like to see the best in people. But Josie creates such tension in me. Just talking about her causes my stomach to jump and makes my chest feel heavy. "She's always trying to come round to ours too." *And get into our family and push me out.*

"I stopped answering the door in the end," says Helen.

I wish bitterly I had created such boundaries earlier. Had I done so, maybe Josie's influence would not be spreading like a cancer within our lives.

"She's obsessed with my daughter," I say suddenly. "And I think possibly with my husband too."

Helen sits up straighter. "She was always offering to babysit. I didn't feel comfortable. I found her too intense. Didn't seem to understand boundaries. One time, for instance, I was annoyed because I saw her giving Amy a couple of sweets in the garden, over the fence. She knew that we'd stopped giving Amy sweets for a bit, as one of the E-numbers was making her hyperactive and she was having tests to see which one."

Helen's face tightens. "I wanted to dash out there. But I waited for Amy to come in. When I asked her what she had been doing, she said, 'Josie said it was our secret.'"

I feel a shot of anger on Helen's behalf. "It doesn't surprise me," I say, wondering if Josie has whispered similar words to Poppy.

Helen smiles bitterly. "Well, when you add Josie to everything we'd learned about the Maynards, I couldn't get out of there fast enough."

"Did she crack on to your husband at all?" I ask.

A smile passes fleetingly over Helen's face. "She might have tried but Jim isn't very attuned to that kind of thing. She did ask him to help her sort out a flat tyre one evening, but he couldn't as he was off to get a flight for a work trip."

Flat tyre. Talking to Helen is making me feel slightly better about Josie. It seems clear that Josie doesn't hold a grudge against my family specifically. She would be making moves on whoever lived next door.

"She's the same with us," I say. "Any chance she ever asked Jim to help out because she was visiting her dying father?"

Helen wrinkles her forehead. "That I don't know." She pauses. "Look, I'm really sorry that you appear to be having an identical experience to mine. I'm sure you're angry with me, but I had to get myself and my family out of there before I lost my sanity."

"I understand." I turn to look again at the small plaque on the bench. "I'll be doing exactly the same thing."

Helen gathers her bag. I know it's now or never.

"One more thing, Helen. Why did you leave the scribbles on Poppy's wall and the crack on the cooker top?"

Helen plonks her bag back down with a thud. "We absolutely did not do that." Her voice, which before had softened, was now hard. "We were really upset to get all that grief from the solicitor, but decided to pay up because we didn't want any more hassle. But when we left, there were no marks on the wall. I went into each room to check they were clean and tidy before leaving and there was nothing. And the cooker top was certainly not cracked. I know because I inspected it. I'm a bit obsessive about cleanliness and making sure everything is as it should be."

I weigh up Helen's words. I'm fairly sure she's telling the truth.

"OK, I take your point. But surely you can see why we thought—"

"Yes, yes," Helen interrupts. "Of course. I'm probably unreasonable to be angry, but it's so frustrating to be accused of something we absolutely didn't do and then have no way of fighting back."

"If it wasn't you, then who do you think it was?"

There's a silence. I'm holding my breath.

"I can only think of one thing behind it. Them. Spirits of the Maynards, or the bad energy in that house. I know I sound batshit, but who else could it be? Who else could be behind the woman I saw, and the ladder to the loft that had been let down?" Helen moves once more to leave. "Sorry. I'm not sure I've helped much, and I'm sorry if I've scared you."

"No, you've helped." I stand up, my legs unsteady. I'm pushing myself too much after my operation. But rather than scaring me, Helen's words have brought me a strange comfort. My overactive imagination was not to blame. Mike should not have dismissed my fears so readily.

But ghosts? Really?

I gesture to the small plaque on the bench. Helen leaps up, startled. "Can't escape them," she gasps, shaking her head.

"My exact feelings," I reply.

Helen moves quickly away from the bench, eager to bid farewell.

"Helen, did you give Josie a key to the house by any chance?"

Helen's answer is instant.

"No."

CHAPTER 28

I creep down the stairs. "I've got Poppy down," I say in a stage whisper to Mike. "She's not asleep, but at least she's lying quietly."

Mike is chopping onion with a flourish. Pulverised garlic lies in a neat pile on the side of the chopping board and a dish of potato gratin has been placed by the side of the oven.

"Wow, this looks really good," I say appreciatively. "Thanks for doing this, Mike."

Mike is making his signature dish for dinner: chicken in garlic and white wine.

He waves airily. "No worries. I'm enjoying it, actually." He takes a swig from a beer bottle to the side of the chopping board as he hums along to the radio.

This is doing him good, I think, watching as he measures the wine needed for the dish. He's glad to be having guests round. We've cut ourselves off since moving here, I realise. At least I've seen Layla regularly, but Mike has barely seen any of his friends. Time for that to change.

It's our dinner party tonight and Mike has gallantly taken on the cooking, brushing off my efforts to help.

I wander over to the fridge, then pause. I need to swallow my cocktail of tablets. I hesitate, then pour myself a glass of wine anyway, taking a swig to swallow my pills. I need some Dutch courage. It feels like snakes are writhing around in my belly. The thought of Josie in my home again, within yards of my husband and my daughter, makes me recoil. I remind myself I'm doing this for Mike, and our marriage. This is the evening we will get back on track. Maybe then I can persuade him we should sell the house.

I acknowledge to myself that I'm not keen on Belinda. Mabel is a closed book. Throw in Layla and Callum and I'm nervous about how the evening will unfold. I take another sip of wine.

I try to raise my spirits by looking beyond the dinner party. Next week I'll be back at work. Just dipping my toe in the water, anyway. My boss insists I should work only if I feel capable, but I'm more than ready. Though I still feel a little delicate, I need a distraction from the Maynards, Josie and this house. More importantly, I have to prepare for my interview for the deputy managing editor's job.

"Mike, I heard from Jake again about the interview and honestly, it sounds like it's a done deal. He implied very strongly that it was just a case of tying up a few loose ends. He was hinting the job is mine."

I sound a little boastful. *Who cares? It's about time something good happened to me.*

Mike lays down his knife and squeezes my shoulder. "Well done," he says. "We'll have to celebrate when you get the go-ahead."

His voice is warm and his eyes twinkle again, in contrast to the icy stare of recent days.

I want to wrap his affection around me like a blanket, to ward off the coldness between us. Things are still not right, though. One foot out of place and the pack of cards could come tumbling down.

I need to smile, to be attentive, polite and friendly, no matter what happens tonight. Then I can slam the door shut on it all.

The doorbell rings. I sigh. "Whoever is here is here early," I grumble, glancing at the clock.

"Ah, well." Mike shrugs and returns to his chopping board. "I'm just going to slice the halloumi for our starter."

He's in such a good mood and I know I mustn't upset him. I march to the door and to my relief Layla is standing there.

"Hello! Are you going to let me in?" Layla clomps across the threshold, making an elaborate display of wiping her Doc Martens on the mat. She thrusts a bottle at me. "How are you feeling, darling? I've been worried about you."

"Much better." I plaster a grin on my face. "Come through."

Layla glances around. "Anyone else here?" she whispers conspiratorially. "Josie or Callum?"

She pulls self-consciously at the deep V-neck of her dress, exposing an expanse of cleavage.

"Just you." I'm leading her to the kitchen when a little figure appears at the top of the stairs.

"Layla!" screams Poppy, bobbing up and down excitedly. She's alert and awake. Nothing about her suggests that she's ready for bed.

"My gorgeous girl," croons Layla. "Let me pop up and see her."

I'm frustrated but at least Layla is handling the situation. I open the fridge and place Layla's wine inside.

"Layla's here," I announce. "And dealing with Poppy, luckily."

"Let's hope she hits it off with Callum," says Mike merrily, taking a swig of beer. "Right, I've done as much prep as I can do for now."

The door bell goes. "I'll get it." Mike dashes to the hall and flings open the door.

"Hi, Josie!" he gushes. "Thank so much for coming."

I stomp to the kitchen door and glare across the hall.

Josie steps in, a blur of blue, and embraces him warmly. "I've been really looking forward to this," she murmurs.

She buries her head in Mike's neck as he lays a hand on her shoulder.

I grip the kitchen counter, focusing on its pattern. Mike's voice breaks my concentration.

"Clara! Josie's here!"

So? I want to scream. *Why do you expect me to be happy about it?* What has happened to my sensitive, emotionally intelligent husband?

I grit my teeth. *Just get through tonight.*

"Hi, Josie." I inject as much warmth as I can muster into my voice.

I draw myself up, expecting Josie to be in a tiny figure-hugging dress. Instead, she is wearing a prim, buttoned-up dress that covers her from mid-neck to her ankles. I almost breathe a sigh of relief, then I realise that the turquoise colour of the dress brings out the beautiful gentian hues of Josie's eyes and forms a wonderful contrast against her flaxen hair.

It also sculpts her tiny waist. I glance down at my own outfit, a voluminous black jumper to encompass my swollen stomach, and baggy cream trousers with ballet pumps. Josie's shoes are pointed, sleek and with a not insubstantial heel. I feel plump, forgettable and at least a decade older than I am when I compare myself to Josie, who is clutching the 1950s doll that she bought for Poppy.

I'm dismayed. Now is not the time to give Poppy a present; we're desperately trying to get her to calm down and go to sleep.

"I'm just dying to give this beauty to Poppy, I know she'll love it," declares Josie, brandishing the doll. It's China blue eyes flash at me. *Creepy thing.*

"We're trying to get Poppy to sleep, so we'll give her the doll tomorrow." I try as hard as I can to keep my voice gentle and relaxed.

"Oh, she's still awake, I can hear her chortling with Layla. I don't think it matters if she has the doll now. It might even distract her from our gathering downstairs and keep her in her bedroom," says Mike cheerily.

He flashes a smile. I force my mouth to turn upwards in response. Then I realise his smile is meant for Josie.

I disagree with Mike but now isn't the time to say.

"Great, I'll go up, then. I can't wait to give it to her." Josie is up the stairs in a flash. I curse Mike under my breath as I quietly follow her. Layla's lying on the bed, reading to Poppy, whose eyes are half closed. I want to grab Josie by the shoulder to hold her back. But I force myself to wait at the top of the stairs as Josie bursts into Poppy's bedroom. "Hi, lovely Poppy, look what I've got for you."

I peer in from the doorway. "Josie!" Poppy is instantly awake and out of bed in a leap. She screams when she sees the doll.

"All yours," says Josie triumphantly.

Poppy cradles her doll carefully, beaming from ear to ear. "She has blue eyes and looks like you," she breathes to Josie. Josie grins back and flicks her hair.

Layla looks distinctly unimpressed. "I'd almost got her off to sleep," she mutters. I'm the only one to hear her complaint.

Poppy coos over her doll and Josie kneels beside her, gently stroking her arm. I resist the urge to slap her hand away and instead continue to hang in the doorway, watching.

Layla stretches her long legs over the bed and wanders over to Josie and Poppy. "You must be Josie," she says. "I'm Layla. I've known Clara since uni."

Josie draws herself up. "Hello." Her voice is cool and detached.

"Clara's been telling me about you, how helpful you've been." I suppress a smile. Layla manages to keep her voice saccharine. "She said how good you've been with Poppy."

Josie runs her fingers through Poppy's hair. "She's a lovely girl. I feel very close to her already."

I want to push her away from my daughter and out of my house, but instead I lay my hands on the wall. I should probably go downstairs as listening in is only inciting my rage, but I'm glued to the spot.

Layla drops her composure for a few seconds with a faint grimace, but then a sweet look is back on her face. She leans in. "I'm so sorry to hear that you've been experiencing some marital difficulties," she says confidingly. "I'm going through a divorce with my husband and it's the most painful thing I've ever experienced. I hope you're OK."

I cringe. I can't decide if Layla is being her usual tactless self or trying to goad Josie on purpose.

Josie tenses and every fibre of her appears to be pushing Layla away. I can almost see a big speech bubble above her head, with *go away* in flashing neon lights.

"It was difficult, but I'm fine now," says Josie through gritted teeth. "I'd rather not talk about it." Polite but icy.

"Sure thing," says Layla casually. The doorbell slices through the tension in the air. "Right, Poppy, me and Josie need to go down for dinner now." She kneels down next to her. Poppy is crooning to her new doll. "Wow, your doll is ace, isn't it? Why don't you cuddle up in bed with her and then I'm sure Mummy and Daddy will come up for a goodnight hug."

There are voices in the hall downstairs. I can hear Callum's easy-going Scottish tones. Mike's voice is light, and he's laughing. I can't remember the last time he laughed so easily and uproariously. Instinctively my muscles relax.

Poppy pouts. "Me want Josie to stay." She tugs one chubby hand around Josie's leg, the other caressing her doll.

"No, darling, we have to go downstairs. Say night-night to Josie." Layla uses her sing-song voice, which usually comforts Poppy. But this time, a look of thunder passes over her face.

"Go 'way," she snarls.

Layla looks taken aback. Her mouth opens slightly. Poppy has never spoken to her like that before. I bustle forward, fuming at my daughter's rudeness, when Josie says, "I'll stay. I want to be with her." She puts an arm round Poppy and smiles at Layla triumphantly. "I'm happy to get her to bed. I'll enjoy it. You go downstairs."

The last sentence is an order. Layla draws herself up to her full height. I wonder if she will fight back, but she just says shortly, "Fine."

She turns away and heads out of the room. Josie smiles, a slow grin that spreads up her face, creating that sweet dimple in one cheek.

She catches sight of me out in the hall and gives me a little wave. I resist the urge to push her out of the room and scoop up Poppy in my arms. Instead, I stretch my face into a half-smile.

Layla links arms with me as we go downstairs. "I understand what you mean about her," she mutters. "Unfriendly, cold, and so possessive of Poppy. Goodness. I'm like an auntie to Poppy and Josie practically pushed me away. The cheek!" She bristles with annoyance.

"Glad it's not just me," I whisper back. "I just need to get through this evening and then try to get Mike to agree to get this house on the market and get the hell away from her." *And them.*

We enter the living room, where Mike and Callum are sitting chatting, each holding a beer.

Mike jumps up. "This is Callum. Callum, meet Layla, one of Clara's best friends."

"Hello." Callum leans forward and shakes Layla's hand. There's a twinkle in his eye. Layla's own eyes darken slightly but she smiles politely. I sigh to myself. I can see she's disappointed. Callum is well built, with a rugby player frame. Indeed, he's a strong amateur full back. His nose is slightly crooked due to breaking it during a match. He has warm brown eyes, straight white teeth and a ramrod jaw. Layla prefers the computer geek or trendy nerd look. Even though I knew he wasn't her type, I'd hoped that she would at least give him a chance.

I embrace Callum warmly.

"Hello, Clara, so good to see you again," he grins. "It's some pad you've got here. Puts my little flat to shame!"

I take it that Mike hasn't told Callum about the strange goings-on in our house.

"I love your flat," I say meaningfully. It's a sleek, shiny, rather characterless one-bedroom flat with every mod con you could wish for, and not at all suitable for a family, but I would still rather be living there than here. Plus, it's in Balham, just down the road from my old home, and my heart aches for that corner of South London.

Mike bustles in with a white wine for Layla, whose phone beeps. She peers at the screen, engrossed and not engaging in any conversation. I hope it's not her ex-husband.

There's a sharp knock at the door. "I'll get it." As I head out, Callum says to Layla politely, "So, I hear you're in IT, Layla."

"Uh-huh," Layla grunts, tapping away furiously on her phone.

I want to grab Layla's phone and chuck it across the room. Callum's opening line is not the most inspiring, but she doesn't need to be so rude.

I fling open the door harder than I mean to and there are Mabel, Belinda and Teddy. Mabel is holding a cake plate on which perches a perfectly executed banoffee pie.

"Oh, thanks so much, that dessert looks to die for," I gush.

"Thank you," says Mabel stiltedly, looking like a mouthful will never cross her lips with her bony figure emphasised by a tight black dress. Indeed, she's dressed all in black, with black tights and patent pumps, like she's kitted out for a funeral. It puts me on edge.

"Come in, come in," I say, my voice unnaturally loud. *Tone it down*, I urge myself, feeling my cheeks blush.

"How are you feeling?" asks Belinda sympathetically. "I hope your little one isn't running you ragged. I know what it's like!" She rolls her eyes.

"I'm actually feeling loads better," I say, glancing automatically upstairs at the mention of Poppy.

I smile at Teddy.

"My husband, Teddy. Teddy, Clara," says Belinda.

Teddy has a wide smile, but it doesn't quite reach his steely grey eyes.

"Good to meet you," he says, proffering a bottle of fizz.

"We thought champagne was appropriate, to celebrate your recent move to this fabulous home."

I take the bottle, glancing uncertainly at Belinda. The festive drink seems at odds with the newspaper cuttings slipped through the door exposing the dark history of the house, which Belinda is entwined in.

But Belinda just nods, a stiff smile on her face.

I usually love champagne, but the thought of the crisp bubbles on my tongue, the acidic golden liquid sliding down my throat, makes nausea rise.

"Lovely, thanks," I murmur.

Mike bounds through the living room door and heartily shakes hands with the trio. I slip into the kitchen and put the champagne in the fridge, leaning my forehead against its coolness for a moment. I need to get upstairs to Poppy, to keep Josie away from her. I head into the hall to dash up the stairs, but Mike beats me to it.

"I'll go, you sit down. I'll drag Josie away; it's not fair for her to be stuck upstairs." He puts his hands round my waist as he passes me, but in an impatient, practical way, rather than affectionately.

I shake my head, to banish thoughts of Poppy snuggled up with Josie.

I lead my guests into the living room, where Layla is sitting with Callum. She's nodding absent-mindedly to an anecdote that Callum is avidly telling, which involves shipping and drinking, with one eye still on her phone.

I make the introductions, and then disappear to get drinks for Mabel, Belinda and Teddy. I can hear Teddy's booming voice, intoning about the state of the NHS.

I walk out of the kitchen carefully holding a tray of drinks, one ear attuned to upstairs. Silence. My heart pounds uncomfortably. Placing the tray on the coffee table, I mumble an excuse about needing the loo and creep upstairs.

The landing is in darkness and there is silence. An amber glow from Poppy's night light emanates from her bedroom. I peer in. There are three figures lying in bed, three heads close together. Poppy's in the middle, Mike's dark hair on one side and Josie's sleek blonde head on the other. Poppy's arms are wrapped around the necks of both, and Mike's and Josie's arms are around her, their fingers almost touching over my daughter's little body.

I stare at those fingers, just millimetres away from each other, such a contrast to the expansion of space I feel between me and Mike. If I gaze long enough, I'm almost convinced that those fingers will stretch across Poppy's unicorn duvet and curl around each other. I want to step into the room, to march across it and pull Josie away, and to slip into my rightful place.

Instead, I'm glued to the spot as I watch Josie turn her face to Mike. Just as I'd imagined moments before, I watch Josie's hand creep over to Mike's and squeeze his fingers. Mike's fingers stay slack. At least he doesn't respond but he doesn't pull away either.

"We'd better extricate ourselves," he whispers.

Mike seems keen to get moving, sitting up and placing his feet on the carpet. I feel a twinge of relief. But Josie stays lying down, the hand that had touched Mike now stroking Poppy's hair.

"I don't mind staying," she says softly. "It's a treat for me, to be lying here with Poppy."

There is a pause. *Please say the right thing*, I beg Mike silently.

"No, come down. Poppy's asleep. There's no need to be here with her. And we've got your dinner all prepped!" Mike sounds light-hearted, but he lays a hand on Josie's shoulder and pulls her up firmly.

I slink against the wall and sneak down the stairs, cheered by Mike's behaviour.

In the living room, poor Callum is still desperately trying to talk to Layla, earnestly telling her a rugby anecdote that involved a lot of drinking.

"Hmmm." Layla still has one eye on her phone. Mabel, Teddy and Belinda are huddled by the window.

"Any more drinks anyone?" I trill.

Hurry up, Mike. I don't want to carry this evening on my own.

"I think it's time to open the champagne," booms Teddy.

If these people weren't strangers I'd turn on my heel and walk away. I'd challenge the champagne. What is there to celebrate? A maniac killed his family in this so-called family home. The woman next door wants my daughter and husband.

I walk to the kitchen to take the champagne out of the fridge and want to slam the bottle on the floor and break it into a million shards. Instead, I grit my teeth and pop champagne glasses onto a tray.

I walk gingerly into the living room. Mike and Josie have arrived, standing in a corner. Josie is staring at Belinda, Mabel and Teddy, her face tense. Teddy is holding court, droning on about the NHS again.

I watch as Mike strides forward. "Hello, I don't think we've met. I'm Mike." He flashes a smile at them.

His beaming smile is at odds with the stony expression he has on his face with me recently. It reminds me of past times — not so long ago — when he was happy and relaxed. When he looked at me with a twinkle in his eye, his mouth curved upwards. There's a lump in my throat. I miss the old Mike so much.

Josie stands a step behind him. "Hello, Josie," says Belinda. "It's been a while." She sounds cautious.

Josie nods curtly. "Hello," she says shortly.

"My dear, how are you?" Mabel bustles forward and places a kiss on Josie's cheek. "I haven't seen you for ages. I do hope you're OK?"

Josie's expression warms. "Hi, Mabel. Nice to see you. It's been a bit up and down, but I'm all right, thank you."

"Champagne!" I cry, my voice as brittle as glass.

Everyone takes a flute.

Teddy clears his throat. He appears to have appointed himself official spokesperson and master of ceremonies. "Well, can I just say I'm so pleased that you've moved into this wonderful street, next to the amazing Mabel."

I think I see a flash of irritation on Mabel's face.

"Belinda loved growing up here and our girls love to visit. They'd love to meet your little . . . er, Jasmine . . ."

I gasp at his gaffe, as blood and gunshot wounds crowd my mind.

I open my mouth to set him straight, when Josie cuts in. "Poppy."

I snap my mouth shut angrily. *My daughter. It's my place to correct her name, not my next-door neighbour's.*

"Poppy," says Teddy smoothly, giving an airy wave. "Anyway, where was I? Here's to a fantastic life in your new home."

"They've been here a few months now," mutters Josie. He doesn't appear to have heard her.

"To happier times," Mabel mutters at the same time. An image of those words written in Mabel's neat, flowing handwriting floods into my mind.

"Cheers," Teddy continues, raising his glass. Belinda raises hers, her face bland, smiling neutrally. Josie doesn't raise her flute. She clutches it, frozen.

As I raise my glass automatically, I'm sure if I turn around, the other family will be there, shadows in the corner of the room, waiting to pounce.

I take a pretend sip of my champagne. Teddy starts a monologue about the terrible state of the A&E department in his hospital. Mike is nodding, his eyes wide and engaged, leaning towards Teddy as if fascinated by his comments. He's good at pretending, at seeming to hang on to every word when not particularly interested. But maybe he is interested.

All those times I thought he faked it, he may have been genuinely absorbed. The last few weeks have made me wonder how much I really know him.

I glance behind my shoulder uneasily, almost expecting to see an innocent girlish face staring back at me, next to a brooding dark presence. Jonathan Maynard's eyebrows are thicker in my imaginary vision than in the photos of him in newspapers, and his chin squarer, his eyes deeper set. Knowing what he did has made him look more menacing to me. Belinda walks over to me so quietly that I almost jump when I notice her right up against me, leaning in. I take a step back, pushing back against the invasion of my personal space. But Belinda leans in.

"I see them too."

Her breath smells of champagne with an undercurrent of apples.

CHAPTER 29

"Come in, come in." Mike sweeps everyone into the kitchen and through to the dining table. It's a little small — another piece of furniture that we need to upgrade — but we've managed to squeeze eight chairs around it. The lights are dimmed and candles are lit on the table, throwing shadows on the wall. Despite the large expanse, it feels cosy. Mike has done a good job.

Discreetly, I tip my champagne down the sink. My throat closes up at the thought of trying to drink to a bleak celebration. Instead, I tip some water into my glass.

Mike bustles around the kitchen. Fried halloumi is lying on plates and he's adding rocket, tomatoes and a splash of balsamic vinegar.

"Can I help?" I ask.

"No, no, you sit down," says Mike distractedly, giving me a little push towards the table. I long to feel tenderness in his touch, but he turns away from me instantly, buried in his starters preparation.

I see with a sinking heart that there are only two seats left. One at the head of the table, which probably needs to be Mike's since he's managing the whole dinner, and the other by

Teddy. I grit my teeth at having to nod along and smile while he no doubt pompously talks at me though the whole meal.

I slink into my seat beside him, gratefully clocking that Josie is seated at the opposite end of the table to both me and Mike. She's next to Belinda, which she doesn't look thrilled about. Belinda is earnestly trying to make conversation, while Josie stares morosely at the tablecloth, her fingers gripping the stem of her glass.

Layla is still fiddling with her phone. I want to shake her. Callum is gallantly telling her another anecdote. She gives a half-hearted bark of laughter at the end just as she starts tapping away.

"So what do you do, then?" Teddy asks.

"I'm an editor of a business magazine," I reply, surprised that he's asked me a question. "I—"

"Ah, deadline driven. My job might seem very different, but I know what that feels like," Teddy intones, clearly delighted that he's found an angle to drag the conversation back to himself.

I'm resigned to sitting quietly, offering polite questions. But then I sit up straighter. *No, I won't be a people pleaser.* "So, what do you think about the history of this house?" I ask abruptly.

Teddy's eyes bulge as his monologue grinds to a halt. I turn away and watch as Mike places dishes of steaming halloumi on people's placemats. I should offer to help him, but I'm glued to my chair, waiting for Teddy to tell me his thoughts.

"Well . . ." He stares down at the halloumi. "It's obviously distressing, but it's a long time ago."

"It must have been awful for Belinda, living next door to them and having Maynard as her lecturer." I can't bring myself to address him by his first name.

Teddy forks a piece of halloumi and thrusts it into his mouth, a dribble of oil trickling down his lip.

"Oh, she didn't have much to do with him, except at university," he says airily. "So, while it was obviously a horrendous and tragic event, she feels a little shielded from it."

"But I thought that they struck up a real friendship, as she came round here a lot, to babysit for his daughters," I stutter.

Teddy swallows and opens his mouth for another piece of halloumi. "Nope, I don't think so. She admired his achievements in the academic field but that was it." He shovels in his forkful.

Mike seats himself at the table, after ensuring everyone's wine glasses are topped up. He's turned Alexa on, and a Sam Fender song plays softly in the background, filling in awkward pauses in conversation.

Mabel is seated on one side of Mike. She chats away with him, taking large sips of her wine. Mike leans over to pour her another glass. Mabel's cheeks are flushed and her voice ratchets up a notch.

"Oh, you are a nice man," she gushes. "Isn't Clara lucky to have you?"

Am I? I watch Mike, his easy smile and his twinkling eyes staring straight at Mabel.

"You remind me of Ken, my husband," Mabel continues.

In my other ear, Teddy is banging on about a boring hospital topic.

"Oh yes," I say vaguely, in what I hope is the right place, trying to block him out and home in on Mabel and my husband.

"We were married fifty years and we lost him so suddenly last year to cancer." She drains her glass and holds it out to Mike for a top-up.

"I'm so sorry." Mike pours more wine into her glass. "That must have been a terrible shock. It sounds like you had barely any time to come to terms with it."

I like to joke that Mike could be a journalist with his empathetic manner and careful questioning which draws people out of themselves.

It works this time. Mabel takes another gulp of wine. "One month and he was gone. He complained of pain in his back and then he turned yellow. Jaundice, we were told.

Then we had the diagnosis of advanced pancreatic cancer, and before we knew it, he was end-of-life. And then he died."

Mabel's stoic, cool demeanour crumples. "I'm lost without him."

Mike lays down his wine glass very deliberately and touches her hand. "I can't imagine the pain you and Belinda went through. My dad got diagnosed with lung cancer. He's a heavy smoker, so I shouldn't have been surprised. He's made it, touch wood, but I'll never forget how I felt when he was first diagnosed. I was convinced we'd lose him. I think I was more worried than him, as guess what, he's kept on smoking."

"It was the speed of it all," says Mabel. "One minute he was here, and then he was gone." She snaps her fingers. "Just like that."

She pauses. I notice that Belinda has gone quiet, watching her mother.

"You OK, Mum?" she mouths.

Mabel nods quickly. "Ken would have enjoyed coming here tonight. He liked the Maynards. He enjoyed talking to Jonathan."

There's a sudden silence. Even Alexa stops for a few seconds before the next song plays.

"Mum, we're not with the Maynards. Mike and Clara live here now," Belinda hisses.

Layla raises her eyebrow and catches my eye.

"Oh yes, dear, of course. I just felt I'd been transported back to the past talking about Ken." Mabel takes a sip of wine. "I do know that," she adds defensively.

The beginnings of dementia or just that she has had too much to drink? I watch as Mabel takes another mouthful of wine. *Or perhaps it's simply that she has some cognitive decline.*

"Right, I'm going to clear the plates." Mike jumps up and starts bustling round the table.

"That was delicious, mate," says Callum, fumbling around in his pockets. "Have I got time for a vape?"

"Yes, the main will be ready in fifteen minutes," says Mike. "I'll open the doors to the garden for you."

"Want to come out for a breath of air?" Callum asks Layla hopefully.

"Oh no, I'm a little chilly, and I'd like to help clear the table," Layla shoots back quickly.

"I'll step out for some air with you." I can't wait to escape the claustrophobia of the dining room. Mabel sits stiffly in her seat, while Josie broods at the other end of the table. Belinda has given up trying to speak to her and is over with Teddy.

"I'll help clear the table too," Josie says suddenly. She moves to Mike's side, smiling at him. I turn away quickly and follow Callum outside, welcoming the breeze on my face.

"I'm not sure Layla's too impressed with me." Callum exhales, vape smoke wafting around him. He winks at me. "I have an inkling as to what you were hoping, Clara."

"No, I don't know what you mean, honestly," I bluster. "Layla's my friend, you're Mike's, and we wanted a bit of moral support what with having our neighbours over for the first time. And, of course, we wanted to see you."

Callum smiles and waves his vape around. "I think Layla's cute but I don't think she feels the same about me. I've been trying to tell her my most engaging anecdotes, but she's got one eye on her phone the whole time."

"She's going through a messy divorce," I say quickly.

"I remember you saying a while ago." Callum stares out to the end of the garden.

I close my eyes. I'm tired and want this night to end now.

"Mike seems very happy and settled. This house appears to suit him." He tucks his vape away.

I stare at him. *If only.*

Through the bi-fold doors, I see Mike carefully carrying plates heaped with chicken in white wine sauce. Josie follows him, carrying two dishes also. She meets my eyes and turns away, a small smile turning up the corners of her mouth.

I turn towards the back of the garden, towards the tall, shadowy trees. I'd rather lose myself under their widespread branches than go back in the house.

Nevertheless, within minutes I'm sitting at the table, dutifully forking the chicken into my mouth.

Callum tells a witty story involving him and Mike and an ultra-large container ship. Teddy looks miffed that he's not the centre of attention. He morosely spears chicken onto his fork. Josie smiles politely and Layla glances at her phone to the side of her plate. Belinda stares straight ahead, not even pretending to listen.

There's a cackle of polite laughter that Belinda appears oblivious to.

"Gosh, this dining area is different to how I remember," she says almost dreamily. "It used to be so small and pokey. You've had a huge extension." She gestures to the skylights and the large space surrounding the table.

"The extension was done by the family who lived here before Helen and her family," explains Mike.

"Oh yes, I know," says Belinda absent-mindedly. "I'm remembering it as it was when the Maynards owned it." She pauses, a stricken look on her face.

"And you'd remember it very well," Josie says, her voice at once both soft and hard. "You were round here all the time."

Belinda slams her knife and fork down. "As you were too," she retorts. "Always with Lily, like her shadow."

Josie swallows her mouthful of food and sedately lays her own cutlery down.

"And you were Jonathan's shadow," she says, sounding both cold and amused.

"What the hell?" Belinda glares at her.

"Oh, come on, you were always round here, with him," Josie snaps back.

"Belinda saw him at university as he was her tutor, that was it," intervenes Teddy smoothly, readjusting his collar as perspiration trickles down his forehead.

"Her tutor, and also the person she was having an affair with." Josie's eyes are blue flames.

Gone is her demure, quiet voice. Her tone is strident and filled with dislike.

Teddy starts coughing, clutching his throat. Mike leaps up and slams him on the back. Teddy spits up a mass of half-chewed chicken. I feel sick eying it.

I get up to fetch a dustpan and brush, as Belinda says, "Why are you saying this? Who exactly is this helping, or do you get a sick kick out of it?"

"I'm telling the truth," says Josie. "You had an affair with your next-door neighbour and tutor. Jonathan Maynard."

She flashes a triumphant look around the table.

"Now, hang on." Teddy leaps to his feet, his face puce. "Do not insult my wife like that. You don't know what the hell you're on about. Belinda certainly did not have an affair with that man. She barely knew him. He was her tutor and that's it."

Spittle lands on the tablecloth.

"Oh no, she had an affair," says Josie calmly. "You were always round here, weren't you, Belinda, with Jonathan. It really upset Lily. She knew there was something going on, even at her young age, and she felt unsettled and displaced. You used to ignore her or snap at her. As if she didn't have enough crap to deal with in her young life already."

Josie stands up, her body rigid.

The blood has drained from Belinda's face.

Even Layla has stopped staring at her phone and is gazing wide-eyed at Belinda and Josie.

"And tell them your little hobby, Belinda — you know, the one you shared with Jonathan," says Josie, her voice dripping poison.

"No." Belinda tosses her head wildly and stares into Josie's eyes. "Please, Josie, don't do this."

"Tell them your hobby," Josie repeats. Her body is still as she glares at Belinda. "Go on, what hobby did you share with Jonathan?"

"I used to have a firearms certificate." Belinda stares straight ahead. "But so what? I was doing an MA in the history of guns. Of course I've got an interest in it."

"I never knew you had a licence to use a gun," exclaims Mabel. She appears more shocked at that than the accusation that Belinda had an affair with Jonathan.

"And Jonathan helped you get a licence, didn't he? He gave you the reference and you used to go off practising together."

"You never told me about any of this," Teddy blurts out. He grabs his napkin and wipes his forehead. "And you haven't responded to Josie's allegation. Did you have an affair with Jonathan?"

Belinda's eyes fill with tears. "I did," she says quietly. "I was young and naive and really looked up to him. I regret it every day."

"Why didn't you tell me?" Teddy bangs his fist down on the table.

"Because I was ashamed to admit I had a relationship with a killer and devastated that I shared a sport with him that led to the murder of his family." Tears streak down Belinda's cheeks.

Mike stands up and touches Belinda's arm. "Come on now, let's all calm down." His voice is soft, but a vein pulsing in his forehead belies his real thoughts. I feel a swell of sympathy for him. He had been really looking forward to tonight. Now all that positive energy will drain away and no doubt place yet more strain on our relationship. I sigh, but I can't help my fascination with what is unfolding. Josie's demureness and simmering secretiveness have exploded as if from a volcano.

The pieces of the puzzle concerning Belinda's behaviour and her over-investment in the house and its occupants are falling into place.

Belinda moves her arm away from Mike's touch. Her shoulders shake. "Why are you doing this, Josie? Why are you humiliating me in front of these people?"

Josie takes her time in replying. "Because I loved Lily, and I saw what effect that monster Jonathan had on her. You added to her misery. She knew you were having a relationship with him. The two of you barely hid it when Anna went out and you used to come round. You would blatantly kiss and hug him in front of her and Jasmine."

Josie shakes her head. "I can't get over the complete disregard of those girls' feelings. You must have seen how that man treated Lily, yet you continued to have a relationship with him — no, sorry, an affair, I should say."

"I was young, naive and gullible. I looked up to him, with all his maturity and knowledge. He paid me so much attention, telling me how gifted I was and really boosting my confidence," Belinda speaks quickly, desperately trying to put her side forward.

"But you saw how he was to Lily?" thunders Josie. Gone is the muted tone I'm used to hearing.

Belinda shakes her head. "Not really, if I'm honest. I know a lot of things came out after the deaths—"

"Murders," barks Josie.

Belinda carries on, ignoring her. "But I wasn't particularly aware of anything wrong. I saw snapshots of him and his daughters. I knew he wanted Lily to do better at school and pushed for that, but I didn't think that was a bad thing at the time. He was ambitious for her, that was what I thought."

"You didn't hear him yelling at her, berating her? I used to hear him shouting at her through the shared wall with my house."

An image of Josie with an ear up against the wall comes into my mind and I suppress a smile, horrified at myself. This isn't a laughing matter.

"I didn't know!" Belinda shakes her head violently, as if to get rid of a fly buzzing in her ear. "It was years ago, and like I said, I was young and, well, under his spell. I probably should have been more aware."

Josie continues as if Belinda hasn't spoken. "And when he got a gun and blew their brains out, you stayed quiet. You skulked away and just got on with your life."

"What was I supposed to do?" says Belinda. She wipes her hand roughly over her eyes, smudging her mascara. "Nothing I could say would change matters. I made a terrible judgement of character. And I was devastated. I just wanted to get on with my life and get away from it all."

"Come on, let's continue with our mains before they go cold." Mike desperately tries to defuse the tension. No one pays him any attention.

"Going for a vape," mutters Callum weakly, slinking out of the bi-fold doors. He glances conspiratorially at Layla but she has no intention of joining him, staring transfixed at Josie and Belinda.

"I can't believe you didn't tell me about any of this," mutters Teddy. I haven't warmed to Teddy, but I feel sorry for him. All his previous confidence seems to have been squeezed out.

"I'm sorry. Please, Teddy, forgive me. It all happened before we met and I've done my best ever since to block it out."

Belinda is sobbing, tears streaking down her face and into her hair.

"And do you still shoot?" Josie doesn't bother to hide the disdain in her voice.

"No, my five-year licence expired years ago and I never renewed it."

Belinda stares at Josie with hatred.

"I'm not sure what you're hoping to achieve with this, Josie. But since you've been so eager to put your point of view across, let me give mine. You were obsessed with Lily. Everywhere Lily went, you were right there. I clocked the way you used to watch her."

Josie shrugs. "So? I was protective of her, and no wonder, considering what happened. I acted like a mother to her."

Belinda shakes her head. "Mother? Or stalker?"

Josie laughs. "I could ask the same of you with Jonathan," she drawls.

Belinda moves round the table to get closer to Josie.

Josie puts her hands up in front of her. "Get away," she says coolly. "I'm not even going to reply to your comments."

Belinda places her hands on Josie's shoulders.

"Leave me alone," Josie breathes. She wraps her arms around herself protectively.

"Come on, stop this." I hate the way that Mike is at Josie's shoulder, the two of them against Belinda.

I'd almost forgotten about Mabel, who suddenly stands up. "Well, my dear, I always thought you had a bit of a crush on Jonathan," she says stridently, and seemingly unperturbed. "I'm not surprised. Why didn't you just say?"

"I was twenty-one, of course I wasn't going to admit to my mother that I was having an affair." Belinda is anxiously trying to meet Teddy's gaze, but he's staring dourly into his wine glass.

"And the gun licence." Mabel sighs and shakes her head. "Daddy and I wouldn't have minded. You've always been adventurous. We would have understood."

"OK, thanks, Mum." Belinda moves over to Teddy and lays a hand on his arm, but he shakes her off.

"I must say, I liked Jonathan very much," Mabel blurts out, her voice defensive. "As did Ken, and I tell you he was a good judge of character. Ken didn't believe he was capable of doing what he was accused of."

"What, despite all the evidence that he murdered his family? That he made Lily suffer her whole life?" Josie is shouting, tendons sticking out in her neck.

"He was strict with her about her schooling, over the top, I admit, but does that mean he was a murderer?" Mabel is calm, her tone is puzzled but at the same time belligerent.

"The police saw the crime scene, Mum, and said that he killed the family. They had evidence," Belinda butts in, agitated.

"The police weren't there," says Mabel defensively. "Who knows exactly what happened?"

"When are the police ever present when a crime happens?" snorts Belinda. "There'll have been overwhelming evidence at the scene."

Josie chimes in. "Who do you think did it, if not Jonathan? His wife, or someone outside the family who managed to get into the house and out without the police catching them?" Josie's voice drips with sarcasm and incredulity.

Despite the simmering tension between Belinda and Josie, the two women have clubbed together to take the same side against Mabel.

"I have no idea," says Mabel firmly. "But the police have been wrong before."

Belinda emits a strangled cry. Her eyes protrude and she raises her hand before dropping it weakly.

"We need to go," she says.

"Yes, I think we do." Mabel's voice is cool. "You need to pull yourself together. Look at the state of your face! You need to dry those eyes. You have two daughters waiting for you at home. They won't want to see you like that."

Belinda fumbles in her bag and pulls out a tissue which she scrubs at her eyes. It pulls the mascara stains further down her cheeks.

I watch, mouth open. What a scene. Half of me shies away from it, embarrassed by the raw emotions on display. But the other half relishes it, partly due to the journalist in me, but also because it vindicates my own feelings. The history of this house has pulled the foundations from under my feet, and I'm not the only one. There is comfort in the solidarity.

But then I look at Mike. His face is ashen as he surveys the table of uneaten chicken and potatoes, knives and forks splayed across the tablecloth.

My heart aches. The evening meant so much to him. He saw this as a turning point for the house, for us. My stomach sinks as I ponder what this turn of events means for our relationship.

Belinda and Mabel walk to the front door, Teddy marching behind. I follow uncertainly.

"Well, thanks for coming tonight," I say stiltedly.

"I'm so sorry," Belinda says. "I shouldn't have ruined the evening by bringing up this house's past."

I automatically open my mouth to assuage Belinda's guilt but close it again. *No, you bloody well shouldn't have.*

"What a silly tiff blown out of all proportion," mutters Mabel, as if she played no part at all in the events of the evening.

"Thank you for having us," Teddy says quietly, shaking my hand limply.

"We'll make it up to you. You'll have to come over to mine for dinner, and we'll have a really fun evening," declares Mabel. *Not a chance.* Belinda and Teddy don't look enthusiastic about the idea either.

I close the door quietly on the trio.

"You lied and deceived me, how dare you!" Teddy's voice has gone from quiet to thunderous. It blasts through the closed door.

"Disgusting, to have an affair with a murderer," he rants. "You embarrassed me in there. What a fool I looked, having no idea that you had done those things."

"Teddy, please, I'm so sorry. Please let me explain," Belinda sobs, her voice shaking.

"I'll discuss this with you at home, behind closed doors." Teddy's voice has lowered a notch, but I can still hear him. The raw anger has been replaced by seething scorn.

"No. Please, Teddy. I can explain—"

"Shut up." His voice cuts through her sobs, which stop abruptly.

Silence. Teddy's grey eyes and clefted chin merge with Maynard's thick brows and dark hair in my mind. Belinda appears to have a type when it comes to men. Despite my anger and distrust of Belinda, my heart goes out to her. I hope Teddy calms down. Maybe I'll get Belinda's number from Mabel tomorrow and text her to check she's OK.

I turn back to the kitchen. Mike is very still, staring at the dinner table.

"Mate, are you OK?" Callum comes back in after his vape and is patting Mike uncertainly on the back.

"I'm sorry," Josie says. Her voice is back to its usual quiet, diffident tone. "I shouldn't have brought up Belinda's past with the Maynards."

"No, you shouldn't have," Mike says abruptly.

My eyes widen. *Good*. Maybe this will open his eyes to Josie and put a stop to the friendship between them. I realise I'm holding my breath.

Josie looks taken aback. "I'm incredibly sorry," she says. Her voice is calm, but there's an edge to it. "I haven't seen Belinda properly for a long time and it brought back all my anger at how she made Lily feel."

Layla jumps up. "Right," she says authoritatively. "Me, Callum and Josie are going to tidy up in here."

She nods at me and Mike. "You two go and relax in the other room."

A look of anger passes quickly over Josie's face. I guess that she's not pleased to be told to clear up the dinner plates.

We move to the lounge. Mike is brooding, standing by the coffee table. I hesitate. Usually, I would know how to comfort him, would take him in my arms and soothe him. But with things feeling so tenuous between us, I'm not sure how to console him. It makes me sad.

"I'm so sorry," I say gently. "You've put so much effort into this dinner. It's not fair that they ruined it."

Mike picks up a half-empty wine glass from the coffee table and throws it at the wall. It smashes and wine sprays over my top. I stare at the pieces of glass glinting on the floor in shock. His anger on our moving day and his violent throwing of towels in our flooded bathroom flash into my mind. While I always knew he had a temper, until we moved to this house, he kept it under control.

"Sorry," says Mike robotically. Then his face crumples. "I've tried so hard to get on with this house, to get over its history. I wanted this to be a night we put down some roots, got on with the neighbours, for you to bury this feud with Josie."

I stiffen.

"But it was a disaster. What the hell was the point in it? It's just made everything worse."

His eyes are bright and I wonder if he's about to cry. He blinks rapidly.

"You were right. I think it's best we put the house on the market and get out of here." He pauses. "So, well done you. You've got what you wanted."

He turns and walks out of the room. My spark of relief at his agreement to sell the house has quickly been replaced by hurt.

I bend down, wincing slightly at the pain in my scar and start picking up the pieces of glass, placing them carefully on the coffee table. I walk to the kitchen to get a dustpan and brush, but also to check up on Mike.

Layla is rinsing down the dishes before stacking them in the dishwasher. Callum is wiping the dinner mats. There's a companiable silence between them.

"Where's Mike?" I ask. *And Josie.*

Layla nods at the wide open bi-fold doors. "He's out in the garden. She followed him." She raises her eyebrows. "They've been a few minutes. I was about to alert you."

I feel my usual flash of anger at Josie. "I'll go and see him," I say tightly. I creep quietly out. There are voices at the bottom of the garden. I move softly forward.

The end of our garden is a wilderness of overgrown bushes and sprawling trees and I squint into the darkness, unable to make out Josie and Mike at first. But as my eyes adjust to the gloom I spot their figures by the shed, under the willow tree. Except it looks like one large figure rather than two distinct people . . . I inch forward slowly and realise why. Josie and Mike are huddled together, arms around each other.

I freeze. My heart is beating so loudly I almost expect them to look up, to see what is making that sound.

I creep closer and see their heads are as one, their lips locked. Then Mike moves away.

The taste of the halloumi I ate earlier fills my mouth and I wonder if I'll throw up, but instead I hiss, "You lied." I address Mike, staring at him so hard I feel my eyes will pop out of their sockets. "You told me that there was nothing between you and Josie. You betrayed me."

Mike moves Josie's arms from him roughly. "It's not what you think," he says, the words falling over themselves. "I was comforting her and then she . . ."

The devastation that swept over me recedes, overtaken by a tidal wave of fury. "I know what I saw. I think we need space from each other. I'd like you to leave the house for a few days."

The internal me is in awe at this powerful, angry woman who has taken control. It's as if someone else has invaded my body, as if someone has poured cold water on the flames of my earlier despair at my marriage breaking down.

There is silence.

"Fine." Mike stares down at the ground, his hands in his pockets. "You're right. We've been struggling for a while. I'll go and stay with Callum." He pauses. "But I'll be round to see Poppy. Whatever happens, it'll be fifty–fifty custody." His voice is fierce.

A secret part of me had been hoping that he would fling himself at my feet and pray for my forgiveness. Well, he hasn't, and surprisingly I don't care.

I glance at Josie. It's hard to make out, but I'm sure that my neighbour's mouth is stretched into a smile.

"You." I step towards her, my hatred towards this woman making me feel breathless. "Happy now? You can go for my husband now. But never, ever, my daughter. She's mine and I won't let you near her again."

I want to spit in that pale face, to push that frail shoulder with the collar bone sticking out, to stamp on those hands that were wrapped around my husband.

"Stop it." Mike steps forward.

God, you let me down. Even now, when our marriage could be over, he's still taking that bitch's side.

"I'm going to speak to Callum and pack a case."

Mike doesn't look at me as he walks purposefully towards the dining room, Josie following in his wake.

"Callum!" he calls.

I sink down on the grass, its dampness permeating my trousers. I welcome its coolness against my hot skin. I try to think, to analyse, but my mind is a soggy swamp, incapable at the moment of forecasting my future, of assessing what's going to happen. Words like divorce, custody and finances file through my mind but I'm unable to grasp them and examine them fully.

A figure plods out towards me from the dining room doors. Layla pushes back her curls as she reaches me and crouches down.

"What on earth is going on? Mike says he's going to stay with Callum. Are you OK?"

"Not really. I guess you could say we're having a temporary separation."

There's no heart lurch at these words, a contrast to the sick feeling of despair that I was feeling previously.

"Oh, I'm so sorry." Layla grabs my hand in her warm palm. "What's happened to bring it to this?"

"I found him kissing Josie," I reply. I let Layla stroke my palm and feel soothed.

The stroking abruptly stops. "Bloody hell. I can't believe it," Layla breathes. "I know you guys have been having problems but I never expected him to do something like that. He always seemed so loyal. What a let-down. And what a cow."

Layla envelops me in a hug. Her generous bosom digs into my chest and the smell of her floral perfume envelops me and makes me want to gag. I pull away.

"Layla, are they gone?" I ask urgently. I just want to go to bed.

"Josie's gone home — thank God." Layla pulls a face.

"And Mike was just packing a case. But I get the feeling he wanted to leave pretty quickly. I can check for you."

She stands up, dusting her knees down. "But before I do, I have an idea. Why don't I stay with you for a few days? You must be reeling. I can help you with Poppy."

"No." The word fires from my mouth. "Oh, I'm sorry," I say as Layla looks crestfallen. "I just need to be on my own, to get my head around it. But maybe you could come at the weekend," I add weakly.

"OK." Layla says coldly. "I was just trying to help."

She marches back to the house. I follow in her wake. I tense as I enter the house, listening out for signs of Mike and Callum.

"I think they've gone." Layla pulls her bag onto her shoulder. "I'll start gathering my stuff and go."

I walk briskly to the family room. I need to get away from Layla's reproachfulness.

Poppy's magnetic board catches my eye under the lamplight in the corner. I walk toward it slowly, knowing it will give me something to read.

It doesn't disappoint: *itsoneofushere2night*

"Layla!" I shout, hurrying out of the room. "Actually, I've changed my mind. Please will you stay after all?"

* * *

That was a dramatic evening. Finally, Clara's perfect life has gone up in smoke, and I can't say I'm sad. I couldn't resist sticking the boot in. But I'm not as triumphant as I thought I'd be. I've been feeling down recently. My past is all around me and the people from it have burst out of my mind to be in my present. They're with me in real life and I feel in danger, like they're right behind me ready to pounce. I remind myself over and over that they're a figment of my imagination, that they can't possibly be here with me. But I feel unsafe, unhinged, and that I might move on from the things that I've been doing to something larger and more sinister. And to something that I might regret.

CHAPTER 30

"So, Clara, as you know, we're moving to a subscription-based model. Tell me how you see your role in moving this forward."

My boss, Jake, ducks his head forward so sharply that it seems as if he might burst through my computer screen.

I lean back instinctively and grab my cup of coffee with shaking hands.

I've spent hours preparing for this interview, but all my planning slips like quicksand through my fingers. All I can think about is how Mike has packed a bag and left. My bravado about him leaving has disappeared and I have to stop myself texting him to beg him to come back and sort things out.

"Clara?" Jake prompts. Next to him sits David, the company CEO, his face unreadable.

I wish I could press *leave* on my laptop and exit the Zoom meeting.

Instead, I say blankly, "What was the question again?"

A look of alarm passes over Jake's face and David looks puzzled.

Someone might as well have poured cold water over the fire of my ambition. I am not going to get this promotion.

My phone beeps. A text from Mike: *I'll be picking Poppy up from nursery tonight.* No hello, affectionate questions, or kisses. *Is this how it's going to be from now on?*

"Clara?" prompts Jake.

"Sorry, remind me of the question again?" I repeat weakly.

* * *

I'm watching the house next door. I can hear laughter from the other side of the wall. Mike's laugh. He emerges from the house with Josie and Poppy. He and Josie exchange a glance and their hands slip into each other, like a comfy glove. They both stare adoringly at Poppy, who skips alongside them gaily, her hair streaming behind her. "Mummy," she says.

Josie has replaced me. I fall to my knees as Poppy says "Mummy" again, this time more stridently.

"Mummy, Mummy, Mummy!" The screams pierce my brain and my eyes snap open.

Poppy's cries ramp up and catapult me out of bed. I run into the hall and almost collide into Layla, who is sleepily rubbing her eyes.

"Goodness, what's going on?" she asks.

"Night terrors," I say abruptly, intent on getting to Poppy. Layla follows at my heels and we burst into Poppy's room to find her kneeling on the floor, pointing at the door.

"The girl with no face!" she shouts. "She going to get me."

I scoop her up in my arms and cuddle with her in bed. "There's no one here, it's just me and Layla," I say soothingly.

"No, no, no, she here!" Poppy points frantically at the door, tears pouring down scarlet cheeks.

Layla touches my arm. "I'll deal with this," she mutters. "You have enough on your plate."

I shake my head. Layla doesn't understand Poppy's hysteria. But before I can say anything, Layla has leaned across and taken Poppy from my arms. Poppy lets herself be swept up and buries herself in Layla's chest, her screams dying down to whimpers.

I stare in amazement. "Wow. She never does that for me or Mike. She just screams relentlessly."

Mike. He should be here helping with Poppy, not Layla. My heart aches, but then I remember the tension-filled nights, Poppy's constant screams and the sniping between us. It wasn't halcyon days by any means.

Layla strokes Poppy's hair. "But kids always act better for non-parents," she says. "I guess that's at least one good thing I can take from the fact that I'll probably never have my own child, hey?"

I shy away from the brittleness in her voice. "I'll get her some milk," I say dully, rising slowly to my feet.

Layla shakes her head. "Go to bed," she mutters firmly. "I'll sort that out."

Poppy lets out a final whimper and her eyes close, head lolling.

I feel a wash of relief. "Thank you," I mouth, heading swiftly to my room. All I want is unconsciousness, a relief from the aching gap in my heart that Mike has left.

As I stretch in bed and grab the pillow, I hear a scrape above the ceiling. I freeze, hands gripping the pillow hard. I hold my breath, and then there are two more creaks.

Right. I'm definitely going up to the loft tomorrow to investigate. I don't care how scared I am.

CHAPTER 31

I pull the loft steps down with the hook. Layla offered to take Poppy to nursery on her way to work and I'm grateful that I can now investigate first thing this morning. If Mike was still here, he would have been up the ladder, telling me to go downstairs and relax. *Think about something else.*

I plant both feet on the bottom steps of the ladder and take a deep breath.

What if there's someone up there? They could attack me and no one would hear. I banish the thought. As if there would be a person in my loft. *But then why do I hear what sounds like footsteps?*

I have to stop this analysis and get on with it. I place one foot after the other on the ladder, focusing on the silvery colour of the steps, my black socks, the hole that reveals a flash of pink toe.

Finally I'm up there. I fumble about on the wall to switch on the light and gasp. I've never seen so much furniture. Rotten wooden dining chairs are scattered throughout the room. I count at least five. There's a coffee table, covered in cobwebs. Piles of books are heaped up in the corner. I peer at them. Enid Blyton's Malory Towers and Elinor M. Brent

Dyer's Chalet School books are predominant. I manage to smile as I reach out to touch one. I used to love those books as a child. I weave my way to the wall that divides the house from Josie's.

There is a door-shaped panel in the middle, with what looks like a wooden plank fitted in. I touch it. It's flimsy plywood. I push it and it comes away, to reveal Josie's loft, as neat as a pin, with just a few stacked suitcases in a corner, and a shelving unit full of paint tins lined up.

I shove the wooden plank back and collapse on the floor, uncaring that my skirt sinks into a large cobweb. All those creaks and steps I heard up here — they weren't my imagination or rodents. *It must have been Josie.* The letters on Poppy's magnetic board, the flood, even the scribbles on the wall and the broken hob found right at the start — they were Josie's doings. And the lights! My head snaps up. Josie must have meddled with the light control switch in the garage. And the woman that Poppy has been seeing at night. *Josie.* I feel sick as I picture her hovering in a corner of Poppy's room, watching my daughter sleep. What was she hoping to achieve?

The woman is unhinged. I gulp. The thought of her creeping into my house again, meddling with my things, listening at doors and watching Poppy makes me feel sick to my stomach.

Could she be dangerous? After all, she's been illegally entering and damaging our property.

I leap to my feet and rush to the loft opening, almost missing steps on the ladder in my haste to get back to the landing. I head to the kitchen and rummage in a drawer for duct tape, before going to the garage to locate a stepladder. I lug the ladder up the stairs and speedily start sticking the tape round the loft hatch opening. I pull it round the hatch, determined to layer it until I can be confident that no one can get through, when the tape runs out. It's only managed to go halfway round. I sigh. I'll have to go out and buy more. There's no way I can remain in this house knowing that the hatch can stealthily be opened, with someone furtively creeping down the ladder.

The key turning in the front door scatters my thoughts and I drop the empty duct tape roll and half fall, half jump off the ladder.

I run down the stairs and gasp when I see Layla. She drops her bag in astonishment.

"What's wrong?" she asks, alarmed.

"Sorry, Layla. I just got a shock. I wasn't expecting you back at this time."

"Oh yeah, sorry. I should have explained before I left this morning. I had a meeting that I had to go into the office for, but now it's over I can work from home for the rest of the day."

Layla fumbles in her rucksack and pulls out her laptop. "I didn't think you'd be so surprised. Next time, I'll explain my every movement."

I bristle at Layla's sarcastic tone.

"I'm not used to you living here," I say meaningfully. "And my nerves are all on edge after everything that's happened."

"Of course, I understand," Layla says softly. "Let's chat properly tonight. Your emotions must be all over the place."

She touches me on the shoulder. I want her hand to stay there. I want to feel a connection with another human, to be shielded from Josie, and Mike's departure.

But Layla is already treading lightly up the stairs. "Going to work in my room," she says.

My phone pings with a text. It's Mike. *I'll be collecting Poppy again from nursery*

He can't even be bothered to place a full stop at the end of the sentence. I can only imagine that he wants to dash off the text as quickly as possible, to spend as little time contacting me as he can.

Mike and Josie's kiss flashes into my mind. But this time my rage, jealousy and sense of betrayal are laced with fear. Josie, I'm sure, wants to take my husband and child as her own. But what if she wants more than to take my little family for herself? What if she has more sinister intentions than just replacing me? Normal people don't trespass into other people's houses and skulk in toddlers' bedrooms. What if Josie wants to harm them?

I pace to the bay window in the living room and peer to the side, at Josie's drive. *Should I warn Mike?* But then I glance down at his cold text and sigh. *No point.*

A thought suddenly occurs to me. Did Josie make that opening in the wall or was it there already? Sinking onto the window seat, I start to google urgently. Chat forums inform me that it is "very normal — most terraced houses are like this"; that it's "common in 1930s semis", and that "many houses from those times have open loft access".

I read advice about getting it bricked up, and that it's a fire and security hazard. It's certainly the latter, I think grimly, as I start to search for local builders who I can call.

A movement outside catches the corner of my eye. A woman with curly light-brown hair is walking away from Josie's. She's swinging a car key and from the quick glimpse that I see of her profile, she looks to be young, perhaps in her twenties. She hops into her car and pulls out.

I'm surprised. I've never known anyone to visit Josie. The woman seems friendless. I wonder idly who it is, before my mind takes me back to the opening in my loft and the fact that Mike isn't here. I can sense Josie and Mike everywhere in the house, along with the Maynards lurking in the shadows.

CHAPTER 32

"So there you have it." I pause for breath after filling Layla in on the door in the loft.

We're sitting at the kitchen island, plates piled with bacon and vegetable pasta, cooked by Layla. I've taken a few nibbles but can't stomach much more. Mike and Josie fill my mind and it makes me feel sick every time I take a bite. Layla is pushing the food around her plate unenthusiastically.

She shakes her head and her fork clatters onto the table. "That's shocking. I think you're right to get away from here as soon as possible. Get the house on the market and to hell with Mike. That woman is not right in the head."

"I'm worried she's targeting Mike and Poppy, and going to do something horrible to them."

"*He* deserves it," mutters Layla, eyes flashing. I'm comforted by her loyalty. "You have to go to the police. What she's doing is criminal." Layla spears a piece of bacon aggressively on her fork.

"But I have no concrete evidence," I sigh. Footsteps, my daughter crying about a woman in her room at night, the letters on Poppy's board . . . the police would put it down to an overactive imagination. And I have no proof it was Josie who flooded the bathroom.

Layla picks up her fork and traces a pattern on the food on her plate distractedly.

"Layla, what's wrong? I can tell your mind's on something else."

Layla sighs. "Sorry, I know it's self-indulgent. It's just that Max has definitely split up with Celia and she's moved out. He wants to see me to chat."

I bang my cutlery down. "For God's sake, Layla, please don't see him. He's split up with his current squeeze, is seeking a replacement and so calls you up — do you not see how disrespectful that is? Especially after the way he treated you. There's a gap and it's like he's called up Amazon to fill it."

Layla's face darkens. "Thanks for making me feel like shit. It's all very well saying that from a position of privilege, Clara. You've got it all. The house, the husband, and most of all, a child. I have nothing. No husband or child. I don't even have family for support. As you know, they've never cared about me."

She takes a ragged breath. "If I get back with Max, then I have the chance to have a child. OK, he might bugger off again, but I'll have a family. You can't understand my situation."

"Excuse me?" I slam my glass on the table. "A position of privilege? Really? Are you blind to what's been happening to me? Mike has moved out and I might be heading for divorce."

Divorce. I roll the word around my mouth. It feels like a morsel of food stuck in my throat that I need to expel.

"He might be getting together with a madwoman who wants my daughter and who enters my house unlawfully. Hardly the good life."

I scrape my pasta into the food waste. Layla follows me and dumps her own plate of food in the bin aggressively. "I'm going to bed. I'm tired and just want to curl up with a book," she snaps.

I bite my tongue and nod curtly. "OK. Me too."

I don't particularly want to go to bed, but I don't want to stay up either. I don't know what to do with myself. I don't want thoughts of Mike and Josie together, of them with Poppy, circling round and round my head, driving my mad. All I want is to go to sleep the moment my head touches the pillow.

I reluctantly follow Layla up the stairs.

"Night," says Layla gruffly as she closes her bedroom door.

If relations continue like this between us, then Layla might as well return to her flat.

I peer into Poppy's room. Her elephant night light creates a soft glow around her as she cuddles up with her giant unicorn soft toy, her thumb stuck firmly in her mouth.

When Mike dropped Poppy back tonight, Layla answered the door while I fussed in the kitchen. A tiny part of me wanted to see him, to grab him and beg him to try again. But then I pictured his lips locked with Josie. It was so vivid I was transported straight back to the moment and the fury I felt.

At the same time, hearing his deep tones in the hall created such a hollow feeling in my stomach I wondered how I would ever eat again.

Poppy's been told that Daddy has to work away for a bit. But she doesn't really understand. I can still hear her cries when Mike left tonight, causing my eyes to sting.

Bending down to gently kiss Poppy's rosy, rounded cheek, I spot Josie's doll nestled in the bedding. Its eyes are wide open, the glassy blue orbs shining under the night light.

Creepy, horrible thing.

Poppy has named her doll Jojo, after Josie. I carefully extract the doll from the duvet, and creeping across the room, shove it on the highest shelf of the cupboard.

Poppy will undoubtedly ask for her in the morning but maybe I can help her forget Jojo by buying her a new, enticing toy.

I'm walking to my bedroom when my eyes automatically rise to the loft hatch. I gasp with dismay when I see the silver tape only surrounding half of it.

Damn it, I forgot to pop out and get some more tape. Idiot!

I hesitate, wondering whether to go to the local newsagents now.

I glance at my phone. Five to nine. It closes at nine, so I won't get there in time. I'll have to leave it as it is, but I'll go to the shop as soon as it opens tomorrow morning.

Unease gnaws at my stomach as I pass underneath the loft hatch and into my bedroom.

CHAPTER 33

Bang. My eyes snap open. Every limb tenses as I stare at the ceiling, unsure as to whether I wish my eyes could bore through it or not. Do I really want to see if my next-door neighbour is up there?

The silence is heavy. I start to count to myself. *Let's see if I can get to one thousand and fall asleep again.* It's a device I commonly used in my childhood.

98, 99, 100, 101 . . . There's a creak and I look up again. A split second later, I realise that the noise came from downstairs and not the loft. Confused, I freeze, straining to hear another sound.

102, 103, 104 . . . My mind keeps chanting.

Bump. The noise is muffled, but it's definitely from downstairs. Has Josie managed to get through the half-taped-up loft hatch and get downstairs? My heart beats so fast I'm dizzy. I take a deep breath. Maybe it's Layla. That makes much more sense. Maybe she can't sleep and has gone downstairs to get a glass of water.

I hesitate. It's most likely Layla, but I want confirmation. The thought of Poppy and her flushed cheeks, sleeping innocently, propels me like a magnet out of bed. I need to check she's OK. I tiptoe onto the landing. Layla's door is firmly shut. My heart sinks. I was hoping to see Layla's door open — evidence that she's gone downstairs. I hesitate, then dash over to Poppy's room, relief welling up as I see her sleeping peacefully, her thumb still in her mouth. She emits a gentle snore.

Buoyed by relief that Poppy is OK, I descend the stairs slowly. Halfway down, I curse myself that I didn't switch on the landing light. It's pitch black. I can't wait to get to the bottom and snap on the hall lights. At the foot of the stairs I pause, straining my ears.

Maybe the sounds were in my imagination, I think hopefully, edging slowly towards the light switch.

I slide the switch down. Nothing. My heart lurches as I snap the switch up and down again. Just oppressive darkness, like a black glove covering my face. I let out a moan and clatter up the stairs, flying over to Layla's room.

"Layla!" I push open the door and burst in, optimistically trying the light switch. Nothing again. But even without the light I can see that not only is Layla not in her bed, but the covers are neatly made up. It looks like Layla never went to bed.

Where is she? A jolt rips through me as I realise that it's just me and Poppy in a house that potentially has someone else in it. Someone who has deliberately turned the lights out.

I literally don't know what to do. I'm not sure whether to bury my face in Layla's duvet and hope I'm imagining the noises or go and investigate downstairs again. Every fibre of my being screams at me not to go downstairs. What if Josie is waiting in the shadows? But then I think about Poppy and brace myself. I stumble out of Layla's room, arms outstretched, and dip into my bedroom, feeling about on the bedside cabinet for my mobile phone.

I flick it onto torch mode gratefully and exit onto the landing, flicking my phone straight up at the ceiling. The loft opening is closed, the tape untampered with. I take a breath of relief. But if not Josie, what was it? Could it be the house's history coming to life? I whisper the word. *Ghosts.*

No such thing as ghosts. When you're gone, you're gone. My dad's confident, loud voice ringing in my ears soothes me. That's what he always told me whenever I had a nightmare or asked about the afterlife.

Pushing my phone light in front of me, I descend the stairs. In the living room I try the lights but am met with the same darkness as the rest of the house.

Please let me have imagined the noises. Or maybe they were the pipes.

I remember hearing that houses — especially old ones — often made weird creaks in the night.

I flash my torch in front of me as I walk through the kitchen into the family room. There doesn't appear to be anyone here. I pause, listening intently. All I can hear is the sound of my own heavy breathing.

The control to the lights is in the garage. If someone has turned the lights off, then they could still be in there.

I turn this way and that. Where do I go? I'm too scared to go to the garage but I can't stay here. I need to seek help.

I turn around and slowly creep towards the hall. I'm going to run outside and scream for help. *But what if I'm imagining all this? I've heard a few bangs and bumps. Maybe this time it's a fuse or a power cut.* I could embarrass myself. But I keep walking, past the door to the garage. There's a groaning sound like a rusty gate swinging shut.

"We really need to oil the hinges," Mike said last week when Poppy crashed through the garage door to get an ice lolly from the freezer.

I pause and crouch down, suppressing a scream. I turn off my mobile phone torch and lean against the wall, wishing I could disappear into it.

There are no footsteps, no rustlings. I stand up shakily and put one foot in front of the other to continue my journey to the front door.

Then footsteps pound behind me. There's sudden pressure on my hair and my head jerks back. I twist round and there's a torch light shining in my face, momentarily blinding. My eyes readjust. I'm staring down the barrel of a gun.

I raise my eyes above the rifle. In resignation, my mouth forms the word "Josie". I search the face above the gun, seeking the familiar straight, flaxen hair and large blue eyes. But a thin face framed with curly, mousey-brown hair meets my gaze. Josie's name dies on my lips. *I recognise you.*

I desperately try to work out how, when the woman opens her mouth, gasping heavily. "I'm going to get you," she snarls.

"Who are you? What are you doing here?" I stammer.

Then with a jolt I realise that it's the woman who was swinging her car keys outside Josie's house yesterday — this is her. My mind races as I try to process what this means. *This is something to do with Josie. Somehow she's involved.* My thoughts shatter as she waves the gun and prods it against my temple, the cold of the metal reflecting the icy feeling in my heart. I gasp for air. This woman is clearly not right. I need to try and calm her down before she pulls the trigger on me and seeks out Poppy.

My nerves are on fire. Fear threatens to overwhelm me as I think about my innocent daughter upstairs. I have to protect her.

"Jasmine. My God, I've hated you since you were born!" the woman shrieks. *Jasmine.* Shock courses through me.

"Always little miss swotty, little miss bloody brilliant at school. I was always inferior at everything in Dad's eyes. It ruined my life. You watched as Dad goaded me."

With a sickening lurch, I realise who this stranger in my home is.

"Lily." I try to speak slowly and gently, even though my tongue feels as heavy as a brick. "You've made a mistake. I'm not Jasmine. I've never met you. I moved to this house years after you left."

Lily moves the gun from my temple to prod it against my stomach.

"Don't move," she warns.

A bang from the upstairs landing cuts through my thoughts. It causes Lily to start momentarily and raise her eyes up the stairs.

Was that Poppy waking and getting out of bed? I freeze. I'll have to try and grab the gun from Lily if so. I don't fancy my chances, but I'll do anything to protect my daughter. I remember my taekwondo lessons at the age of ten. I'm sure the instructor told us to poke our fingers into someone's eyes as self-defence.

I desperately try to listen for more sounds upstairs as Lily continues with her monologue. From what I can tell in the gloom, her eyes are glassy and staring ahead, as if looking into a different place.

"And Mummy dearest, you let me down. You saw him prod me with his gun, terrorise me, intimidate me. Deny me stuff like showering, a basic human right, if I didn't get eighty-five per cent minimum in an exam. You were frightened, I get that, but you let me down big time."

I watch in terror as a shadow creeps down the stairs. I hear rhythmic, stealthy creaks as the figure approaches us.

The erratic waving of Lily's torch reveals a flash of flaxen hair.

Josie.

I didn't think it would be possible to be more frightened. A second flash of Lily's torch reveals a grim expression on Josie's face. She stands silently as Lily continues to speak about her contempt for her mother.

Josie and Lily are in on this together. My body shakes as the realisation washes over me. They were probably planning it when Lily visited Josie earlier. In fact, they've probably been planning it for a long time. Josie wants my life, my husband and my child. What better way than to bump me off?

Lily moves closer. "And as for you, Dad, after everything you've done to me. Tormenting me, frightening me, making me think my life was in danger with your gun. Well, guess what I have now. One of my own."

She holds it against my temple again. A kaleidoscope of images flood through my mind. Poppy screaming in the hospital after being born, Poppy being cuddled by Mike, the three of us collecting conkers on Tooting Common, moving to this house, me and Mike hugging each other and looking forward to a lovely life in this family home, Poppy's rainbow-coloured suitcase.

I close my eyes and wait for Lily to pull the trigger, Poppy's face tattooed across my eyelids.

Josie says quietly, "Lily."

There is a silence.

"You've come," Lily says. I can tell she's smiling.

Snapping my eyes open, I scan Josie for a weapon. Sure enough, Lily's torch reveals a glimmer of silver. Josie is gripping a carving knife.

That's it. Game over. I'm struggling to breathe. What if they attack Poppy after killing me? But surely Josie wouldn't do that to the little girl she seems to adore. I cling on to this tiny scrap of comfort as Josie continues to descend the stairs, heading straight for me. I hope that Lily finishes me off with the gun before Josie uses the knife. At least that would be a quick death compared to the knife plunging into me, my body draining of blood.

I'm dizzy and I clutch the wall as Josie walks over to stand with Lily. Both of them facing me. Two against one. They must have planned to dispose of my body together.

"I'm going to protect myself, stand up to Dad at last," Lily says. "With your help, Josie." Her eyes bulge as they bore into me.

"That's what we always talked about, isn't it? Me standing up to Dad."

"We did indeed." Josie's voice rings out confidently. She holds the knife straight ahead as she steps towards me.

I close my eyes. I hold the image of Poppy in my mind as I wait for the cool metal to plunge into me, or the crack of the gun, whichever comes first.

And then the knife is touching my chest, Josie's arm pressing on mine, her lips on my ear. I wait for a final, poisonous message.

"Go into the living room and call the police," Josie breathes.

I hesitate. *Is this some kind of pretence? They might be tricking me, getting me to let down my defences, only to pounce upon me.* But I realise I have no choice. I start to walk unsteadily.

Josie addresses Lily. "Lily, your dad, sister and mum are dead. They can't hurt you anymore. Remember what happened? They've been gone a long time. You're free from them."

Josie steps towards Lily slowly. "There's nothing to fear, nothing to worry about," she croons.

There's a spark in Lily's glassy eyes. Her face slackens. "Really?" she says uncertainly.

Josie moves forward again and gently touches Lily's arm. "You're safe," she says. "I'm here."

I close the living room door as softly as possible and with trembling fingers stab 999 into my phone.

"Emergency. Which service do—"

An explosive bang tears through my ears, followed by a terrible scream.

I drop my phone and run blindly to the door, and freeze when I see the scene in front of me. There's a woman lying in the hall, the front door wide open. Blood forms a halo around her head. It's spattered up the door and sliding down the walls.

Josie. The name fills my mind. *You saved my life and now you're gone.* It takes me a second to realise that Josie is standing stiffly at Lily's side, her hand on her shoulder, her mouth open and eyes wide with horror.

My eyes swivel back to the woman on the floor. Golden-brown waves span a face that is familiar. *Layla.* My mouth opens to scream but no sound comes out. I drop to my knees as Layla opens her eyes and stares at me, before they close slowly.

"Serves you right, beloved mother," hisses Lily. "That's for neglecting to stick up for me."

A cry pierces the air. It comes from upstairs. *Poppy.* I'm up like a rocket, my heart pounding.

Lily points her gun up the stairs. "A-ha, that's my sister. You deserve what's coming to you."

Josie pushes Lily's gun down forcefully. "Your sister and mum are dead." She enunciates each word.

I run to the stairs, hell-bent on getting to Poppy. I expect a crack to pierce the air as Lily fires her gun at me, but I have to try and make it to my daughter.

Out of the corner of my eye I see Lily take a step towards the stairs. I pause. I will fight her with my bare hands rather than allow her any further up the stairs.

And then blue lights flash round the room.

Overwhelming relief that the police have arrived fights with my fear that their presence will push Lily over the edge.

They burst through the open door.

"It's the police. Put the gun down."

I hold my breath. Lily sinks to the floor, her gun at her feet. Her eyes have lost their glazed stare. She looks around, confused.

A mob of police, their stomping boots, hard hats and shining guns are everywhere.

"I'm just protecting myself against my family," Lily says in a small voice. "They were here just now, but where have they gone?"

The police surround Lily, one of them taking her gun, another slipping handcuffs on. And then more sirens wail. I hesitate. Poppy continues to scream but now I know that she's safe, I have a primal urge to check that Layla is taken care of. There's an icy grip on my heart as I remember that our last words this evening were cross and aggressive. I can't tell if Layla's chest is rising and falling.

"Please don't die, you're my best friend." My words are crushed by the crisp shouts of the police.

A trio of paramedics erupt through the front door and then they're surrounding Layla, one clamping an oxygen mask on her, another bearing down on her bullet wound with a piece of gauze.

"Is she going to be OK?" My faltering voice is drowned out again by the police. I raise my voice, repeating myself as they efficiently manoeuvre Layla onto a stretcher.

"She's breathing, and her stats are stable," says one of them gently. "For now. But she needs medical help urgently."

Lily is pulled out of the door by a throng of police while others stampede through the house.

I hesitate. Poppy continues to cry but I can't bear to leave Layla on her own.

"I'll go with her in the ambulance," Josie says quickly. Her face looks as if it's been drained of blood.

"Thank you." And then I'm running upstairs, two at a time. All I want is to curl up against Poppy and never let her go.

CHAPTER 34

"Layla." I lean by her bed, reaching for her hand. It's cold and limp. Her face almost matches the white of the pillow. I've never seen her look so vulnerable.

But Layla's eyes are open and she smiles faintly at me.

"Are you OK? Sorry, silly question."

"Actually I am. I've been really lucky, the doctors say."

Layla gestures to her arm, which is strapped up. "The bullet hit my shoulder, broke a bone and has caused some nerve damage. But it could have been so much worse."

The blood fanning out around Layla fills my mind. The bullet could so easily have lodged in her heart or her head.

I sink into a chair next to Layla, my legs weak with relief. Josie is sitting quietly at the other side of the bed, huge bags under her eyes.

"I'll need physiotherapy and I'm on strong drugs for the pain," Layla continues, "but all in all, I'm doing OK."

"Thank God." My grip tightens on her hand. "Look, do you want me to call your parents to tell them what happened? I didn't like to last night. You know, waking them in the middle of the night, and I didn't want to call them until I had concrete news."

"No, don't bother. They're off jaunting around Europe on a cruise. I don't think they'll be cutting their trip short."

I know that Layla isn't close to her parents. But I'm shocked that she doesn't think they'll be bothered. She was *shot*, for God's sake. She could be lying in the morgue now.

"What happened last night? You weren't in the house," I ask, picturing Layla's empty room and made-up bed.

"I popped out to see Max on a whim. I didn't like to disturb you. I got back and opened the front door and all I could see was a gun waving around. The next thing I know there's a bang and I'm on the floor. Then it's all hazy."

Layla closes her eyes. "The fact that I almost lost my life in the process of seeing Max . . . well, I think that's a bad omen for patching up our relationship."

She gives a dry laugh and winces as she gingerly moves her injured arm.

"Your next-door neighbour has been wonderful. She's been with me all night, talking to me, reassuring me. It's been such a comfort."

Josie smiles faintly. "I'm so pleased I've been able to help." I swallow as she stands up. "I'd better get going."

I wait as she gently hugs Layla. "Can I have a quick word, Josie? I'll be back in a minute, Layla."

Josie nods slightly and I gesture to an empty bay, pulling the curtains round us. I stare at Josie. The woman who I've hated with all my might has saved my life, and offered huge support to my best friend in her moment of need. Those blue eyes that always looked so glacial have now taken on a warmer, cornflower blue. The angles of her face, usually so prominent, seem blurred now. Her sharply cut hair seems softer.

"Thank you."

Josie gives a half-smile. "You're welcome."

I sit down abruptly on the bed. My legs are trembling. "When I saw you, I thought that you and Lily had hatched a plan to kill me together," I say.

"I know things have been fraught between us, but I didn't think it was so bad that you thought I was a murderer," Josie says, standing awkwardly in the corner of the bay.

"I went into the loft yesterday and saw the gap in the wall. I assumed it was you coming into our house and doing sinister things, like writing on Poppy's magnetic board and flooding our bathroom. I saw Lily visiting you yesterday and then you appear in my house, presumably from the loft." I shrug. "What was I supposed to think?"

I should be falling over myself to thank Josie. But the about-turn in Josie's character is so abrupt I can't fully let my previous feelings about her go.

Josie sighs. "I understand. That gap has been there since before Steve and I moved in. I discovered it when I first went to put some stuff in storage in the loft. It came in very useful when I got friendly with Lily. We used to meet up there. One of us would push through it and we'd sit together and talk. It was a really good way of supporting her. But I've never used it since. I can only presume that Lily has somehow been getting into your house and has been going up there."

"How did you know Lily was in my house last night?" I'm trying to process the facts that Josie is giving me, but my mind feels like sludge.

"I heard her shouting through the wall. I recognised her voice. I was worried as I know she's had huge issues after what happened, so I grabbed the knife for self-defence and came down through the loft, the easiest and quickest way, despite the tape around it. I was worried you wouldn't be able to answer if I knocked on the front door."

"How do you think she got in there?" I ask.

The questions fire from me like bullets. I need answers.

Josie is quiet. "That I don't know for sure," she says. "But I suspect that she has an old key for the house."

It can't have been through the front door as I changed that lock. As I think about which door Lily might have entered, my jaw starts clattering, joining the trembling in my legs.

"Goodness, are you OK?" Concern fills Josie's eyes as she moves forward and lays a cool palm on my forehead.

"It's just panic after what happened," I answer. It's hard to get the words out. Pins and needles prick at my tongue. I take a deep breath, trying to focus on my breathing.

"I thought Lily was in a psychiatric hospital?" I say, moving my tongue slowly and deliberately.

"She was, but she was deemed fit to leave a few months ago. I didn't tell you because I didn't want to unnerve you." Josie hangs her head briefly. "Not that I ever thought in a million years that she would do something like this," she adds quickly.

I should be apologising to Josie for everything that has happened between us and thanking her effusively. But Josie's face squashed against my husband's, the tips of their noses touching, Josie's hair brushing his shoulder, is burned into my mind.

"Why did you kiss my husband?" I ask, my words staccato-like.

"Because I feel a connection to him, because I felt sorry for him, because I'm lonely," she says. "I didn't plan it, I just suddenly found myself doing it."

"I feel you've been chasing him, wanting to destroy my marriage, take my child," I continue.

Josie's cool demeanour slips. "I've been so lonely since my marriage ended and I've desperately struggled to come to terms with not having a child. You're a happy, cosy family, I just wanted to be part of it and that led me to behave inappropriately.

"Sorry." Josie's final word is so quiet that I'm not sure if I heard correctly.

Josie's voice shakes slightly. "I won't do anything like that again, I promise. I'd love to be a part of Poppy's life still."

The need to hold in my feelings and be calm for Poppy numbed me last night. But now Poppy is safely in nursery, the full enormity of what happened hits me. The trembling that is in my legs has spread to my hands, shoulders and arms. I can't stop it.

CHAPTER 35

"Are you OK?"

Mike is sitting in the car outside the police station.

The flash of Lily's gun is superimposed against his mouth.

No, I'm not OK.

I get into the car and buckle my seat belt in, staring straight ahead.

"They say that they think Lily had a panic attack that caused hallucinations. She thought that she was back at the night her dad shot them. That's why she turned up threatening us with a rifle. She thought we were her parents and Jasmine," I say to Mike. But really I'm explaining it to myself.

I hated Josie and feared Jonathan Maynard but felt nothing but compassion for his daughters. It spins everything around that Lily, who had been through so much, and who was definitely a victim, could intend to mirror her father's murderous actions.

"Her gun belonged to Jonathan Maynard. He had several and that one somehow slipped through the net."

"I'm so sorry. You must have been terrified. To think that she could have killed you and Poppy . . ."

Mike has tears in his eyes. I wish my first feeling wasn't anger.

I had to call Mike last night as the house is now a crime scene and Poppy and I had to leave for the police to get on with their work. *My dream home, how could it now be a crime scene?* Mike dashed over and drove us to Callum's, and we spent the night crammed into his small flat.

He would normally be the first person I turned to — because I wanted to, not because I had to.

After seeing Layla, I had to go to the police station to give a statement. Mike insisted on taking me and fetching me afterwards.

We drive the rest of the way to Callum's flat in silence. Once we're in the flat, door closed, Mike turns to me.

"I was in the wrong, and Clara, I am so sorry. Please can we put this behind us?"

"You kissed someone else," I say, proud I've mastered an even, calm tone. "You took another woman's side over me. Is that still the case?"

"No. And I need to explain to you exactly what happened. Josie was trying to comfort me. She kissed me. She caught me off my guard. I was stunned and was about to pull away when you appeared. It was a matter of a few seconds, if that."

"But that's just the tip of the iceberg. You chose to take her to see her dad and then go for a cosy drink at hers afterwards. You knew it upset me but you continued your friendship with her and completely disregarded my feelings. I feel so let down."

Mike's face is pale, his mouth drooping.

"I'll hold my hands up. I've really struggled with the problems in this house. And I'm not proud to admit this, but I've resented you for pushing to buy it. I felt like you got us in this muddle." He pauses. "Which I know is unreasonable. I have a voice, I could have told you my reservations. I also thought Josie was a nice neighbour. Lonely and a bit intense, but caring and kind to our daughter. I thought you were behaving irrationally." He pauses.

"I'm not pointing the finger at you," he adds quickly. "I'm just trying to explain why I acted as I did. Clara, the thought of that woman taking her gun to you and Poppy rips my heart out. When you told me, I wanted to wrap my arms around you and never leave your side."

He stares into my eyes. I've always loved his multi-coloured eyes, the greens, greys and browns in them, the way they emanate warmth. Or used to. I hesitate.

I want to fall into his arms, to bury my head in his shoulder and have my little family back. But I hold back.

"I want to work it out," I say at last. "But I want to take it slowly. Please can you still stay at Callum's and let's take it day by day."

Mike reaches over and touches my hand. "That's good enough for me."

CHAPTER 36

I hear Poppy's giggles drifting in from the garden as I plod up the drive. It's uncharacteristically hot for April, and my feet are sweating in their boots, with perspiration sliding down the side of my face.

Josie's voice carries in the air, her tone light and happy as she chats to Poppy.

I smile slowly. It's still hard to feel completely at ease with Josie's relationship with Poppy, but I can't deny that my neighbour has been incredibly helpful.

I'm arriving back from my offices in London. After fluffing my interview for the position of deputy managing editor, I explained to Jake the whole saga, and as a result I was called in to my company's offices for another interview. This time, it went well. Jake was suitably sympathetic to my home ordeal, and I'm quietly confident I'll be given the role. Josie offered to collect Poppy from nursery due to my city trip, as Mike is working late. He's spending more and more time at home, and we're slowly rebuilding our relationship.

I slip round the side gate into the garden to see Josie pushing Poppy on the swing we've had installed. Poppy is screaming with delight, her head swung back and pigtails flying behind her. Josie is laughing.

"Go, go, go," she chants.

The sunlight bounces off both Josie's and Poppy's blond locks, and their blue eyes flash. I'm conscious of my contrasting dark curls and mahogany eyes.

They look like mother and daughter.

I give myself an internal shake. *Stop it.*

Josie sees me and walks over.

"Hello," she says gaily. "All's good here. I've given Poppy her tea."

"Me had pizza from Pizza Express! Yum!"

I compare Poppy's glee to her downcast face when I cooked her boring old baked beans and toast last night.

"I do hope that was OK to get her a takeaway?" Josie asks quickly. "It was just a margherita."

I rearrange my face. "Of course. That was so nice of you."

"And me had choc fudge cake. Me going to help her make that cake soon!"

Poppy slows down on the swing and jumps off, running to Josie and burying her head in her chest.

The only cakes that I've made with Poppy are cornflake cakes. *Can you even call them cakes?* A wave of nausea crashes over me at the thought of cornflakes and chocolate. I don't have much of a sweet tooth.

Poppy bounds over to me and pulls me over. "Group hug," she says.

Group hugs used to consist of me, Mike and Poppy. I try to banish the bitter, little thought. Josie saved my life. Without her, I'm convinced that Lily would have pulled the trigger on my daughter.

My stomach is empty and I consider what to eat. There's some chicken in the fridge but I don't fancy that. Or what about an omelette . . . my stomach turns and I almost gag.

And then it hits me.

"Josie, I need the toilet and to pop some food on for myself for tea. Would you mind staying fifteen minutes more?"

"Of course," says Josie promptly. "Take your time."

She turns to Poppy. "Hide and seek. I'll count to twenty."

I dart into the house and straight up to the bathroom. While I'm not keen on sweet food, it's unusual for me to feel sick at the thought of it. And to feel nauseous at the thought of savoury food, well, that has only happened once before, when I was pregnant with Poppy.

I open the bathroom cupboard, and there are five pregnancy tests lined up. I extract one, my heart beating. *Please let it be positive. Please.*

Five minutes later, I'm holding the stick. The slightest tinge of blue appears and rapidly develops into a dark line. Positive. I almost drop it.

I can't believe that it's possible, after everything that's happened and the wedge driven between me and Mike. We've barely been trying for weeks.

I pull out another test. I'd better try again, in case that was a false positive.

"Comin', ready or not!" Hollers Poppy as I waft downstairs and to the garden in a dream-like state.

Mike has arrived in from work. His face is flushed, and he's struggling with his tie. "Blimey, it's boiling. I need to get out of my suit," he puffs.

He sees me and we kiss a little self-consciously. Things are much better between us, but there's still a little gap there, something holding us back.

Poppy bounds over and flings her arms around Mike's legs. Josie stands close by. She and Mike smile at each other pleasantly. They are oh-so-polite and slightly cool around each other now. There's no more flirting, no glances and touching. Everything is above board. The way it should have been from the start.

Mike picks up Poppy and swings her in his arms. My heart soars. I can't wait to tell him my news.

***

I lie cheek to cheek with Mike in bed, his arm flung over me. He's snoring heavily. Normally, I would be pushing him crossly onto his side. But tonight, I don't care. Mike was ecstatic when I told him that I was pregnant.

Any last bridge between us melted away and I told him to leave Callum's flat and move back in permanently.

Could Mike and I give it a go in this house after all? He gives a particularly loud grunt as I consider it. We had planned to move as soon as possible after the Lily incident. But we're safe here now. Lily is in a psychiatric hospital and Josie is now a friend, not a foe. I still feel uneasy about her, but she's been so helpful with Poppy and respectful of my relationship with Mike that I think maybe I can put up with her.

I shudder as I picture the garage and the hall that awful night, a flash of blonde hair and a glint of metal in my mind. I still feel traumatised by what happened with Lily. But it brought matters to a climax and maybe that event, as horrifying as it was, has drawn a line under the tragic history of the house. Our family can fill Number 5 Lunn Road with happiness and banish the Maynards for ever.

No more words on Poppy's board, no more unexpected events like the lights going out and flooding. No more thudding footsteps in the loft.

A high-pitched shriek sends my thoughts flying. *Not again.* I turn to look at Mike. As usual, Poppy's cries haven't penetrated his sleep and he emits a peaceful snore.

I sigh and pad out of bed. I had hoped that these "night terrors" would have eased now that Lily isn't entering Poppy's room to cause them.

Why was she doing that? I shudder. It was so creepy. Maybe it was part of her hallucinatory psychosis. Perhaps Lily thought that Poppy was Jasmine, or herself as a young child, and that's why she felt the need to dwell in my daughter's bedroom.

Poppy shrieks again and I hasten to her.

Poppy is crouching on her bed, eyes half open. "Mummy, Mummy, tell her to go away! Go away, now!"

I wrap my arms around her and try to stroke her hair, but Poppy wriggles out of my grasp.

"I want out, out! Mummy's room!" she screams.

Mike dashes in, rubbing his eyes. "What's going on?"

"Night terrors. Again," I say pointedly.

"Who do you want to go away, Poppy?" I ask gently. But Poppy just screams and writhes until Mike scoops her into his arms.

"Come on, love," he coos. "I'm taking you to Daddy's and Mummy's room."

He whisks her off and Poppy's screams subside. I follow them, pausing under the loft hatch. I can't hear anything.

"Girl-with-no-face won't come in here, will she?" Poppy asks Mike.

A wave of nausea washes over me and I run to the toilet. *It'll just be morning sickness.*

CHAPTER 37

Poppy is curled up in bed with my phone, enraptured with *Peppa Pig*.

I press pause. "Poppy, you were very upset last night," I say gently. "You seemed to see something, maybe a person in your room. Can you remember?"

Poppy moans at the screen being stopped and prods it with her finger. "No. Me don't like being by my own. Me want to be with Mummy and Daddy."

I sigh, trying to hide my frustration. "Did you see a big girl in your room?"

"Don't know. Me want Peppa now!"

I slide the phone over to her.

Mike looks up from his own phone, where he is busily tapping out an email.

"I know what you're thinking," he says. "You're worried that she's seeing an actual person in her room, and that it wasn't Lily after all, it's someone or something else. That there's something sinister in this house still."

I nod, grateful he's understood. "Yes, it really worries me. I was even thinking we could stay here, give it a go and not dash to put the house on the market. But after this, well, I'm uneasy."

Mike's face has brightened, ignoring my last words. "I was thinking exactly the same, that we should give it a go. It's the perfect family home, if only we can put those Maynards out of our minds."

His face tightens.

"Clara, I've been thinking about Poppy's screaming last night. I was unsettled too. But honestly, I reckon that she's been having night terrors as you said all along, and it's not linked to Lily coming into the house."

I consider. "Maybe. I had them as a kid." Perhaps it's just a total coincidence. Maybe Lily was never in Poppy's room after all. My heart lifts at the thought. I grip Mike's hand.

"Let's give it a go here," I murmur, banishing Lily's wide, staring eyes and her gun from my mind. I erase thoughts of Lily creeping up behind me and hands jerking my ponytail back.

Mike kisses me. "I'm so pleased to hear that. Obviously if you can't bear the memories of what happened that night we must move. But I'm hopeful we can replace those memories with happy family times."

He lays a hand on my stomach.

I grin at him as the *Peppa Pig* theme tune plays in the background. I stretch and get out of bed.

"I'm just going to get Poppy's clothes for the day."

I wander into Poppy's room and rifle through her drawers, selecting some leggings and a T-shirt. Turning to face the room, I sigh at the mess. Poppy has a habit of causing chaos in her bedroom when she can't sleep. Dolls, books, hairbands and cuddly toys have been pulled from her shelves. Her duvet is a twisted mess.

I march over to straighten it. As I lift it up to shake it out, a familiar-looking doll falls out. Its glassy eyes look like they're boring into me.

I suppress a cry. Jojo. I open the wardrobe to observe the shelf I put the doll on. There is no way Poppy could have reached it. I fling the doll over on its front, so I don't have to see its icy eyes.

"Poppy, your doll Jojo is on your bed. Where did you get her from, please?"

Poppy is cuddled up in Mike's arms. She looks at me briefly before leaping up and running to her room. "I get her."

"Mike," I say urgently. "That dreadful doll that Josie bought has turned up back in Poppy's room. I hid it on her top shelf, and there's no way that she could have reached it herself."

I can tell from Mike's poker expression that he thinks I'm making something out of nothing. Poppy comes back in cradling her doll.

"Jojo," she croons. "My pretty doll."

I want to throw it across the room.

CHAPTER 38

"How are you doing?" I fling open the front door to let Layla in.

"Better than I was," says Layla, following me to the kitchen. She touches her arm in the sling. "The pain is much better, although I've got really annoying pins and needles. Work have been really good about it and there's no rush for me to go back until I'm ready."

"I'm glad you're feeling better physically, but mentally?" I ask, as I scoop some coffee into a single cafetière.

Layla hesitates. "I get flashbacks," she says at last. "I've been having nightmares about the gun, and in them it fires through my chest and then I'm watching my own funeral."

I pause. "I dream about that night too," I say.

"I'm thinking of having counselling. And you should too," she adds.

"Yes, maybe. What's happening with Max?" I ask, remembering that Max was the reason Layla found herself face to face with Lily at the front door.

Layla hangs her head. "You were right," she says quietly. "I laid all my cards on the table, wanting to give our relationship another go. But he became elusive and distant. I don't want that crap anymore. The playing games. So I blocked him."

"Layla, I'm so pleased." Finally, my friend has done the right thing. I pour her coffee. "Here you go."

"Where's yours?" Layla looks surprised. Everyone knows that I love coffee. The stronger the better.

"I've had loads today, so I'm all coffeed out," I lie, grabbing a mug and heaping a spoon with hot chocolate powder. The truth is, coffee turns my stomach. But I don't want to reveal I'm pregnant as it's still early days, and also, I don't want to upset Layla by telling her the news. Layla looks suspicious, but then her mind moves to another topic.

"Good news about Lily, isn't it?" she says. "Hopefully they'll throw away the key," she adds, her voice hard.

Lily has been detained in a high-security hospital with a string of charges to answer in court.

I nod. "Yes, not only is she being charged for what she did that night, but also for trespassing numerous times into our house previously. She held on to a key to the garage from when she lived here. So it was her behind the letters on Poppy's board, our lights going out and, I believe, the flooding of the bathroom. Sorry if we blamed you for that," I add quickly.

Layla shudders. "The thought of her creeping around the house with me in it, and more to the point with you three living here, is horrible."

"Hmmmm." I try to dispel that unwelcome thought, scared that if I think too much about it I'll never feel at ease in this house, always fearing someone is up in the loft or hiding behind a door.

"It's likely that she's too mentally ill to appear in court. If she's found guilty, she'll stay in a high-security psychiatric hospital, rather than go to prison," I say. "But the police have no doubt told you that too."

I hope I've got it right. I felt overwhelmed by all the information the policeman gave me rapidly over the phone a few days ago.

"Yes. And that makes me angry, if I'm honest. She deserves everything she gets. I know she was hallucinating when she shot me, but I still think she deserves prison and a lengthy sentence too," Layla says fiercely.

"Hopefully she'll be locked up for a long time and can't harm us again," I say. "We're thinking of staying in this house after all. Lily being arrested and charged hopefully closes the door on that chapter."

Layla nods. "And at least you know that after all the anguish, Josie is generally a good person." She sips her coffee. "Honestly, Clara, I was so grateful to her at the hospital. It's made me see her in a whole new light."

"Yep."

I banish Jojo and her glacial eyes to the back of my mind.

"Layla, that's reminded me, can you give me our key back please? My mum and dad are coming next week and we want to give it to them."

"Don't worry, I'll get them some keys cut from mine later," says Layla, running her hand along her injured shoulder.

I'm uneasy. I want Layla's key, and not just for my parents' sake. "I'll take it now, if you don't mind," I say abruptly, mumbling, "It's probably easier."

Layla frowns. "Oh, OK, fine. Problem is, I don't have it on me. I'll have to find it at home and get it to you."

She implies that it's an imposition.

"Thanks, if you don't mind. The next few days would be OK."

After Lily, the thought of anyone having a key to our home is unbearable for me. Even one of my best friends.

"Thanks for coming over." I'm hugging Layla goodbye on the doorstep when Steve's van pulls into the drive next door.

"Who's that?" Layla peers over curiously.

"Josie's ex," I mouth.

Steve spots us and pushes through the bushes dividing our drive.

"I hope you're OK," he says to me. "Josie told me what happened with Lily. In a rare moment of talking to me," he adds dryly.

He glances at Layla.

"Steve, this is Layla, one of my oldest friends," I say.

"I guessed," says Steve. "I heard about what happened to you, Layla." He assesses her injured arm. "How are you doing? Is your arm any better?"

Layla dives into a response, clearly grateful to be asked. I notice them appraising each other as Layla talks. Steve takes in Layla's golden-brown curls and wide hazel eyes. Layla's eyes flit over Steve's chiselled figure, his biceps bulging under his T-shirt. *Shame he's not Layla's type.*

My phone goes and Jake's number flashes up. "Excuse me." I bustle into the house. "Hello?" I cross my fingers. *Please let me get the promotion.*

Twenty minutes later, I'm rushing outside, opening my mouth to apologise for being so long. But it doesn't look like I've been missed. The conversation has moved on from Layla's injury and Lily's act of violence. Instead, Layla is in the middle of a lively anecdote to Steve. He throws his head back and laughs with abandon, Layla joining him, her chuckle carefree and happy.

"Sorry for being so long," I say nonetheless. "I've just been offered a promotion at work and was ironing out the details with my boss."

After congratulations and pumping hands from Steve and careful hugs from Layla, Layla says she has to go.

"Great to meet you." Her eyes linger on Steve before she walks down the drive.

"So, are you OK?" Steve turns to me. "It must have been terrifying. But it seems Josie turned out to be a bit of a hero."

I strain to spot any sarcasm, but he sounds genuinely admiring.

"I thought I was going to be killed," I say. "Josie saved my life, and I can't thank her enough. She's also been so helpful since with Poppy, which we really appreciate, especially as it must be hard for her given her situation," I babble then pause abruptly, giving myself an internal shake at my tactless words.

Steve nods. "Laying aside my feelings for her, she's certainly stepped up. I imagine she adores Poppy, although it's probably bittersweet."

I nod. "She's been through a lot. Especially with her dad currently being on end-of-life care."

"Her dad? He died two years ago. They weren't in contact. Although I appreciate that it was still hard for her," he adds hurriedly. "He practically washed his hands of her after meeting June, her stepmum, and all they cared about was the daughter they had together. When she heard he died from dementia it brought back all those troubled feelings. It made things even harder between us, to be honest."

He looks out over the garden. "Sorry, I sound selfish." His voice is so quiet I wonder if I heard him correctly.

I tense as if waiting to start a race. *Ready, steady, go.* Adrenaline courses through me. Josie lied. *Because it was a way of getting close to Mike. To steal him away from me.*

I persuaded myself to get over Josie's lie about miscarrying twins, but this is too much. Added to the reappearance of the doll and Poppy's declarations about someone being in her room again, I'm scared that it wasn't just Lily who's been trespassing into my home.

Steve cuts across my mumbled goodbyes. "I don't suppose I could have Layla's number, could I?"

I hesitate, wondering if I should give her number out without her permission. But then I remember Steve and Layla's easy comradeship and happy laughter.

"Of course."

As I read Layla's number out, I experience a flash of disloyalty as I imagine how Josie would feel. But then my heart hardens as Poppy's cries echo in my ears.

As soon as Steve ambles down the drive, I shut the door and pound up the stairs. I'm going into the attic again.

CHAPTER 39

I hesitate at the bottom of the ladder. Jojo's glassy eyes bore into my mind and a sense of foreboding washes over me. I give myself a shake and put one foot determinedly on the lowest rung.

The room is the same as when I first went up. Crammed with furniture, dust everywhere and cobwebs winding around me. I walk to the plywood cut-out in the wall, but there's no change since I last saw it. It doesn't look to have been moved.

I sigh. I had hoped to see a concrete sign that Josie had been coming into our loft and down into Poppy's room. I'm about to turn away when on impulse I press the plywood to peer into Josie's loft. Like last time, I note the neatness, the paints lined up on shelves.

Nothing to see here.

Then I spot something on the floor. Pushing through into Josie's loft, I pick it up. It's a black face mask with holes for the eyes and mouth.

She has no face.

Poppy's voice echoes through my mind as, with a scream, I drop the mask and frantically push through the plywood to the safety of my loft. In my haste to get away I trip over a pile of board games towering precariously. The boxes crash down and the top comes off one of them. The Game of Life. I'm transported back to being ten years old again, whiling away a Sunday afternoon with the game. Memories of my childhood crumble when I see on top of the gameboard and coloured pegs a blue leather-bound book. I hesitate, desperate to get down the ladder and out of here, but curiosity gets the better of me. Quickly, I pick it up and open it.

Lily Maynard's Diary is stencilled neatly on the front page, and then sheets of writing in spidery black biro confront me. I feel guilty that I'm planning to read someone's personal thoughts. *But it might help me understand more about her.* The woman who attacked me with a gun. But deep down, I know there's also a good dollop of morbid curiosity driving me to read it. I hesitate. I'll just read the last entry, I tell myself, not acknowledging my whispered thought, *In the first instance.*

Dear Diary,

No one might ever see this, so maybe this is just a confession to myself. But I'm going to write this down nonetheless.

In four hours, I'm going to take my Dad's gun and shoot him, my mum and my sister dead.

I will place the gun on my Dad's body. I'll wear gloves so that the police can't find my fingerprints. Then I'll curl up in my closet, cowering. That's how the police will find me.

And I won't regret it a jot.

My dad's a monster. He loves to press the gun up against me and intimidate me with it. When his girlfriend comes round, that Belinda from next door, they like to go shooting or fool around with the gun, and Dad flaunts their relationship in front of me. Weirdly, despite what I'm intending to do, I'm not a violent person.

But even though my dad taunts me with being thick at school, the total opposite to my fabulous sister, I observe and learn quietly. I've picked up the art of shooting, by watching him and listening to him.

Aside from guns, all he cares about is school and exam results. I'm not academic. My talents lie in different areas. I'm a really good runner, and I love woodwork. I'm helping my uncle make some decking at the back of his house. But these things mean nothing to my dad. I'm not like my sister, who is total perfection when it comes to school, and everything else for that matter. He tells me all the time that I'm useless, that I'll never amount to anything.

Well, I'm going to show him, and that sister of mine. You're meant to love your siblings. Well, I don't. All she does is revise and revise and spend hours over her homework. When Dad has a go at me for bad results, I can see the gloating look on her face. She denies it, but I know she enjoys being so much better than me. Well, she'll get her comeuppance tonight.

As for Mum, I should feel sorry for her. Dad's vile to her. Not only is he having an affair, but I can hear the way he speaks to her. It crosses between contempt and rage. But she never stands up to him, either for her or for me. When he gives me grief about my school reports, she stands there silently, tears rolling down her face. What's the point of that? I want to scream at her. Why don't you stick up for me?

It's coming to a head tonight. When I told Josie my plan, she agreed. They deserve it, she said. She's an adult, and so if she says my plan is OK, I need to believe it and bury any doubts.

I'll smuggle one of Dad's guns out, hidden in my belongings, after I'm rescued. You never know, I might need it again one day, as I'll never let anyone treat me like that again.

I just need to wait a few more hours, and then finally it's bye-bye.

I stare at the letter, my hand shaking. I should go to the police. Josie and Lily should both be charged. But I don't want any more dealings with Josie, I just want to get away from her and erase her from my life. I carefully place the letter back in the board game box and close the lid.

I collapse onto the floor, uncaring that cobwebs creep up my legs. I know what Mike and I need to do. And I won't be breathing a word of it to Josie.

I dig around in my pocket and stab the estate agent's number into my phone. "Press one for sales, two for lettings," intones the welcoming message. I press two.

"Hello, I would like to rent out our house."

After my call, I extract Jojo from our bedcovers and march down to the kitchen, plunging the doll in the bin. I catch a final glimpse of its staring blue eyes as I slam the lid shut.

CHAPTER 40

"Sit on the suitcase Poppy!" I shout, fumbling with the zip. "There, done it." The case is bulging, but I've managed to close it.

"Are we done?" Mike is anxiously glancing at his watch. "The removal people will be here in ten minutes."

"All finished," I say. I look around the room, at our suitcases and boxes crammed with belongings, and smile. I can't wait to get out of here.

It only took five weeks for the whole renting process to go through. The second viewing led to an immediate offer, which we accepted, and in record time we found a house to rent on the other side of Twickenham.

It's not ideal. We'll need something else by the time the baby arrives as there are only two bedrooms. But Mike agreed with me that it was important to get out as quickly as possible, and then find something more suitable. Our long-term plan is to release equity from this house and buy another property, but that can wait.

I glance down at the slight curve of my stomach and smile. I can start getting properly excited about our new arrival.

The speed of it all and the fact that only two families viewed the property means that Josie is oblivious to anything going on. Mike and I have kept up a carefully friendly if slightly distant profile. She still comes over and spends time with Poppy, but we've made ourselves less available and accepting her offers of help less.

I was desperate to brick up the gap in the loft. I was frantically looking through builders on Checkatrade when suddenly I remembered that Steve is a builder. My shoulders sagged with relief. Even though his diary was full, he managed to find time to come the very next day.

"I always wanted her to block this gap up and she resisted fiercely. Now I know why," Steve said wryly after I explained what was going on.

Since then, there's been no sound from the loft, and no night terrors from Poppy. I've wondered if Josie has tried to get in and found the gap blocked, but there's been no sign of anything amiss with her. She's been nothing but pleasant and helpful.

I've also wondered if I leaped to conclusions too quickly, that maybe Poppy's night terrors were coincidental, as Mike suggested. But then the doll and face mask pop into my head and I know I'm not wrong. Lily might have been responsible for most of the sinister events, but she's not the shadowy person who creeps into Poppy's room.

At least our tenant won't have to cope with Josie potentially sneaking down into her children's bedrooms.

There's a knock on the door.

"The removal van's here!" Mike picks Poppy up and swings her around as she giggles.

He flings open the door, and Mabel is standing on the porch, clad in skinny jeans and ballet flats. But while she's dressed about twenty years younger than her age, I note that a few grey roots are inching through in her hair, and there are dark circles under her eyes.

"Ah, Mabel." Mike doesn't sound altogether thrilled. "Sorry, I thought it was our removal guys."

"I won't keep you long," says Mabel. "I just wanted to wish you luck in your new home." She thrusts a bottle bag at me. The top of a bottle of champagne peeks out.

"Oh, Mabel you shouldn't have," I say politely, reading the gift tag.

To happier times.

Mabel's card from months before flashes into my mind. *Can she not come up with a different phrase?* I'm torn between laughter and irritation.

"I really hope you're happy there," says Mabel sincerely. "And also, I want to thank you for your help with Belinda. We appreciate it so much."

"Oh, it's no problem," I say uncomfortably.

We say our goodbyes.

Mike turns to me and mutters, "To be honest, Belinda is doing us a favour."

Exactly.

We squeeze arms.

My phone beeps and a text from Layla flashes up. *Good luck with your move, Clara! Hope it all goes smoothly. Give Poppy big kisses for me xx PS I'm going on another date with Steve tonight — our third!*

I smile. I'm thrilled that Steve and Layla have hit it off. He's a far cry from her usual type, but that's a good thing — Max and a succession of faceless online dates parading through my mind. I had to work hard to persuade Layla to accept Steve's offer of a drink, as Layla felt disloyal after what Josie had done for her that night she was shot. But she got over her feelings when I explained that actually, Josie was not so innocent after all. But despite what Josie has done, I still have to suppress a flicker of guilt as I read the text.

The next time the doorbell rings, it's the removal company. I let out a sigh of relief. Soon we can get away.

I glance over at next door's drive. "Oh no," I breathe. Josie is walking up our drive, staring at the removal van, forehead furrowed.

I want to run inside and hide like a five-year-old but force myself to stay put.

Mike is speaking to the removal men when Josie walks past. They smile stiltedly at each other.

"What's going on?" Josie asks, a trace of anxiety in her voice.

"Josie!" Poppy flings herself delightedly at our neighbour.

"Darling, can you go and get your suitcase and your remaining toys," I ask Poppy. Poppy kisses Josie on the cheek before running inside.

A jolt of guilt rushes through me. Poppy doesn't really understand we're moving to a different house. It's partly down to her age, but also, we haven't told her explicitly that we're moving, for fear that she'll say something to Josie.

Josie stands frozen like a statue, her eyes boring into me.

"We're moving, Josie," I say blandly. Platitudes about not wanting to but needing to, about missing Josie, about keeping in touch bubble up, but I close my mouth tightly. It's uncomfortable, but I need to be honest with this woman, to cut all ties.

"Why?" Josie's usual demure, cool tones are gone, replaced with bewilderment and shock. "You said you were going to stay here and make a go of it."

"That was before I found out that Lily killed her family."

Josie's eyes widen and her face pales.

"What?" she stammers.

I force myself to look her straight in the eye. "And I know that you know that she was the killer, Josie. Don't deny it, I have proof."

"I . . . I . . ." Josie stammers. Her previous contained self has vanished.

"He deserved it," she bursts out. "He was evil."

"And poor innocent Jasmine and Anna?" I retort.

There's a silence. There is of course another reason for me and my family leaving.

"Josie, I know that it was you that Poppy was seeing in her bedroom. You're the person that caused her night terrors."

"No." Josie shakes her head frantically. "It would have been Lily. It wasn't me."

"And your doll?"

I see a flash of understanding in Josie's eyes, but that is quickly replaced with incomprehension.

I try again. "And your face mask?"

Josie gasps. She struggles to regain her composure.

"Sorry, I . . . I don't understand," she stutters.

"Oh, I think you do," I say.

"All OK?" Mike slips an arm around me as the removal people file into the house.

"I'm heartbroken that you're moving." Josie fixes her blue eyes on Mike. "Mike, I thought we had a bond, a connection, but you did all this behind my back, when I've done my best to help your family."

"I'm sure Clara has explained why we felt forced to do this without your knowledge," Mike says calmly. His eyes look anywhere but at Josie. "Look, I've not handled this at all well and I've obviously upset you, and for that I'm truly sorry. But my loyalty is with my wife."

"Please, at least let me see Poppy still. Please, we love each other." Josie is begging, her eyes suspiciously glinting.

I start to feel guilty, to wonder if I'm in the wrong. But Mike squeezes my waist reassuringly.

"I don't think so," he says quietly.

"Can I have your address to write to her? Or at least your email," begs Josie.

I turn away, guilt tugging with my desire to get away from Josie.

"No, Josie. I don't think it's a good idea. I'm sure Poppy will remember you for a long time and we very much appreciate your help," Mike replies.

Josie grabs me. "Are you going to tell the police that it was Lily that shot her family?" Fear laces her voice. *For herself.*

"Not if you leave us alone and never contact us again," I reply.

Mike grabs my hand and we walk into our house.

"Goodbye," Mike says, adding quietly, "I'm sorry."

Poppy is dashing towards Josie, dragging her rainbow-coloured suitcase in one hand and in the other clutching her cuddly dog.

Mike swoops her up and I close the door.

CHAPTER 41

Josie

I'm sitting at my living room window. My body is starting to ache as I've sat here for over an hour. But I'll sit for as long as it takes. I continue to stare out of the window.

How on earth did Clara find out? Lily must have left some clue. I wildly try to think what happened but draw a blank.

"I even bloody saved your life, Clara," I speak aloud, bitterly. Despite my jealousy about that woman and her perfect family, I couldn't have stood aside and let Lily fire that gun at her.

Finally, I see their car pull out and drive past. I glimpse Poppy in the back, her curls wild, her face pressed against the window.

I want to run after the car and keep on following until they get to their new house. But I stay frozen in my position. I'm fighting a losing battle.

If it hadn't been for Clara's threat, I would have tracked them down. I know where Poppy's nursery is. I could have waited there and followed them back home and . . . my mind races with how I could have traced them and forced my way back into Poppy's life.

But I never will. I can't risk Clara telling the police and implicating me. I could be in serious trouble for concealing the truth.

Clenching my fist, I slam it against the window in frustration. *There is nothing I can do.*

I really like Mike, but I like Poppy more. After it all exploded when Lily threatened Clara with her gun, I knew I had to give up on my dream of taking Mike for myself, to stay in with their family. And I could cope with that because what I wanted most was to be close to Poppy. In fact, it was even better after the incident because Clara accepted me, and so I saw Poppy more and felt like part of their family. Now the rug has been pulled from under my feet.

Being with the next-door neighbours helped me forget about being completely alone in the world, with no family, and now no Steve. The house is empty without him. It's still strange to see his favourite armchair empty. The ashtray filled with cigarette stubs he left in the utility room used to drive me mad, but now I would give anything to see it there again, to smell its stale smoke.

On the coffee table is a letter from the lawyer he's instructed about our divorce. I haven't opened it yet, and now isn't the time when I'm feeling so crushed. I pick it up and shove it behind some books on the shelf.

Out of the window, a car pulls into next door's drive, and as a statuesque figure steps out, I see a flash of red hair. *Belinda.* She must be here to see Mabel, but why is she parking on Clara and Mike's drive? A prickle of hatred runs through me.

I watch, expecting her to walk over to Mabel's, but a van pulls in behind her car.

My mouth drops open. Two burly men start to lug out furniture and suitcases. Belinda's two girls exit the car. Grabbing their hands, she takes them to the front door.

I fly out of my house and march over.

"What on earth are you doing?" I gasp.

"Moving into our new home," Belinda says coolly, inserting the key in the lock.

"But . . . but . . ." I stutter.

"We're renting it from Clara and Mike." Belinda lowers her voice. "I've decided to divorce Teddy, and this seems the perfect solution. I can be next door to Mum and have some help from her with the girls."

"I can't believe you're going to move into this house after everything that's happened," I cry.

Belinda shrugs, but concern flashes in her eyes. "I have to put that behind me. This is the most practical solution."

Not only has my lovely Poppy gone, but she's being replaced by a woman that I cannot stand. For the second time today, I clench my fists. And then I home in on Belinda's daughters.

They are petite, with large eyes and clad in adorable flowery dresses. The younger one even has blonde curls, like Poppy. And like Lily when she was a girl. Her eyes are also blue, although a darker shade than both Poppy's and Lily's.

"How old are your daughters and what are their names?" I ask.

Belinda looks surprised at the sudden change of subject. "Pippa is seven, and Ava is five," she replies.

The girls smile. "Hello," says Ava shyly.

"I love your name," I smile. "Like the movie star Ava Gardner."

Ava grins, although it's clear she has no idea who I'm talking about. *Oh! She even has one dimple. Just like me.*

Belinda clears her throat. "Anyway, we'd best be getting on. We need to get unpacking."

I flash a huge smile at Ava and turn back to my own house. Once inside, I'm running up the stairs, dragging the loft ladder down with my hook and clambering up its steps. *It's a drug I can't resist.*

I curse myself as I haul myself into the loft. It's been so good the last few weeks with Clara and her family. Even though I was dying to slip though the wall and sneak into their house, and into Poppy's room, I stopped myself. It was important that they thought Poppy's "night terrors" were down to Lily. But then I cracked one night. I couldn't resist slipping my mask on, creeping down and staring at Poppy's peaceful, slumbering face, imagining that she was my little daughter.

Poppy told me over and over that she couldn't find her precious dolly, and I had a hunch what might have happened. It was pretty obvious that Clara wasn't keen on it. I had a look in Poppy's room, and I quickly managed to locate it in the top of the wardrobe.

I tried to drop the doll quietly on the bed, but its hand tapped Poppy's face, and that was it. The little girl peeked out under her eyelids and uttered a wail as I rushed from the room and up to the loft before Clara and Mike could catch me.

It was a silly thing to do, and I promised myself I wouldn't do it again. It wasn't worth risking the fragile truce I had with Clara. I spy my mask on the floor and grab it. How on earth did Clara find out about it? *She must have entered my loft through the opening.* I curse myself for my carelessness. I was usually so careful to hide it behind the paints, *just in case*. Poppy is back in my thoughts and I'm full of regret even as I slip my mask on and push against the adjoining wall, to drive back the plywood.

But rather than flimsy wood, a rock-hard surface lies beneath my hands. I push hard and then frantically feel about. There's no soft board ready to move under my hands. I haven't bothered to turn the light on, in my eagerness to hotfoot it into my neighbour's home, to quietly observe where Ava's bedroom is going to be.

I slam on the light switch, and sure enough, no flimsy, cut-out plywood meets my eye. Rather, what looks like thick oatmeal has replaced it. I thump my palm against it. It feels, as before, impenetrable.

I'm all alone now, there is no outlet for me. Ava's sweet little face with its dimples merges with Poppy's in my mind, and then breaks, as if made out of glass.

I slam my hand again and again against the new cement filling. My skin is crimson and sore, but I don't care.

I sink onto the floor and wail, keening for what I've lost, and for what I was hoping for.

* * *

They keep telling me that there are various things wrong with me.

Psychotic, suffering from paranoid delusions . . . she needs new medications, more medications . . . new therapies . . .

In my head my spirit rises from my body when they give me their laborious explanations. I hunch up tight in the corner of the ceiling. I'm floating and I like it. They look so serious when they describe me. Is that all I consist of — cold, medical words?

I can barely remember the night when I entered my old home and threatened Clara with a gun and shot Layla. The main thing that sticks with me is all those policemen charging at me, their footsteps sounding as loud as a stampede of bulls.

I wish I hadn't done it. But the main thing is, it wasn't my fault. And that's not just me saying that. A team of psychiatrists say a panic attack brought on hallucinations.

Unfortunately, while that is true, it doesn't account for the other charges against me, that I trespassed into my old house. I've tried to pass that off as hallucinatory too, but I don't think that cuts it. They look at me suspiciously, eyebrows raised and mouths in thin lines.

I shouldn't have done it, of course. But I became fixated with the people in my old house. How that little girl was living the dream childhood I should have had, how Clara was living the life with her perfect little family that I wanted but was unlikely to achieve, tainted by what happened, and in and out of psychiatric hospitals all the time.

I do my best not to think about that night ten years ago, because just one nanosecond, one glimpse sends me straight back there and I feel the horror, despair, shock and, conversely, satisfaction, all rolled into one. But of course, while I shouldn't, I do think about it. It flashes into my mind every few minutes. Especially since that night I entered my old home with a gun.

I've been deemed too unwell to be tried in person in court. While the case will go ahead, I feel grateful that I don't have to be there.

I'm entering a plea of diminished responsibility. Whatever the outcome, I know I'll be detained in a high-security hospital. My lawyer acts like I should be grateful that I'll avoid prison. But I've been locked up most of my life. I don't have any freedom. The words "high security" drill into my brain. It might as well be prison.

Josie has come to see me. Amid all the bleakness of my current situation, my heart gives a little jump. Josie is the closest person to me. The sister I never had. I delete Jasmine's big, dark eyes from my mind, her studious face buried in a book. There have been times when Josie hasn't visited me regularly, but I forgive her for that. I know about her struggles for a baby, the difficulties with her husband. She's taking their split badly.

Josie is down in the mouth. She wears her bleakness around her like a cloak.

"What's the matter?" I ask.

Josie is quiet for a long time. It looks like she's weighing up what to say to me.

I stiffen and am about to tell her to blurt it out, when she mutters, "They left. Clara, Mike and Poppy." Her voice trembles over the syllables of the little girl's name. "They've rented their house out and have moved elsewhere. They're never coming back."

I feel both a pang of disappointment and relief. I became obsessed with that family. It's probably a good thing they've moved so that I can wipe the slate clean. No knowledge of the inhabitants of my old home is power. I need to move on from it, not give a thought to who is living in my house, licking the jealous flames of my mind.

It has really affected Josie though. She obviously grew close to them, especially the child. Another little girl pops into my mind. One with honey-blonde curls — and who saw Josie as an escape from her family, from her cruel dad, her perfect sister who could do no wrong, and from her mum who couldn't stand up for her.

Josie speaks, shattering my thoughts. "It's bad enough that they've gone. But even worse is that they've rented their house out to Belinda."

My mind freezes, and then the gears start moving.

"My dad's Belinda?" I gasp.

"Yep." Josie is curt, unhappy about this too. Then her eyes soften slightly. "But her daughters are very sweet. Especially the youngest one."

I have no interest in that woman's children.

I'm transported back to a decade ago. Belinda and my dad are earnestly looking at his gun. He's giving her a tutorial on how to use it.

Mum is at work, on her shift as a nurse.

He slips an arm around Belinda, both of them cradling the gun, their hands touching over the smooth metal.

Dad glances up and catches me watching them from the hall.

"Jasmine got top marks for her French project, any such news for you?" His voice is cold.

Belinda smiles blandly. And then her and Dad start kissing, not caring that they're in full view of me.

I hate her.

I'm back in the present, my face is hot and my heart is pounding. Despite her selfish disregard for me, she ends up all cosy in my family home, while I'm going to be incarcerated in hospital.

My plans to leave that house well alone when I'm finally released fall down like a pack of cards.

It was kind of Josie to obtain the key to the garage of my old home for me, just after I was released from my latest stint at hospital.

I'd told her I wanted to go into the house to "get something", and "for old time's sake". Luckily, Josie's not one for a lot of questioning.

She said it would be easy for her to find a key by slipping though the dividing wall in the loft. And sure enough, on her next visit to me, she was gripping a large silver key.

With regret, I think about that key now firmly in the hands of the police.

"I'll need another key," I say.

Josie sighs. "I'm afraid that won't be possible. Clara and Mike have closed up the loft wall opening with cement."

Something akin to grief breaks over me. I'm back in Josie's loft having slipped through the opening, sipping hot chocolate and chatting with her. It's where I briefed her about my murderous plans, and she encouraged me to go ahead.

Anger quickly takes over. How dare they?

I'll just have to find another way.

"No matter how many years my sentence is, as soon as I'm out, I'll find a way to get into that house and punish Belinda. And I'll track Clara down and make her pay," I spit.

Red-hot spikes of anger pierce me when I think about that woman blocking up my little escape route, the one glimpse of happiness I felt in my childhood. And crucially, creating a big obstacle to me easily being able to get into the house and wreak vengeance on my dad's girlfriend.

Josie beams. Usually her smiles are diffident, but this one is wide, her mouth fully turned up.

She takes my hand.

"Count me in."

THE END

ACKNOWLEDGEMENTS

So many people have helped me with this book. I am very grateful to them all and there are some to whom I owe a special mention.

To my friend Charlene, for helping me settle on this theme and for giving me the confidence I needed to push ahead with it.

To my husband Tom, for his endless patience, encouragement and feedback.

To my late mum, who gave me my love of reading and always believed that I could one day become an author.

To Joffe Books and Kate Lyall Grant, for believing in me in the first place and for all their support and expertise.

Above all, I am so grateful to the people who have taken the time to read my books.

THE JOFFE BOOKS STORY

We began in 2014 when Jasper agreed to publish his mum's much-rejected romance novel and it became a bestseller.

Since then we've grown into the largest independent publisher in the UK. We're extremely proud to publish some of the very best writers in the world, including Joy Ellis, Faith Martin, Caro Ramsay, Helen Forrester, Simon Brett and Robert Goddard. Everyone at Joffe Books loves reading and we never forget that it all begins with the magic of an author telling a story.

We are proud to publish talented first-time authors, as well as established writers whose books we love introducing to a new generation of readers.

We won Trade Publisher of the Year at the Independent Publishing Awards in 2023 and Best Publisher Award in 2024 at the People's Book Prize. We have been shortlisted for Independent Publisher of the Year at the British Book Awards for the last five years, and were shortlisted for the Diversity and Inclusivity Award at the 2022 Independent Publishing Awards. In 2023 we were shortlisted for Publisher of the Year at the RNA Industry Awards, and in 2024 we were shortlisted at the CWA Daggers for the Best Crime and Mystery Publisher.

We built this company with your help, and we love to hear from you, so please email us about absolutely anything bookish at feedback@joffebooks.com.

If you want to receive free books every Friday and hear about all our new releases, join our mailing list here: www.joffebooks.com/freebooks.

And when you tell your friends about us, just remember: it's pronounced Joffe as in coffee or toffee!

www.ingramcontent.com/pod-product-compliance
Lightning Source LLC
LaVergne TN
LVHW031659170725
816442LV00013B/102